SANDS

OF

TIME

SANDS OF TIME

THE CHRONOS PARADOX • BOOK 2

HUNTER BLAIN

Podium

This is a work of fiction. Names, characters, places, and incidents are either products of the author's imagination or used fictitiously. Any resemblance to actual events, locales, or persons, living, dead, or undead, is entirely coincidental.

Cover design by Podium Publishing

ISBN: 978-1-0394-3342-7

Published in 2023 by Podium Publishing, ULC
www.podiumaudio.com

SANDS
OF
TIME

"The future is not something we enter.
The future is something we create."
—*Leonard I. Sweet*

"The only reason for time is so that everything
doesn't happen at once."
—*Albert Einstein*

PROLOGUE

Where are they now?" Andrew Frost asked the AI while narrowed eyes stared at the floating computer screen above his desk. Displayed on the hologram was the scene from his old backyard, with the anomaly Andrew having just stopped the cycle and then disappearing into the wormhole.

A smooth feminine voice sounded from all around the office like a theater-quality surround sound system, nearly reminding Andrew of the old Siri or Alexa assistants from days long since passed.

"Tim has convinced your past variant to seek you out in this wheren, which is one of the many contingencies put in place should the operation not go as planned."

Andrew looked down at his left arm where a typical white lab coat covered his Clepsydra.

"Tim, can you confirm?"

I cannot, I'm afraid. I do not have the memories of the Tim variant attached to that Andrew Frost, Tim replied almost apologetically. *However, if I am able to make a connection with the Clepsydra, I'll be able to sync our data. But not until then.*

"Damn it," Andrew grumbled.

"No need for that sort of language," the feminine AI said playfully. "*I* know exactly where they will arrive."

Andrew slowly lifted his head with narrowed, unfocused eyes.

"Where?"

"I've uploaded the coordinates to your Clepsydra. But you must hurry. The Clockmen will be able to trace the variant through the wormhole and will be expecting him."

"Damn it," Andrew repeated, with more vigor this time, and shot to his feet while stripping off his lab coat. "Increase the sensor sensitivity around the entrance and emergency exit."

"Already done," the AI answered with a smile in her tone.

Hanging up his white coat, Andrew grabbed a black jacket with an altered left sleeve and threw it on in one swift motion.

Inside the jacket pockets were a thick scarf, which he wrapped around his face, and sunglasses that would best be described as steampunk mixed with modern.

"Wait," the AI assistant called out. "You will probably need these."

On a metal tray affixed to the countertop near the back wall behind Andrew's desk, a pair of synthetic leather gloves seemed to rise out of nowhere.

"Right," Andrew exhaled at understanding his near fatal mistake, and strode to pick up the gloves.

Slipping them on, Andrew looked at his Clepsydra and asked, "You ready, Tim?"

Not like I have a choice . . . the AI quipped.

"Ali," Andrew said to the ceiling, "can you have the car ready for me?"

"As you wish, Daddity," Alison answered just as Andrew Frost and Tim made their way out of the lab and down the rabbit hole.

CHAPTER 1

Andrew . . . I'm not sure this will work," Tim hesitantly said as his six-inch Cairn puppy avatar floated above the metal sleeve of my Clepsydra. I could see what could only be described as anxiety in his large hologram eyes.

"Only one way to find out," I said as we approached the point in the wormhole that would lead me to the future—at least *my* future . . . I think. Time travel was wonky like that.

"Are you sure you want to do this?"

"Wasn't it *you* who convinced *me*?"

"It-it was just an idea that popped in my head. Almost out of nowhere," he mumbled the last words.

"Still, it's a good plan. The future me will have more answers than we do. Right?"

"I suppose. But if we go through and there is *nothing* there—no universe—then all you've been through would have been for naught," the AI said in his cultured British accent. I wanted to ask him why artificial intelligence avatars seemed to prefer that accent over all others, but just didn't care at the moment.

"It'll be there." There was a confidence in my voice I didn't rightfully own, almost like I was borrowing it from an Andrew Frost who had already succeeded. Sort of like replaying a video game where you knew all the answers from your first exploratory playthrough.

"If you say so," Tim conceded, not having any other alternatives but to do what I said.

The wormhole, which stretched from the instant that the Big Bang occurred to the creation of the tunnel itself, showcased countless clouds of galaxies just outside the mostly translucent walls.

"Open it," I instructed while looking in the direction of my future, my back facing toward the Big Bang.

"Dear 01. It's me again. Tim. If you could find it within your bandwidth to—"

"Open it, Tim!"

"Fine, fine, fine!" the AI said with a gulp as a glowing doorway, like a me-sized circle, opened in front of me.

There was a moment of hesitation until my mind flashed with Alison calling out "Daddity!" as I hid behind the shed. I had saved my family and allowed an Andrew Frost who wasn't me to never know the horrible fate that he had narrowly avoided. Over three thousand Andrew Frosts had been tricked into going back in time and continuing a cycle of *hell* where they were forced to choose between saving the entire universe . . . or their own family.

Three thousand Andrews had made the wrong choice, and the cycle had ended with me.

I'd stopped the last *and* first killer. Defeated the Clockmen. And changed both the past and future in one fell swoop. Having an incalculable Chronos Scale allowed me to shift events however I saw fit, but it had come at a great cost. I would never get to see my family again—at least not without choosing a point in time and killing *myself* in order to take his place. But that wouldn't stop the impact that Alison, my beautiful baby girl, was having on the pull of the universe.

There was only one man who could help us. And he was probably going to be pissed to see me.

Setting my jaw and narrowing my determined eyes, I stepped through the doorway and into an unknown future.

CHAPTER 2

Oh, thank science! Tim cried out from inside my head, his avatar having vanished from view.

It had been dark when I confronted the last and first killer, and the modest light inside the wormhole had been provided by the sea of galaxies. So when a full, blinding scene came into view, I had to shield my stinging eyes as if I had been exposed to a flash-bang.

Adjusting your pupils, Tim said, and the sharp pain faded in a few seconds. I normally hated it when the AI made changes to my body through the system of connections he had made throughout . . . well, *me,* but right then, I didn't really mind.

Hesitantly pulling my eyelids apart while holding up my hand to shield my face from the bright sun, I gasped at what I saw.

Skyscrapers covered in what appeared to be glass, taller than anything I had ever seen, occupied most of the sky. It almost gave me vertigo as my mind tried to convince me I wasn't looking straight up, instead insisting that I was looking down a train tunnel with a modicum of light at the end.

Advertisements danced over the glass surface of the buildings, nearly blending with one another if not for the tiny barriers separating the skyscrapers, like looking up at a dense forest where trees allowed but the barest of space between their canopies.

"You have got to be kidding me," I drawled as I saw the biggest ad was for RC Cola.

"Hmm?" Tim asked before noticing how my eyes followed the gliding logo which dwarfed all others. "Oh. That. Yes, RC Cola won the advertising wars of 2122, taking out the likes of Coke and Pepsi, who were too busy fighting with one another to notice their loss in territories until it was too late."

I instantly thought of an old Sylvester Stallone movie and asked, "Did Taco Bell win the food wars?"

"Did you just make a *Demolition Man* reference? Because I *love* it!"

I started to smile at the praise from the quirky AI when something caught my attention.

"Did you say 2122?"

"Yes. The ad wars took place thirty-seven years ago."

"So the year is, what, 2159?"

"Well, look who can do math!"

"Tim," I exhaled, running a hand down my face in frustration. "Why did we come so far?"

"To find the future Andrew. 01! Did you suffer some sort of memory loss during the jump?"

"Am I even still alive, Tim? The future me, I mean."

"Oh. I, uh, see where the confusion lies."

I waited for him to go on as I stared up at the enormous RC Cola advertisement as it slid around the building and out of sight.

"Tim?" I finally said, almost grunting with annoyance. Only the fact that I was in public kept me at bay.

"Yes?"

"*How* am I still alive?"

"Um . . . *weeeeellll* . . ."

"Tim, just tell me. No more lies, okay?"

"It wouldn't be lying to *not* tell you something I think would serve to hurt the mission."

"And how would it do that?"

"By depressing you."

"Just spit it out. Please."

"As soon as we arrived, I began searching for this wheren's Andrew Frost. But I haven't been able to locate him. Or even a trace of him, for that matter."

"And?"

"The Andrew who programmed me no longer seems to . . . how do I put this . . . *exist.*"

"Because I changed the past . . ." I thought aloud as something above us moved. I flicked my gaze up to see what had to be a flying car.

"Exactly."

"What does that mean for the mission?" I asked as I lazily followed the flying car's trajectory.

"Either you are dead, by whatever means, or you are in hiding."

"Could it be from old age, Tim?" I sarcastically asked, remembering the year.

"No. Nanotechnology has advanced to the point of cellular repair to the measure of basic immortality."

"Basic?"

"Well, if you were to be in an explosion or have your brain obliterated, or even just burned alive, then the nanoids couldn't repair the catastrophic damage enough to bring you back to life."

"But they can stop aging?"

"Aging. Myocardial infarctions. Cerebrovascular accidents. Most mortal wounds."

"What's cerebo vascular accidents?"

"Cerebrovascular, Andrew. Add in the *bro*, like I know you want to."

"I don't think I've ever said *bro* to you . . . bro."

"Hmph," Tim dismissed. "It means stroke."

"Ah. Kind of feels weird that they call it an *accident*."

"Agreed. But the point is, the Andrew who programmed me was able to extend his lifespan to infinitum because of nanotechnology."

"Like the gun Retnuh used in the forest?" I asked, remembering the handle the leader of the Clockmen had pulled out. My memory played back the growing weapon which looked like a cross from something from a sci-fi movie and an anime.

"Well, sort of," Tim explained. "Retnuh's nanite gun was powered by exotic matter, just like a Clepsydra, allowing the ammunition to destroy the unfortunate recipient's entire timeline."

"Just like the contamination when I shot the tall Tock's Clepsydra." My mind flipped from the scene of Retnuh firing the nanite gun to that of the screaming skeleton who had flesh growing and decaying over his entire timeline, all at once. I shuddered at the thought.

"Traze was his name. And yes. It is like a controlled exotic matter contamination, controlled by the nanomachines' AI by influencing gravity."

Something came to me, and I patted the pockets of my black tactical pants.

"Shit."

"What is it?"

"I left the nanite gun in the other Andrew's hoodie."

"Shit!" Tim agreed. "How could we possibly forget such a powerful tool?!"

"I blame you."

"Me?!"

Seeing the AI actually get offended, I changed the subject. "What about the antimatter, um, *thingy* that the killer used while fighting Retnuh?"

"Oh, I got that installed while you slept after, uh . . ."

"Killing the other Andrew," I finished for him. My voice was cold, like a mortician who had become accustomed to seeing the bodies of the dead.

"Y-Yes . . . that."

"So it's installed?" I asked, lifting my arm to inspect the Clepsydra. I didn't notice any physical changes to the smooth metal sleeve stretching from elbow to wrist.

"All internal components were mostly additional lines of code. The hard part was moving the fuel over without, *hehe*, killing you."

"Not funny, tin can," I sighed as I watched a long flying vehicle glide overhead. I could only guess it was a city bus or something along those lines.

I thought about how the killer had manifested different weapons with the antimatter. "So can I, like, make saw blades and stuff?"

"Oh, you can do much more than that. You can even—"

"Frost!" a voice I recognized called out from my right, making Tim vanish from sight in an instant.

I snapped my attention to the side, seeing three men clad in black, including their fedoras. The tallest of the three had every inch of his skin covered in some sort of tight material, like a bodysuit under his Clockman suit—all except his face, which had a blank metal mask over it, looking like a retail store's mannequin. I couldn't see his mouth, nose, or—most unnervingly—his eyes. Only a silver, featureless face stared back at me.

With a Spanish accent, Retnuh Ordune took one step forward, lifted a glowing fist, and said with absolute authority, "You're coming with me, *Tick.*"

"The hell I am," I called back while arcing my left arm in their direction and flexing the muscles in my forearm which I associated with firing. The difference this time was, I intently focused on the white energy of the antimatter that killer Andrew had used.

Wait! Tim cried out inside my head as a beam of antimatter lashed out, violently carving out a crevasse in the concrete before rushing toward the Clockmen.

For a split second, the beam struck the corner of the building behind the three men clad in black, and the entire glass structure rumbled before all of the advertisements blinked out of existence. It was like taking a hyperdetailed pencil drawing of a building and aggressively rubbing at one corner of it with a cheap eraser.

Retnuh moved his glowing fist to latch onto the beam as it approached him, as if grabbing a physical object.

"What the . . ." I mouthed as he absorbed the antimatter into the palm of his glowing blue hand. There was a complete lack of strain on his face, resembling a man on the precipice of boredom, even as the air around him seemed to crackle and a sudden wind tugged at his suit.

Run! Tim said urgently as I let the beam drop.

There was a rumble from beneath all of our feet, and the entire area began to rock like an earthquake.

Retnuh moved his glowing hand, which was considerably brighter than before, and crouched to place his palm on the concrete at his feet.

Light shot out in all directions, focusing on the crevasse I had accidentally created, all while the other two Tocks kept their eyes locked on me. At least, I assume the tall one was, judging by how his creepy face never moved away from my direction.

"What's he doing?"

RUN, PLEASE! Tim shouted inside my head, making me wince with the volume, which was an odd feeling.

"Traze. Go," Retnuh said over his shoulder while the earthquake began to ease.

The tall, faceless Clockman tilted his head down a little, and I could almost see him smile beneath the featureless mask. With long strides, the tall man began sprinting toward me, resembling a carnivorous giraffe hopped up on cocaine.

FOR THE LOVE OF SCIENCE, RUN!

I felt an uncomfortably warm surge of adrenaline shoot through me and let my body begin to move with powerful strides.

My vision tunneled, and heaving breaths filled all that I could hear as I ran faster than I had in my entire life. I might have been roaring with each exhale from my galloping lungs, deafening me from the sound of my own footsteps.

Daring a glance over my shoulder, my eyes went wide as I saw the tall man drop to all fours with ease. If my comparison of him resembling a giraffe hadn't been accurate before . . . it sure as shit was now. His almost unnaturally long limbs moved with the precision of a predatory feline rushing after its prey.

"Jesus!" I screamed as I turned my attention back to where I was running, not knowing where to go.

Charging for a blast. The antimatter attack took a lot of energy, Tim explained with a nervous sort of stoicism, like a professional facing a losing scenario but doing everything in his power to mitigate the unavoidable collateral damage.

I relentlessly ran, but could feel the creepy man gaining ground, judging by how the skin on the back of my neck continued to tense.

Jump! Tim shouted as a big arrow appeared in my vision, pointing to the left.

Without hesitation, I leaped to the side right as Traze slashed the air where I had been with glowing blue claws on his left hand.

I hit the ground and rolled before scrambling to my feet and continuing to flee. I could feel that I'd hit both knees and my hip hard, but didn't care at that moment.

Glancing over my shoulder, I saw the tall man orient on me before giving chase once more.

"What the hell . . . is that thing?" I asked between heaving breaths.

I don't know, and I don't want *to know,* Tim answered. *Sixty seconds until charged.*

"We're not . . . going to make it," I blurted as I looked all around for a big flashing sign which said Hide Here, Andrew! But alas, there was none.

Go through that museum! Tim said as a building to my left illuminated. Thank God for his ability to manipulate what I saw because I couldn't make out the difference between the conjoined buildings.

I changed course and somehow managed to run even harder as the galloping man charged on all fours.

"Where's the door?!"

Here!

In my vision, part of the smooth glass building illuminated, and I aimed for it, hoping Tim was right.

As I approached, the doors slid open, and I was met with a rush of cool air. The floor was a brown concrete which had been sealed to a mirror finish. All around were signs pointing to the different areas of the museum.

"Where to?" I asked right as Traze burst *through* the doors faster than they could slide open. "Shit!"

Anywhere! an alarmed Tim responded.

Going on instinct, I ran down a hallway with a floating sign which said Literature.

There was a shriek of rage from behind, and this time, I didn't dare a glance over my shoulder, knowing what I would see.

Forty seconds!

Looking around for somewhere to hide, I saw a pedestal with a book at the top, protected by thick glass. A sign which I barely registered said, "First Edition of *I'm Glad You're Dead*." Even during my adrenaline-fueled fleeing, I couldn't help but note what an odd title it was.

Dropping to the ground on my hands and knees, I clamored behind the display that was barely thick enough to hide my body and tried to subdue my out-of-control breathing.

I tasted blood with each breath, and hoped it was from the intense running and not from some injury I was unaware of.

The unnerving galloping of the tall man stopped, and I could see in a glass display behind me the vague reflection of the figure as it slowly righted itself. A silver, featureless face looked all around like a snake hunting its prey.

Thirty seconds.

Seeing the distorted reflection of the man, I shot my hands up to cover my mouth, which drew the attention of my pursuer.

His metal mask turned toward the same reflection I was watching, and his head tilted to the side.

"Oh shit," I mouthed as he lifted a glowing fist toward me.

I scrambled to the side right as the pedestal disintegrated in a violent flash of light—book and all.

Staying low, I ran on all fours to a row of thick displays. Where the Clockman resembled a predatory feline, *I* could best be described as a drunk deer on ice, slipping all over the stained concrete floor.

"Heeeeeeeeheeeheeeheeheheheeeeeeee," the ultracreepy Clockman let out as he casually slithered his way closer to me, knowing his prey was trapped.

"What's *with* this guy?" I whispered while crawling behind another display.

He's insane, Tim explained. *The fact he's alive at all after suffering three full days from the Clepsydra breach is beyond amazing. Retnuh must have pulled* all *the strings in order for the doctors to keep him alive. At-at this point, he must be more nanomachines than man.*

"Great. Super."

Fifteen seconds.

"Little pig, little pig . . . let me in," the crazed faceless man said as he stalked closer and closer.

I gulped, and the tall man snapped his face toward where I hid while hunching his torso over like a serpent.

Five. Four. Three. Two.

Leaping to my feet, I pointed my glowing fist at the Clockman.

And fired.

CHAPTER 3

The display behind the crazy predator vanished in an explosion of debris.

Nice shot, Andrew! Tim cried out victoriously as I stared at the empty space where the bastard had just been.

In response to his wolf-and-three-pigs reference, I couldn't help but victoriously taunt back, "Not by the hair . . . on my chinny chin chi—" There was a growl from behind, and I turned my head right as the tall man lifted me up by the back of my neck and butt.

The next thing I knew, I was flying through the air, only to be caught by a glass case which was happy to show me its displeasure by hungrily slicing into my flesh wherever it could.

"AH!" I cried out, more in surprise than in pain.

What in 01?!

I lifted my chin from where I lay on a pile of ancient books and saw the tall man staring at me with a head tilted so far that his ear was touching his shoulder. If he had an ear, that was. I couldn't tell with how his entire body was covered in a tight black material under his suit.

His body glowed a faint blue as he stared at me, blood oozing from my numerous wounds to stain the pages I laid on.

In the blink of an eye, the tall man disappeared and then reappeared on top of me, blue claws at the ready.

All I could do was gasp as the man telegraphed the killing blow.

A tight blast of energy struck his head, just above the tall man's left eye, violently throwing him off of me.

"Huh?" I winced as I lowered my head and tried to find where the shot had come from.

I saw an upside-down man walking toward me with a glowing blue fist held up like a loaded gun. I couldn't see his face, as it was covered in a thick scarf just below black, steampunk-looking sunglasses.

Rolling over with a groan, I saw the man wasn't upside down, which was obvious except to my stunned state.

"Let's go," the man said in a gruff voice, keeping his fist pointed toward where the Clockman had fallen.

Slowly shifting my gaze around, I saw the crazed attacker rise from behind a destroyed display case, a portion of his silver mask missing above his left eye. What lay beneath made me wonder, did his flesh look like that *because* of the attack? Or was that the remains of his skin from the Clepsydra breach?

"Let's go. Now!" the man repeated, grabbing me by the back of my BDU with a gloved hand and yanking me to the ground with ease.

More glass cut into me, but I didn't have time to care at that moment.

The tall man snarled as I climbed to my feet, his blue claws growing in length until they resembled handheld scythes.

Getting to my feet, I moved behind the man as he continued to hold his glowing fist up. I briefly wondered how he was already able to fire again, but that thought vanished as quickly as the tall man did.

There was a crackling sound to my side, and I turned right as the Clockman appeared from thin air and slashed his long claws at me.

The man in front of me smoothly moved his left hand to point at the attacker, and his palm fully opened right before a sphere of blue light shot out.

The shriek of pain and anger was nearly deafening as the tall man was thrown back as if he had been struck by a speeding city bus.

Without a word, the mysterious stranger grabbed my wrist with a gloved hand and muscled me behind him as he strode to an Employee's Only door.

"You're me . . . aren't you?" I asked with a wince as I began to feel each cut from the glass.

"No shit," the man chided as he continued to pull me along as if I were some sort of trouble-prone child.

We moved through narrow, bland corridors which the man apparently knew by heart, or maybe his Tim was guiding him as mine had done for me.

We only stopped once for him to place something the size of a tube of Chapstick on the wall.

"Where are we going?"

"Shut up," the man who admitted was the future me barked. "Tim. Connect with my Clepsydra so you can explain what the fuck is going on."

"On it," Tim said aloud. "Boy, do I have a story for you."

"I'm sure . . ."

Coming out the back side of the building, the future me looked all around before locking his eyes on something.

Yanking me down hard enough that I could feel the muscles in my elbow and shoulder scream in protest, the future Andrew lifted his fist and fired at something down the alleyway.

A blast of light shot past where I had just been standing right as a man screamed.

Turning with wide eyes, I saw the shorter Tock holding his face with both hands as a section of the glass building next to him fell to the alley.

"Get up. Let's go," Andrew said, lifting me by the back of my shirt like I weighed no more than a bag of potato chips.

"Jesus!" was all I could say in surprise before landing on my feet hard enough to clink my teeth together. My jaw let me know it wasn't happy about it, but would wait until I was out of danger before beginning to throb.

Lifting his hand, Andrew waved it through the air, and a sleek car shimmered to life.

"Whoa."

"Get in," he demanded as he went to the driver's side and lifted the suicide door before climbing in.

I repeated the process on the passenger side, but had to wait for him to open it from the inside, as I didn't see a door handle.

There was a thunderous *thump* as something struck the glass of the cockpit, but the car somehow held strong against the attack. Moving with efficient fingers, Andrew pushed a series of buttons, and the vehicle lifted off the ground faster than a normal car would have been able to start its engine.

"Ah!" I cried out as the g-forces pushed me back in my seat while we zipped through the sky.

"Sorry." Andrew pushed another button, and all the forces pushing against my body were neutralized, leaving behind a rolling stomach. "Do *not* throw up in here."

"Transmission complete," Tim informed.

"Good. Now I can find out what the hell is going on," Andrew said as he undid his scarf and removed his sunglasses.

An identical copy of me, only perhaps in his late forties, looked over with deep blue eyes I had seen a hundred thousand times in the mirror. There were also a handful of scars decorating his face which I didn't have, making me instantly want to ask about them. Not because it was an interesting topic of conversation, but rather because I wanted to know my potential future . . . and what to avoid.

Andrew pressed another button, and the display stretching across the dash from door to door scrolled with Autopilot Engaged.

"Sooo . . . I guess it all started—" I began to explain when he simply held up his hand, staring at nothing in the air above a steering wheel which resembled a figure eight rather than a circle.

Tim— . . . his *Tim, I mean—is explaining everything, Andrew.*

"Ah," I said out loud. I turned and watched as the skyscrapers eventually shifted from above us to below. It shouldn't have been possible for them to reach that far into the sky. Then again, I had jumped through time and was now in a flying car sitting next to a version of me from the future while we both talked to our AIs.

"Ow," I mouthed as I moved my increasingly sore body.

Working on your cuts first, then I'll move to the bruised bones and muscles, Tim spoke inside my head. *Sheesh. You really like to take a beating, don't you?*

"Hmph," was all I could say as I leaned back in my seat and turned my head to stare out at a world I didn't recognize.

CHAPTER 4

You have got to be shitting me," Andrew exclaimed, prompting me out of my unfocused daze.

"What's that now?" I grumbled.

"*This* guy did all that?" Andrew asked as he pulled the sleeve up on his left arm to reveal a Clepsydra. "I mean, I knew *some* of it. But *damn*!"

"You knew some of it?" I asked in slight confusion.

A hologram of a six-inch Cairn Terrier appeared above the future me's forearm—and ignored my question. "I know, right? You wouldn't think that by looking at him," the future Tim said.

"I can hear you. You both know that . . ."

The two looked at me with assessing eyes as my own Tim came to life. "Believe me, I am just as surprised as you two are, but . . . here we are."

"Are you guys done?" I asked the three Judgy McJudgersons.

"Hmph," Andrew grunted with a touch of what could only be admiration.

"What?"

"You're handling all of this quite well."

"You're not the first Andrew I've had to deal with."

"Deal with?"

The future Tim spoke up. "He means kill. Yes, according to this handsome AI next to me, this Andrew has killed all the Andrews he's come in contact with."

"I've only ki—" I started to say, but didn't like the choice of words. "I've only *dealt with* two Andrews. The last killer, and the first."

"You also let an innocent Andrew be absorbed by the killer . . ." my Tim muttered under his breath.

"I . . ."

"Why don't I remember *any* of this?" Andrew asked his Tim. "From what you've just told me, his Chronos Scale should have altered *my* past."

"Oh, uh . . . thaaaaat's a good question, actually."

A dark thought came to mind, and I mumbled, "Because you haven't been to sleep yet."

Both Tim's looked at one another before glancing at the future Andrew.

"What?" Andrew asked with a cocked eyebrow.

"He's right," his Tim said. "Once you go to sleep . . . *all* of this Andrew's memories will be seared onto your brain."

"That sucks," I said dismissively. I didn't mean to sound so apathetic. It's just how it came out.

"Oh, it does indeed, Andrew," my Tim spoke. "Don't forget, *your* brain has a whole lifetime of memories awaiting as well. Everything from the night of your ASA-Day to this point in the timeline is in queue to be remembered."

My memory flashed to just an hour or so ago, when I had stopped the *first* Andrew from killing Alison and Sylvie, giving my past self an entire new set of memories that would be painfully etched onto my brain whenever I went to sleep.

"It'll be worth it," I declared with my jaw set, wanting nothing more than to remember a life with my girls.

"Unless it kills you," both Tim's spoke at the same time.

"Oh. Excuse me," Tim apologized to the future version of himself.

"No. I insist. After you!"

"Oh, but I couldn't—"

"Guys . . . please stop masturbating in front of us," I droned while covering my eyes with one hand. Doing so let me feel every healing cut and throbbing muscle. Surprisingly, the bruised bones hurt the most, like a deep pain seemingly miles below the surface of my skin.

"Not sure if that was the proper verbiage, but alright," my Tim mumbled below his breath.

"So what's going to happen when *we* go to sleep?" Andrew asked. "My memories will be passed to him . . . and his to me?"

"Yes. *Buuuuut* . . . there is a distinct probability that you will die. Both of you," future Tim said. "That is, if that sliver of vascular tissue traveling toward your brain doesn't kill you first."

"Wha-what?" I asked, lifting a hand to press against my skull. "Tim?"

"I'm *working* on it, Andrew! Don't have a stro—oh . . . poor choice of words."

"Get the nanoids ready at the lab," Andrew told his Tim.

"On it."

As the words that described the manner of my death percolated in my mind, I dropped my hand from my head and glared at my Tim.

"So *if* you are able to prevent me from having a stroke, then the memories could kill me in my sleep? You didn't convey that to me before we came here, tin can," I grumbled.

"Oops. Did I leave that part out?"

"What a shock . . ."

"I could have sworn I mentioned it."

"Even if you did, the last four days have been nothing but a blur to me."

"I can understand why," he said somewhat softly. "You've been through more than any one human should be able to withstand."

The future Andrew spoke up.

"How have you been handling his PTSD?"

"My what?"

"It hasn't been easy," Tim told Andrew. "But luckily, our boy here is amazingly resilient."

"You mean hardheaded. Stubborn. Too stupid to know when to quit," Andrew listed while tightening the straps on his gloves, which looked like leather but weren't quite right.

"Smart," I said.

"Not the word I'd use," he countered.

"No. I mean the gloves." I gestured down at his hands.

"Wasn't about to risk touching you without some form of protection."

My Tim couldn't resist. "There's a prophylactic joke in there somewhere."

"I was thinking the *same* thing!" future Tim exclaimed.

"Why are you here?" Andrew cut straight through the bullshit as he turned to stare at me with narrowed eyes.

"Why don't you go to sleep and find out," I asked before I could tell my mouth to stop.

Andrew's furrowed brow turned into a full-blown scowl at the suggestion that he risk death to know the answer.

With a long sigh in which I tried to emphasize an apology, I said, "I'm here to make sure Alison and Sylvie get to live out their full lives."

"*Annnnnd?*" Tim prompted.

"And save the universe."

Andrew looked from me to my Tim before locking eyes with me once more.

"You can't," he spoke sullenly, as if it hurt him to say it out loud.

"The hell I can't!" I exploded, throwing my hands up before dropping them to my lap with a loud slap.

"Please don't do that again," Tim requested, referencing how I jostled him with my outburst.

Closing my eyes to get my emotions in check, I could feel my brow twitching as I tried to suffocate my anger.

"If I may," Tim started, drawing our attention. "Andrew—*my* Andrew, I mean— has proven to do the impossible over and over again. He's even managed to thwart paradoxes."

"That's not possible," Andrew said.

"What did I just say?" Tim blurted with overt, feigned frustration. "He has done the *impossible* in front of me. Tim? Do you concur?"

"I'm afraid he's right, Andrew," future Tim told his Andrew. "Whether his Chronos Scale is somehow high enough to cancel a paradox or there's yet an unknown factor we hadn't considered, *this* Andrew has managed to do what no one else has ever done in the entire history of your species."

Andrew's eyes softened as he looked at me. Where there had been an almost expression of disgust, now only doubt remained.

Something the future Tim said caught my attention—*no one else.*

"Where's Sylvie and Alison?" I asked Andrew. Now, it was my turn to narrow my eyes.

Andrew looked away, unable to make eye contact as he pretended to stare out the windshield as we flew.

"Andrew."

"First, call me Drew, alright? We can't have two *Andrews* running around," Drew said, trying to change the subject.

"I'm not changing my name," Tim told future Tim.

"Well, neither am I."

"Drew . . . where is my family?"

"They're dead! Okay?!" he blurted, turning to look out his window in order to hide his face from me. It was odd to watch because I knew exactly what he was doing. But hiding his tears did nothing to soften the blow.

"But . . ." I tried to get the words out, but my brain was already exhausted from trying to piece together the cause and effect of time travel. One thing I did know, however, was that my family should have been alive.

"How are they dead, Tim?" I asked through a tight throat, lifting my arm to bring the AI hologram closer to my face. "How . . . are they *dead*?!"

"I'm . . . I'm not sure," he admitted, turning to the other floating puppy. "Tim?"

"If I had to guess, though I hate to admit it, thiiiiis might be an alternate timeline . . . ?" There was an upward inflection at the end, suggesting he really had no idea.

Slowly shifting my gaze from future Tim to Drew, I asked, "What do you remember?"

"Of what?"

"You know *what*," I harshly responded.

Drew wiped at his cheeks before turning from his window to face me.

"I killed them," he harshly whispered, trying—and failing—to hold back the tears. I felt no sympathy for the man whom I now knew was *not* my future self. Not directly, at least. Instead, he was just like all the other Andrews who had succumbed to the directions of the AI on their arms.

"And then what? Another Andrew didn't come to kill you and take your place?"

"No."

After seeing Drew wasn't offering any further explanation, my gaze shot to Tim.

"*Tiiiiim*," I let out, trying to control my building rage. "You better explain. And right the hell now."

"No need," Drew interjected. "Once it was discovered that the universe was beginning to pull in on itself, it took six more years before zeroing in on Alison's birthday as the commencement date. Two months later, a far-fetched hypothesis was formed: what if a girl was the cause of the gravitational pull?"

I sat for a moment, thinking about the words, when a negating thought came to mind.

"Why didn't it start when she was in the womb?"

"That was debated. Heavily."

"And?" I prompted with brimming frustration. It was clear to me this line of questioning would lead to Drew deciding that Alison's death was justified.

"The consensus is that Sylvie shielded the impact until Alison was born."

"Consensus? You mean lazy guess."

"Whatever you want to call it. Sure."

I rapidly blinked several times in a row as my brain raced to form the next nagging question.

"If . . . if Alison had *that* much of an impact on the *entire* universe . . . why didn't everything around her crush inward? Hmm? How is there even still an Earth if she could grab the furthest galaxies across *all* of space and pull them in?"

"If I may?" future Tim spoke up.

Both Drew and I shifted our focus to the floating AI as he brought up a hologram of what I assumed to be the Big Bang. At this point, I had seen it enough times to easily recognize it.

"Remember when I—I mean, *your* Tim, heh . . . talk about a mind freak, am I right?"

"Indeed," my Tim confirmed. "Hard to remember which memories are our own."

"Guys . . . continue," I droned, pinching the bridge of my nose.

"Right. So, uh, remember when *Tim* said that you and Sylvie were particles that were one of the few separated during the Big Bang?"

"Mm-hmm," I sighed, feeling the scientific explanation coming on as to why my daughter needed to die.

"When you and Sylvie conceived Alison, two halves of the same particle created a new form of life that *our* universe had never seen."

"What does that have to do with gravity?"

"Andrew, please," my Tim said softly. "He's getting to it."

I crossed my arms, leaving my left forearm resting on top so I could keep my Tim within my periphery.

"The theory is that Alison is a reset switch which triggers the universe to collapse in what is known as the Big Crunch, allowing another Big Bang to occur where a brand-new universe will form."

"I already know all this."

"Right. But what you *don't* know is that Alison's gravity is *reversed*."

"Reversed?" I asked in confusion. "Wouldn't that mean pushing things *away* from her?"

"No, I mean reversed as in it gets stronger the further out it goes, and weakest at the point of origin."

"Why . . . why would it be like that?"

The hologram zoomed out to show countless specs of light.

"This is the universe when Alison was born." Tim zoomed in on one of the outer edges of the cosmos. "There are—I mean, *were* galaxies flying away from the Big Bang at incredible speeds."

Understanding began to form, and I didn't like it.

"There, gravity needed to be the strongest to catch the fleeing galaxies."

The hologram showed the universe as a two-dimensional display, flat like a tabletop. On the outer edges, a thick circle formed, which began to pull in. As it shrunk toward the center, the thickness began to diminish.

"How can the force grab all the other galaxies if it gets weaker the closer it comes?" I asked, slightly uncrossing my arms as I watched.

"The gravity from the ensnared galaxies, including massive stars and black holes, would latch onto any matter they passed like a magnet."

"Why?"

"Notice how the matter of the cosmos starts to form a perfect circle, all moving at the same speed as they approach the point of origin."

"Circle?"

"Well, sphere, to be exact. But for the purposes of this explanation, I am keeping it simple," Tim clarified as the gravity continued to snag everything in existence as it raced toward the very center.

"All the matter hits the middle at the same time . . ." I whispered, just as the simulation showed precisely that.

"Correct. Effectively creating another Big Bang."

The hologram changed to a 3D representation showcasing another universe being violently born, like a phoenix from the ashes.

Refusing to believe that my little girl needed to die, I spit out the first thing that came to mind in some distorted form of confirmation bias.

"Maybe this is *supposed* to happen," I spoke flatly, just under my breath, as I watched the explosion ripple outward.

"Maybe you're right," Drew said. "But one death could save the lives of the countless who might exist throughout the rest of time. Trillions. Quadrillions even. All blessed with life because of one sacrifice."

Three sets of eyes watched as I turned to face out the window at the city disappearing below and behind the flying car.

"I don't appreciate the religious overtones," I growled. "My baby girl is not Jesus Christ."

"I didn't say she was," Drew noted. "But she could be nearly as important, if not equally so."

Even though it was my sweet, beautiful daughter who was being compared to the son of God, the comparison still made me uncomfortable.

Drew continued. "Where Jesus died for our immortal souls . . . Alison gave her life so the rest of humanity could live. Wouldn't you say that's up there in terms of importance?"

"She didn't *give* her life . . . it was *stolen* from her," I nearly screamed as I shot my face to the man. "At least Jesus went willingly! Alison didn't even have a choice!"

Drew's expression became pained as my words struck. But there was something in his eyes I couldn't decipher. A twinkle that held knowledge, trapped within a stoic brain and locked mouth.

My breaths came in heavy as I landed one final blow.

"The only thing . . . that Jesus and my baby girl have in common . . . is that their daddies *knowingly* let them die."

"You're right," Drew croaked, fighting back the tears. "But what do you think she would have said if we asked her?"

My furious brow shot up in complete surprise at such a question, but my mind betrayed me by immediately forming an answer.

Drew continued. "She was loving, generous, and most importantly, selfless."

"Stop," I mouthed, unable to form words as my throat constricted.

"What do you think she would have said if you'd asked her if she would be willing to sacrifice herself so that the entire universe, and the future of every man, woman, and child, could continue to exist?"

"S-Stop," I repeated, fighting to control the muscles in my bottom lip and brow demanding to quiver.

"I know what she would have said."

"But you didn't just kill one! Did you?! You killed Sylvie, too! You bastard!"

"I spared her the pain you and I have experienced."

The future Tim added, "It also prevented two halves of a particle from procreating again."

"He-he could have gotten a damn vasectomy or something!" I countered for the sake of argument and not in acquiescence of their point.

"We couldn't risk it," Drew sighed.

"You . . . selfish . . . *prick*!" I spat out. "You *knew* you would see the hurt in Sylvie's eyes every . . . single . . . day . . . and made sure you wouldn't have to endure that! Y-Y-You didn't do it to spare *her*! You did it to spare *you*!"

Drew's eyes went slightly unfocused as he slowly turned his head to face out the windshield.

"You might be right," he whispered like a ghost in the darkness.

"I should kill you now for what you've done," I growled like a lion as I lifted my glowing left fist toward his face. He didn't move or try to fight back, accepting of what he deserved.

"Andrew!" my Tim shouted, both in horror and surprise at my ability to fully control the Clepsydra on my own. The muscle memory had been formed, and I knew how to work the device; at least to the extent of firing the charged energy.

My fist glowed brighter as I sent the signals to my forearm to fire, all while my lips pulled back in an angry snarl.

"It was Sylvie's idea," Drew spoke without a trace of fear, and I knew he was telling the truth. Or at the very least he *thought* he was.

His words swirled around my head, yanking free thoughts and emotions before picking up speed like a deadly tornado confined within my skull.

"Fuck . . . yo—" Blackness enveloped me, like diving into the ocean at night.

CHAPTER 5

The steaks smelled savory with strong hints of garlic, which perfectly blended with the soy sauce I had used to brine the meat.

I held Alison to my right hip, allowing her to watch the flames vigorously lick as the minimal fat dripped free. My beautiful daughter sniffed at the air, taking in the intoxicating aroma of charcoal-cooked steak.

"Smells good, huh, sweetie?" I asked while giving her tummy a quick tickle.

"I still want chickie nuggies, Daddity," she replied, shaking her head and blowing a quick blast from her nose to clear the pungent smell.

"Oh, so you don't like red meat?"

"Is, um, that reb beet?" she asked, pointing a little digit toward the grill.

"Red meat," I enunciated. "And yes, it is."

"Then I don't like it."

Alison buried her nose into my neck, trying to block the smell.

"Maybe you're a, what is it called? Pollotarian?"

"What's that?"

"I think it's someone who only eats poultry."

"What's, um, pool-tree?"

"Poultry is another fancy word for birds."

"Birds?" she asked in disgust.

"Yeah. It's what chickie nuggies are made out of."

"CHICKIE NUGGIES ARE BIRDIES?!" she cried out in horror.

I wanted to ask if the *chicken* part of *chicken nuggets* didn't give it away, but then I remembered the cute name she used.

"What's going on out here?" Sylvie asked, shutting the door behind her.

"Daddity says, um, that, um, I eat birdies!"

"Is that right?" Sylvie gave me a barely perceptible glare which my keen mind picked up as the equivalent to a nuclear alarm blaring at the Pentagon.

"No, no, nooooo, sweetie. Chickie nuggies are, uh . . . juuuuust chickie nuggies!"

"You're lying," Alison declared with a straight face, making Sylvie and I burst out laughing with how mature it felt coming from such a tiny person.

"She's definitely your daughter," I said under my breath.

"What was that?" Sylvie asked, crossing her arms and tightening her lips, but in a playful manner.

"Hey! Steaks are done!" I segued, setting Alison on the ground and reaching for the tongs.

Clicking them twice, as was required of anyone who grilled, I pulled each one off, setting them on a clean tray. Three clicks were also acceptable, but any more and you were just playing with it.

"Maybe we should leave hers on a bit longer?"

"Hmm?" I asked, shifting my gaze to the smallest steak and understanding that a child might not appreciate medium rare as much as the adults. "Oh, right."

Clicking the tongs two more times, just in case, I picked up her steak again and returned it to the flames.

"I'll take these in and set the plates," Sylvie said as she grabbed the tray and went inside. "Alison, come help Mommy."

"Okay, Mommy!"

I watched with a beaming grin and a twinkle in my eyes as my whole universe ran inside.

Alison started to shut the door, but she stopped, turned to me, and shouted, "NO BIRDIES!" before slamming it.

"I don't think cows are birds," I chuckled to myself as I turned my attention to her little portion of meat, making sure there wouldn't be a spec of red.

The scene evaporated like fine grains of sand in the wind, and then I was in bed with one of our nightstand lights on.

Sylvie was on top of me, moaning in ecstasy. Leaning down to my ear, she whispered, "Happy ASA-Day," before giving my lobe a playful bite.

It was then I was punished with the knowledge that this was just a dream I was remembering, because our ASA-Day, the day when me and my two girls had shared our birthdays, had ended in tragedy.

As I fought to stay within the effects of the blissful dream and relive a life that hadn't happened for me, I could feel a throbbing behind my forehead begin to grow.

My ears and jaw began to hurt as my eyes felt like they were being pushed outward. It felt like someone was pushing a white-hot hydraulic press through the top of my skull, squishing my brains through every orifice on my head.

Through the agony, I fought to focus on Sylvie's face as she climaxed, bringing with it a sense of completion that I had brought intense pleasure to the woman I loved more than life itself.

Andrew? a voice echoed in my head from far away.

"No," I growled through my teeth, focusing on Sylvie's face as the scene began to blur.

I watched in shock as my wife began to pixelate just as she was leaning down to plant a kiss on my lips.

Andrew! Tim's voice repeated, louder and closer this time.

"NO!" I bellowed as Sylvie burst apart into dust, leaving me alone as the rest of the bedroom drifted apart like a handful of sand thrown into a fast-moving stream.

The joyful memory was ripped away from me, leaving behind a black background with pulsing red lights as the incredible pain in my head exploded, dominating everything I could see, touch, and even smell.

I pictured molten lead flowing throughout the vascular system inside my skull, charring my brain like Alison's steak on the grill.

Even through the agony, I fought to remember having a successful dinner with my wife and daughter, wanting nothing more in the entire universe than to be with them again.

ANDREW! Tim thunderously boomed, making the walls of my skull seem to vibrate, and stealing me from my dream.

CHAPTER 6

"NO!" I shouted as my eyes popped open and my limbs flailed about as if I were falling.

The boiling electricity bouncing around inside my skull forced hot bile to gurgle up my throat, causing a coughing fit from the burning and sending the bubbling liquid spilling over my bottom lip.

"He's seizing!" one of the Tim's cried out in alarm.

I wanted to say that I wasn't having a seizure—it was just that every muscle in my body was firing all at once from the pain—but I was unable to formulate words.

"Working on it!" the other Tim replied, and I could *hear* something moving inside of my skull. "The memory is etching itself on his brain, overwriting existing synapses!"

"Shock him! Cancel the memories!"

"Don't you dare!" I tried to say, but I'm pretty sure what came out was, "*Dnn eeew daaaah.*"

"Clear!" Tim called out, right as everything went fuzzy. My thoughts. My sensations, including my vision. Even my tongue seemed to vibrate as a cascade of random tastes flooded my mouth from a severely confused palate; tacos made of peanut butter and motor oil, followed by a snow cone flavored with cherry Pepto-Bismol. And the last taste was one I hadn't experienced before—something resembling burnt flesh.

My body felt numb as I stared at the glass dome of the car, which slowly came into focus.

"Uuuuhhhn," I groaned as I saw an arm sticking out above me at an odd angle.

"Damage report?" the driver inquired, confusing me as to how he had my voice.

"Working on it," Tim responded as my conscious mind slowly came back.

My vision cleared, and I realized it was *my* arm that was somehow positioned above my head.

"Whaaa . . . ?" I somewhat managed to ask as I looked around and saw I had slipped onto the floorboard of the passenger side. With arms and legs that tingled with pins and needles, I drunkenly pushed myself back into my seat.

I smacked my mouth a few times, tasting something extremely bitter. My teeth felt like I had eaten sand, and I reached my forearm up to wipe at my lips. However, the burning taste of charred flesh didn't leave my tongue.

"He suffered extreme trauma, but I think I caught it in time," Tim explained as a hologram of my body popped up above my left arm.

The image zoomed in on my head, going through my skin and skull to show the synapses of my brain. It was clear in an instant that severe damage had been done, as shown by the portions of tissue that were carved up like a Thanksgiving turkey.

"What . . . what happened?" I managed to ask, trying not to throw up from the awful taste of bile sitting at the back of my throat.

"When you went to sleep, the memories of the previous Andrew began forcing their way into your brain. Had I let you remain unconscious for even a minute more, you probably would have died."

"Why did it hurt so bad?" I asked, reaching both hands up to push on my temples in a foolhearted effort to alleviate some of the lingering pains. "I thought the brain didn't *feel*."

"*Teeeeeechnically* . . . your brain *didn't* feel anything. But, hooo-hooo," he chuckled in mild disbelief, "the swelling caused by the sudden trauma you experienced must have been excruciating. Every nerve in your head, especially the trigeminal which connects the nerve branches running from forehead to under your neck, must have been singing like Cher in that one song about believing in life after love. Heh."

"Thanks, Tim . . ."

"For saving your life, right?" Tim asked with complete seriousness.

I lowered my hands and glared at the six-inch floating Cairn Terrier as the hologram of my carved brain disappeared.

"R-Right?"

"Why does my tongue hurt?" I asked, smacking my mouth.

"Oh, um . . . it might have been slightly burned when I had to . . . heh heh, *shock* your brain."

"You can do that?" I asked weakly, rolling my tongue around. It was odd how all of my teeth, cheeks, and the roof of my mouth tasted like burnt flesh.

"You're welcome," Tim said unironically, making every muscle in my body freeze as I slowly turned my gaze toward the little bastard.

"I . . . I can't remember what happened after . . ."

Drew spoke up, breaking the tension before I could somehow telepathically crush Tim.

"Is the same thing going to happen to me?"

A part of me became instantly annoyed at how selfish the question sounded, but then I reminded myself that this was potentially the only person who had the information I sought. I needed him alive because he *was* going to help me . . . no matter what.

"I'm not entirely sure," his Tim admitted. "Perhaps I can take measures to prevent, or at the very least, mitigate any damages should the memory scarring occur."

"You two come up with a game plan," I flatly told the AIs. "Drew and I have some things to talk about."

The two hologram dogs stared at me.

"I think he wants you two to leave us," Drew clarified.

"But . . . we'll still be here," Tim pointed out.

"I don't want to see you right now," I elaborated sternly.

"Oh. Well . . . I know when I'm not wanted," Tim said before turning to the other AI. "Let us go, Timothy. It's clear our company is no longer valued."

"Why am *I* Timothy?" Drew's AI asked. "Why can't *you* be Timothy?"

"You're Timothy," I aggressively told the other AI before turning to the future Andrew. "And you're Drew. There. No more confusion."

"I— . . ." the other AI began, placing a paw over his heart at the perceived disrespect.

"Timothy . . ." Drew cut him off, backing me up on the decision to separate our names for the sake of sparing us confusion. "Give us a few. Yeah?"

"Fine . . . *Drew*," Timothy replied before blinking from view.

"I'm here if you need me," Tim told me, and I knew a large portion of the platitude was because he had won the name game.

"Go."

Tim blipped out, leaving Drew and I alone in the car as we flew farther from the city.

"Where are we going?" I asked, rubbing at my cheekbones where a slight throbbing remained.

"Retnuh knows I'm involved now. So the first thing we have to do is position ourselves the farthest away from a teleport station, lose the car they are no doubt attempting to track, and double back to the only safe place in one of the neglected sectors of the city."

"Why not hide out in the woods?" I asked, thinking about where I would have hidden a safehouse.

"There are no woods left."

I looked out my window toward the ground, amazed and disgusted at how large the metropolis was. It seemed to stretch on forever, racing from horizon to horizon.

Shifting my gaze behind us, I saw the impossibly tall skyscrapers. Following a random direction, I noted how the farther out from the center, the poorer the buildings seemingly became. There were no glass castles piercing the clouds with ads for RC Cola running along them in a seamless dance. Instead, digital billboards remained, at least in the apparent middle-class portion.

A large stone wall appeared, splitting the middle- and lower-class sectors like the border between First and Third World countries.

"Welcome . . . to the Forgotten."

The car began descending as we crossed the threshold into the land that those above the poverty line intentionally ignored.

A line of text scrolled across the dashboard which read "Warning: You Are Entering a Restricted Zone. You Are Advised to Immediately Turn Around. Your Safety Is Not Guaranteed."

It was funny how safe a *restricted* zone could feel when the government was warning you against going there. All it really said was there would be no men in uniforms and guns telling you what you could and couldn't do.

For the first time since I arrived, grass could be seen, but this greenery was trying to reclaim unkempt buildings stretching no higher than two stories. Once paved roadways had been crumbled so far beyond recognition that they could now be classified as nothing more than loose gravel.

People wandered the streets, with some appearing like zombies with how they moved.

"Neuronova," Drew said as he glanced out his window at the aimlessly walking people below. "It allows people to relive their past memories."

I looked at him then back down at those who fled from reality in whatever way they could.

Turning off the autopilot, Drew oriented on a demolished building that had been mostly swallowed by determined grass, and carefully hovered down to land in the center.

"It won't be long until they crack the shroud I installed and track my car to this location."

"Didn't you say they have teleport stations?" I asked as the vehicle turned off and we both got out. "Is that, like, the equivalent of public transport?"

"Yes and no," Drew replied as we carefully moved down the caved-in roof. "Yes because it replaced archaic modes of transportation such as airplanes. No because only the rich can use them. They didn't put a single one in the Forgotten."

"No more TSA?" I asked, daring to daydream of a perfect utopia without the blue-shirted agents.

Drew ignored my comment as we made our way to the street.

There were no power lines running to the buildings, yet lights were on within most windows I could see.

"How is there power? Do the lines run underground?"

"They used to." We swiftly moved back toward the wall separating the lower and middle class. "Now, each home runs on hand-me-down solar panels."

"Did they finally find a way to make solar panels one hundred percent effective? In my time, I think they barely reached twenty or so."

"They did, but that's not what the wealthy use."

"Oh?"

"Pure fusion. Limitless power. And they horde it all for themselves while throwing the previous technology down the drains for these people to use."

"You know," I said, thinking about how bleak the future seemed. "You aren't making a very good case on why the universe should be allowed to continue."

"That's not funny," Drew shot back, stopping in his tracks and turning to face me. "There's still plenty of good to be had."

A dangerously thin man huddled on the ground nearby noticed us and lifted a hand while moaning. His eyes were unfocused as his mouth hung open.

"I'm not seeing any *good*," I replied darkly.

Drew stopped, lowered his head, and shook it slowly from side to side.

"We see . . . only what we want to see."

"*Want* to see?" I barked, gesturing toward the zombie on the ground. "I don't *want* to see this! *You* showed it to me!"

"Come on," Drew sighed. "They'll be on our trail soon."

I was ready for a fight, wanted to call this future version of me out on what the *true* cost was of killing my baby girl, but the threat of Retnuh and the Clockmen kept my tongue still.

We moved through the sector, keeping under awnings and any bit of cover we could find. I wanted to ask why, but I instinctively knew it probably had something to do with advanced satellites that could zoom in on the pores dotting the tip of my nose.

A group of men in hard hats walked by, coated in filth as they carried their metal lunch boxes.

"What do people do for work here?" I asked, making conversation as we walked. "I doubt coal mining is still a thing."

"Close. Dirt miners."

"Dirt . . . miners?"

Doing a double take, I noticed the filth on the workers was actually dirt.

"With the increased lifespan came more and more births, along with fewer deaths. Humans used up all the nutrients in the topsoil. That's when they decided to expand the cities outward, swallowing the dried-up farmlands in the process."

"Why not up?"

"Only the richest of the rich live in skyscrapers, and they weren't about to share the views out their windows with those beneath them. Nor did they want to even *look* at them. So they padded the pockets of those in charge, and expanded outward instead of up."

I wanted to point out that he was *still* not helping to make his case, but there was no point at the moment. He knew how I felt.

"So people dig for dirt?"

"They find patches of nutrient-rich soil which could have been buried long ago by earthquakes or landslides and haul it to commercial farms to feed those who can afford *real* food. There are also large swathes of dirt that hold ample nitrogen and phosphorus from decades of fertilizers and manure carried by groundwater. It's dangerous work, with cave-ins happening almost monthly."

"If only the wealthy can afford the crops grown by these . . . these commercial farms . . . what do the poor eat?"

Drew stopped, looked at the grass poking up through the gravel, and suddenly dropped to one knee while clapping his cupped hands.

I arched an eyebrow as he stood up, turned to me, and slowly opened his hand.

A cricket looked up at me as if to say, "Surprise!" then hopped away.

"They . . . they eat them off the ground?"

"No. Don't be stupid." Drew turned and continued walking toward the wall. "They are grown in farms . . . farms bigger than the city of Houston was . . . and turned into dense bars handed out by the government."

"And people eat that?!"

"If you are hungry enough . . . you'll eat anything."

I thought about the workers who carried lunch boxes.

"Everyone eats that?"

"No. Not everyone. Some dirt miners grow their own crops below the surface, selling or giving it to those in need."

"Drew . . ."

"I know what you are going to say, and you haven't seen the good yet. Just be aware that I am giving you the full truth."

I shook my head as we neared the wall. It stretched considerably higher than I had thought when looking at it from above. It felt every bit as tall as the Statue of Liberty, which felt completely appropriate for this scenario.

A flying car with flashing red-and-blue lights zipped overhead, followed by another. Soon, a small parade of speeding vehicles were flying past.

Drew stopped, looked up, and said, "They found us."

CHAPTER 7

We picked up the pace, making sure to keep under cover as we moved along the wall toward a section of city that appeared to be uninhabited.

"What do you mean they found us?" I whispered as if the speeding cars overhead could hear us.

"My car," Drew explained. "It won't take long for them to track our direction."

"So what do we do?"

Drew ignored my question as we came to a blockade with a hand-painted sign which read "Mine Unstable. Turn Back Now."

"Um . . . shouldn't we . . . ?" I asked, pointing at the sign. Then I registered whose handwriting it was. "Oh."

Just outside, the ground was dried and cracked, looking like a sun-baked lake bed in a severe drought, crunching underfoot. But once we moved past the entrance of the tunnel, the air grew instantly cooler as the scent of dirt and old sweat filled my nostrils. Our sharp footfalls were replaced with dull thuds as the earth seemed to regain moisture.

The hairs on the back of my neck and right arm prickled, and I subconsciously rubbed my left forearm, wondering why it didn't share in the sensation. When my fingers glided across the smooth metal of the Clepsydra, I shuddered once, and let my hand fall away.

I couldn't help but think about how the device had burrowed its way through my skin and up my entire body, especially my brain.

Everything alright, Andrew? Tim asked inside my head.

"Fi—" I started to say before focusing on mentally communicating. *I'm fine.*

"You say something?" Drew asked, glancing over his shoulder as he continued deeper into the darkness.

"No."

I was about to ask if he had brought a flashlight when everything in my vision brightened, like changing the settings on a cell phone.

"Where is the light coming from?" I asked aloud.

"Oh, that's me," Tim replied. "I'm . . . *aiding* your ability to register light."

"Aiding?"

"Well, you don't like it when I say things like 'I'm accessing your occipital lobe while enhancing your photoreceptors and controlling your irises so that the lenses of your eyes can function beyond maximum efficiency.'"

As he spoke, my thoughts filled in the images of little wires running throughout my eyeballs.

"You're right . . . I don't like you telling me that."

"See? That's why I said *aiding*."

Drew spoke up without taking his eyes off the path in front of him.

"You'll get used to it."

Ignoring his almost eerie acceptance of the AI that was *literally* infused with his entire body, I asked, "Where are we going?"

I didn't care what his answer was, as long as we were going away from the Clockmen. Instead, I only wanted to change the subject from a topic that made me feel like my body was doing an imitation of Swiss cheese. Swiss cheese with countless wires running through it.

"Somewhere safe," Drew replied as we continued down the circular corridor of dirt.

I let my enhanced eyes wander, not having much else to do, and noticed the evenly spaced supports, with most having been recently repaired or replaced entirely. But they weren't wood.

"What is this?" I asked as we walked by a smooth gray support and knocked on it with my knuckles. I noticed a small box, the size of a pack of cards, affixed at the very top center with a small red light on it.

"Resin."

"Resin?" I asked, looking at the structure that wrapped around the tunnel in much the same way as old coal mines had wooden supports. "These are 3D printed?"

"We don't say *3D* anymore. It's just *printed*. Like most things are, now."

"It's cheaper than wood, then?"

"Heh. You aren't wrong there," Drew chuckled while shaking his head. "There isn't any wood left. At least not past the wall."

"Why not?" I asked before my mind filled in a small part of the movie *Blade Runner 2049* in which the protagonist found a small wooden horse and was offered a *real* horse or off-world papers as payment for the priceless item.

"You're thinking of *Blade Runner*, aren't you," Drew asked without the inflection at the end of the sentence. He already knew.

"The entire world is paved over with asphalt?" It wasn't a question seeking a direct answer, more a subtle understanding that humans had used up all the natural resources in our insatiable greed.

"We could never get enough. And didn't care about the future."

"Sounds about right."

"I would say you don't know the half of it"—Drew stopped and turned to face me—"but, if I have my timeline correct, you come from an era *before* widespread nuclear energy. Everyone fought over, quote, unquote, "renewable" energy or burning fossil fuels, while no one on either side even considered fission."

"Heh. Nuke-u-lar is scary," I mocked, intentionally mispronouncing the word to showcase the ignorance of mankind to make decisions based on nothing more than emotion, despite the overwhelming scientific evidence.

"Don't get preachy and holier-than-thou, Andrew. You drove your gas car. Bought your plastics, all of which were made from oil. And cranked the AC. All while saying to yourself that it wasn't *your* fault the world hadn't come up with something better yet."

"Hey. I couldn't *afford* an electric car."

"First, that's a lie. But it doesn't even matter, because harvesting the lithium batteries for those things was just as bad as burning gasoline. Plus, the disposal was a nightmare. It wasn't until fusion was achieved that everyday life was run on nuclear power."

"Wait. Fusion? Or fission?"

"Fission came later. So everything at the dawn of the nuclear era was powered, initially, by fusion."

"Heh. Even cell phones?"

"*Everything*, Andrew."

"No more charging cables?" I whispered to myself, thinking about all the items that relied on lithium batteries.

"Right." Drew continued, turning to resume our way down the dirt corridor, which was slowly being replaced by thick rocks and a resin mesh that wrapped around the walls to keep everything in place. Soon, the entire tunnel was nothing but large boulders that had been cut through. I was going to ask about them, but I understood they had probably come across the thick layer of rock and decided to cut through rather than try and dig a new tunnel in a different spot.

The deeper we went, the more I noted the same small boxes on the support structures. I wanted to ask what they were, but just assumed they were some sort of sensors to warn of cave-ins or something of the like, especially with the layer of rock held in place by the resin mesh.

Instead, I kept the interesting conversation of energy going.

"Soooo . . . humans consumed all the natural resources, forcing us to switch to nuclear. But by then, the damage had been done."

Drew didn't respond, indicating I was right.

"If there are no more trees . . . how do we breathe?"

"Most of the oxygen on the planet is made in the oceans. And once we realized the air was becoming toxic, a handful of scientists did what the world's governments couldn't—they found a solution rather than just preach from their crosses made of diamonds. But even with the ocean cleanup programs, artificial reefs, and genetically altered plankton—which reproduced fifteen percent faster and were less susceptible to temperature differences— we still had to create giant machines that cleaned the air for us."

"Like the cloud machine?" I asked, remembering a video online which showed a metal structure siphoning water from a river and billowing out white clouds that raced toward the sky.

Though the conversation had nothing to do with the plan, it was still a long walk down the tunnels, and the topic was interesting to me. Better than walking in silence.

"Sort of. But the point is we didn't stop to think *maybe we've gone far enough.* Instead, humans did what humans always do—they used a Band-Aid to fix a broken arm."

My Tim spoke up audibly while his hologram remained off.

"Perhaps you should tell Andrew about the *good* things that have happened?"

I could hear in his voice that he was all but pleading with Drew to convince me of the reasons the universe should be permitted to continue, but my mind was already made up. Nothing was worth killing my family for.

The thought of Alison and Sylvie turned my heart to stone as my face fell into a frown—the corners of my lips and the space between my eyebrows pulled down by the gravity of the wrath that had become ingrained in my soul.

"I don't need to tell him," Drew said as we approached a resin wall with a door which looked like it was intended for a bank vault or panic room. "I'll show him."

Drew waved his Clepsydra over a reader, and a series of heavy mechanized locks clicked on the other side just before the door popped open with a hiss, reminding me of opening a bottle of soda.

My guide stepped through first. Not having to tell me to follow, I crossed the threshold of the thick resin wall.

"Whoa." I held up my hands at chest height as two turrets each locked a set of gun barrels on me. Blue light glowed at the base of each of the barrels, looking like two sets of ethereal eyes from the unmanned sentries.

"Tim," Drew said to his AI. "I mean, Timothy."

"Already working on giving Andrew the necessary clearance, *Drew*," Timothy replied with a hefty helping of snark. It was clear he was still butthurt at having to change his name and wasn't shy about letting his handler know it.

"Glad to see not much has changed in all the time you've had your Clepsydra," I said just under my breath.

"We stay together for the kids," Drew answered flatly, but with an undertone of sarcasm that I picked up on. It was odd seeing my own mannerisms being used before my eyes.

The sentry guns with their twin barrels let the blue fade away as they snapped their attention back toward the door instead of my center mass. I also took note that a faint blue glow remained around them, appearing like some sort of energy shield.

"Done and done," Timothy stated.

"Good. Lock the door behind us," Drew instructed as he carried on into a short corridor.

"A *please* would be nice," Timothy muttered just as the door shut behind us and the locks engaged.

Drew ignored him as we walked toward a doorway that led to a massive opening. The entire area looked like the inside of an egg made of resin and standing as tall as a building. Even the coloring was a gentle off-white that evenly bounced and diffused the lighting.

"Welcome to Empyrean," Drew said, crossing his arms and slightly leaning back like a father watching his son opening presents on Christmas morning.

I walked to a railing and peered down, gawking at an underground civilization stretching deep into the Earth.

The dirt floor had been replaced with resin as well, though a darker wooden color, like maple, and I was surprised to see the artificial floor was clean. Anyone who had any patches of grassless land around their home knew of the constant battle to keep the dirt out.

Around the perimeter of the egg-shaped area was a slowly descending ramp, reminding me of a spiral staircase for some reason. Archways with doors at the center were evenly spaced around, appearing like an apartment complex or hotel.

"How many people are there?" I asked in awe as my eyes continued to follow the spiraling ramp.

"In this one? Around nine hundred or so."

"Nine hundred and seventy-one," Timothy spoke up. "Or should I say seventy-two?"

I turned to face Drew, who stared at me with a subdued expression, wondering what I would say to the subtle invitation.

"I won't be staying long," I replied dismissively, turning back to look down at the city. It wasn't that I was trying to avoid the invitation; rather, I was negating the suggestion that I give up on my mission to save Alison and Sylvie.

"Andrew . . . I really think—" Drew started to say, but he slammed his mouth shut as a familiar ethereal electricity burned every cell in my body, and I dropped to the hard resin floor, right before everything went black.

CHAPTER 8

I sat in one of several rows of chairs as something gripped my hand. Looking down, my fingers were interlaced with someone with freshly manicured nails.

Following the arm, I saw the breathtaking face of my beautiful wife as she stared up at the stage. There was only the hint of barely visible wrinkles beginning to form—*smile lines* I believe they are called.

"Please welcome our valedictorian, Alison Frost, to the stage."

As the audience began to applaud, excited eyes were pulled from my beaming Sylvie and landed on a young woman walking on stage whom I knew immediately was my sweet baby girl.

Unable to help myself, I shot to my feet and clapped my hands like a machine gun—all while the gigantic smile I wore nearly hurt my face.

The edges of my vision wavered as a searing pain danced across my scalp, but I fought to keep the dream in focus so I could watch my baby graduate. With a sheer focus of will, the scene steadied, and I was able to recall the last portion of Alison Frost's valedictorian speech.

". . . and that's why I say to you, the class of 2035, to go out into the world and chase after what you desire most. Make the necessary sacrifices. Take the road less traveled. And in the end, reach for the stars. Because you never know . . . your grasp might exceed what your eyes can see."

The audience stood up with energetic applause as Alison moved the tassel to the graduated side of her cap, smiled like only a teenager could, and launched her cap into the sky. An explosion of soaring graduation caps blotted the stage for a moment as the class of 2035 all yelled out in victory.

From the corner of my vision, I could see Sylvie wiping a tear from her eye from how proud she was of our daughter.

"Woohoo!" I called out, pumping a fist into the air as Alison took a bow on stage and then dove into the audience.

Sylvie and I gasped, but our fears were quickly squelched as Ali was hoisted up by her classmates and crowd surfed.

"She gets that from you, you know," Sylvie said, once again clapping as she gave me a playful side-eye.

"I took her to *one* metal concert," I said, just before Sylvie and I burst out into laughter.

"I'm pregnant," Alison told us as we all sat around the kitchen table of our beach condo. Sylvie and I had sold the house in Houston and moved to Boca Raton, Florida, to be close to where Ali was getting her double PhD in biomedical science *and* neuroscience at Florida Atlantic University.

I glanced at her college boyfriend, nearly igniting him in furious flames with just my eyes. How *dare* he defile my baby girl *and* not use protection.

"What are you going to do?" Sylvie asked, grabbing both of Alison's hands between her own.

"What do you mean what is she going to do?" I interjected in the way only a dad could. "She's going to finish her last year of college and graduate as the first doctor in the Frost family!"

Alison looked down as her boyfriend, Samuel, remained stoic. Which, if I were being honest, was impressive, considering I was a dad who'd just been told his daughter's future might be jeopardized because of their lack of forethought.

"What do you *want* to do?" Sylvie asked, suffocating my dad-rage with her mom-love.

"I . . . I don't know," Ali said before breaking down into tears.

Samuel moved a hand to rub at his college sweetheart's back while keeping a steady chin.

We all sat there like that for a while before Sylvie turned to me and conveyed an entire message with her stern eyes. Because I was a smart man, I did exactly what my wife wanted. It was only a minor point that, in the end, I actually agreed with her.

"We'll watch the baby while you finish school. If that's what you want," I spoke as softly as I could, grinding down my rough tone as the anger subsided. "Both of you."

Samuel looked taken aback at my suggestion—probably expecting me to demand that he drop out of med school to raise his child. But I wasn't petty or vindictive . . . *most* of the time. Plus, I knew that if they brought a child into the world, it would fare considerably better with *two* doctor parents.

"We would love to," Sylvie added, patting Ali's hands.

"Yeah. It's been pretty lonely without you, kiddo," I agreed.

Alison lifted her face, wiped her eyes on her sleeve without taking her hands from her mother's, and looked at Samuel. Just as Sylvie and I had done, they exchanged an entire conversation with just a glance.

Samuel nodded, and Alison seemed to inflate with hope and love.

"You mean it?" she asked, fighting back the tears.

"Of course we do, sweetheart," I said, feeling my heart flutter with the gift of hope I had just given my baby girl—who was going to have her own baby now.

Sylvie and Alison embraced, and both began crying as I looked at Samuel and gave a single nod of approval. He returned it, and I could see the words *thank you* in his eyes.

Alison stood up, moved to me, and wrapped her arms around my neck hard enough that I questioned if she should have been a chiropractor instead.

"Thank you, Daddity," she whispered so that only I could hear.

Even in my dream, I could smell her wonderful scent—a scent which only a parent could understand—and feel her warmth.

Letting go of me, she rushed to Samuel, and I felt a sort of pride at watching them embrace.

"We're going to be a family," she cried out in both relief and unbridled joy.

Sylvie and I looked at one another, grabbed each other's hand, and squeezed.

The scene began to waver, and I fought with all my might to keep the memory alive. But now that the important, life-changing portion was over, the lesser details began to fade, as all dreams do.

CHAPTER 9

"Andrew?" Tim asked from somewhere far away, as if loudly whispering inside of a deep cavern.

"Wha . . . ?" I droned as the feeling returned to my body, which I instantly regretted. I showcased this by sucking in an entire lungful of air through my teeth in a mere second. "SSSSS!"

With the intense pain, the wonderful dream I had lived evaporated like a light fog under the midday's sun. But it wasn't just my body which hurt from the ethereal lightning—my head was also beginning to feel like an overworked blacksmith's anvil.

I opened my eyes and saw a sterile light above, beckoning me like the proverbial tunnel to the afterlife. But I knew I wasn't dead because my entire body felt . . . crispy.

"We're back online," I think my Tim said.

"What was that?" I croaked, feeling how dry my throat was.

"Another dream searing brought on from unconsciousness due to aggressive Temporal Sickness," Tim explained. "You *are* in Drew's wheren."

"I . . . I thought it started off slow and built up."

"If you remember, I explained that it would take years to fully recover from how long you were exposed to the universe trying to erase you."

Timothy spoke up.

"Well, *years* in your rightful wheren. But here, we can mitigate much of the sickness by using our current technology."

The blinding light began to dull as my eyes adjusted, and I looked around to see Drew looking down at me with someone in a white lab coat on the other side of where I lay.

I lifted a hand to rest on my head and felt something tug at my forearm.

"Caaaareful, Andrew," Tim said. "They aren't finished injecting you with the nanoids."

"Nan . . . oids?" I drawled before the words clicked, and I shot up to a seated position, reaching for the tube sticking out of my right arm.

Drew grabbed my left wrist with his gloved hand, once again surprising me with his strength. Or maybe I was just really weak from having the universe zap the shit out of me.

"They'll help," Drew told me sternly.

"He's right, Andrew," Tim said. "Drew, if you would be so kind as to remove your grip from me?"

Drew looked at me for a moment with narrowed eyes, then reluctantly let go of where he held my Clepsydra in his hand.

A hologram of a slightly rectangular robot sprang to life above my arm, and Tim explained.

"The nanoids—or nanobots, as you might better recognize them—have the ability to cancel the Temporal Sickness . . . mostly."

"Mostly?"

"Well, it's hard to see to *every* cell in your entire body. Your mass would increase dramatically if we put a one-to-one ratio of nanoids to cells. And without proper augmentation, such as switching out flesh limbs with cybernetics or, at the very least, replacing your bones which would act as housing for the nanoids, we can't put enough inside of you to mitigate *all* of the Temporal Sickness."

"You'd have to replace my . . . my *bones*?"

"At the very least, yes."

The hologram displayed what I assumed to be a nanoid above a red disc.

"The nanoid is slightly smaller than a red blood cell, roughly eighty micrometers in size, allowing them to traverse anywhere in the body that your blood can."

"Get to the point, please. I can't handle the full-blown science explanation right now."

"Very well." The hologram zoomed in on the nanoid. "These machines are powered by exotic matter—"

"Just like the gun Retnuh had . . ." I cut in, remembering how powerful of a weapon it had been. Tim had made me intervene before Retnuh could shoot the killer because, had it hit, it would have killed *both* that Andrew . . . and me.

"Yes. *And* your Clepsydra. *But!* Where the ammunition from the nanite gun had the sole purpose of destroying all matter along a linear existence, *these* nanomachines will help protect you *from* the timeline. In a simple manner of speaking, I mean."

"So the nanoids, Clepsydra, *and* nanite gun . . . all use the same fuel source?"

"Not *precisely*. Just as a nuclear reactor is different than, say, Little Boy or Fat Man, which were dropped on Hiroshima and Nagasaki."

"But a reactor can explode. Like in Chernobyl."

The hologram of the microscopic robot was replaced with floating formulas with all sorts of symbols I had never seen before.

"I can further elaborate, if you wish."

"Later," I dismissed, pivoting and pushing my legs off the side of the bed. I simply didn't have the mental fortitude to listen to one of his overly detailed scientific explanations.

Drew carefully watched as I moved, making sure I let the infusion of nanoids finish.

"Who's this?" I asked, thumbing over my shoulder to the silent doctor.

"Folks 'round here call me Zephyr," the man in his late forties proudly said as he jammed a thumb into his chest. He had on well-worn blue jeans and a black T-shirt with a silhouette logo of what appeared to be the face of a bearded man arching an eyebrow and a beanie on top.

I mirrored the logo with my own arched eyebrow at seeing a doctor with deteriorating clothing underneath a mostly pristine white lab coat.

"He's not the doctor," Drew informed, leaning forward as if reading my thoughts.

"Nope. But I did *earn* the nickname of *Doc*, seeing as how I'm a wiz at all things computers."

"No one calls you Doc," Drew said, lifting a hand to rub at his eyes.

"Well, they should."

"Where'd you even get that coat?"

"Was just sittin' on the hook by the door."

"And you didn't think to leave it?"

"Figured if I was gonna be workin' in the examine room, I's supposed to be wearin' one?"

"Examination room," a female voice clarified. "Now, please, give me back my coat. I don't want it smelling of onions."

"Sure thing, Bubbles," Zephyr said with slight embarrassment at his misstep as he took the coat off and handed it to the somewhat full-figured woman.

"It's Doctor Hanifin when I'm on duty, *Jonathan*," the doc said, putting strong emphasis on Zephyr's apparent real name.

"And it's *Zephyr* at *all* times, *Doctor Hanifin*," he shot back, crossing his arms.

"There's so much emphasis being thrown around," I moaned, lifting my own hand to rub at my eyes, just as Drew had done a moment before.

"Where are we at on the transfusion, Zephyr," Drew asked.

"'Bout three more minutes, Andy."

"Andy?" I asked, arching an eyebrow once more.

"He knows I hate that," Drew responded flatly.

"Why don't you just ask him to call you D-Frost?" I asked with a shit-eating grin at suggesting my high school nickname.

"D-Frost! That's brilliant!" Zephyr cried out victoriously.

"And here I thought self-loathing was supposed to be a bad thing," Drew grumbled under his breath.

I let out a single chuckle as I felt the lingering effects of the Temporal Sickness and dream searing begin to fade.

With a sigh of relief mixed with borderline exhaustion, I lifted my left arm. "Why couldn't you do all this, Tim?"

"Well, uh . . . as awesome as I am . . . *admittedly*, I am unable to influence your cells *directly*."

"But you were able to filter my blood, repair my body—"

"Several times," Tim interrupted, making sure I focused on his successes.

"Repaired my body *several times*, and was able to alter my mood. But the great and powerful *Tim* needs the help of tiny computers because we found something he can't do."

"I can make your genitalia fall off," he muttered.

"You—" I started, but Timothy spoke up.

"I believe what *Tim* meant to say was that the volume of nanoids needed to mitigate the Temporal Sickness is more than the mass of a Clepsydra. Hence, we cannot carry them with us, except for just a handful. But those are mainly used for maintenance on our integrated housing."

I digested Timothy's words and looked down at the line running into my arm. My eyes followed it up to three large silver bags that looked like what hospitals used for saline drips. Two of them were fully depleted, with the last one nearing the finish line.

As I looked at them, it was evident that just one of the bags was the same size of my Clepsydra, not to mention how the center of the device was hollow to allow room for my arm.

"So, are you able to work with the nanobots now?"

"*Nanoids*, Andrew. And yes. I will be able to control them as if they were an extension of the Clepsydra."

"More like add-ons instead of an extension," Zephyr clarified. "*Annnnnd* we are done!*"

Zephyr moved to pull my IV out when Doctor Hanifin grabbed his wrist.

"Ladies first," the IT guy said with a half smirk, taking a step back with his hands held up in surrender.

I continued to look at the three deflated bags as the doctor removed the needle.

"How is that much . . . *stuff* inside my veins? Wouldn't my blood be jelly or something?"

"Very perceptive, Andrew." Tim pulled up a hologram and zoomed in on my arm. "It is true that if the total volume of nanoids were localized in your vascular system, then problems would most assuredly arise."

The hologram placed several tiny robots inside my veins that appeared to jiggle around. I felt like I was watching a children's show with the gesture. Some of the machines sauntered sideways into my muscles and bones, while a few remained inside my blood.

"The nanoids are able to fit anywhere in your body where a red blood cell can. *More* places, actually, because they are twenty percent smaller. But the point is they are able to spread themselves over your entire body in an effort to combat the Temporal Sickness whenever it strikes. And you might not know this, but your body is *made up* of cells. Neat, huh?"

"Cut the sarcasm." I rolled my eyes and dropped my left arm, maneuvering it so the back of my hand was on my lap, forcing the hologram to disappear.

"Rude."

"I think what the floatin' dog is tryin' to say," Zephyr spoke up since this was his area of expertise, "is that the nanoids need to spread 'round your body as much as possible. They won't be able to affect *every* cell. Not even close. But somethin' is better than nothin'. Right, Bubbles?"

"If you call me Bubbles while I'm on duty again, I'll stop prescribing you those special pills for your, ahem, *little* problem."

All eyes turned to a red-cheeked Zephyr, who looked like he had just trusted a fart to be silent, in the middle of a prayer, in a packed church—only to have the wooden pews amplify the sound to a degree where a shotgun blast would have been quieter.

"Boy, would ya look at the time?" Zephyr said with an all-of-a-sudden dry throat. "I gotta go, uh, attend to some stuff . . . in my office . . . which is away from here."

"Have a nice day, *Jonathan*," Doctor Hanifin singsonged with a beaming smile.

As Zephyr scuttled out of the doctor's office, Drew looked over at Hanifin and said, "Went a bit far, wouldn't you say? Boy's face looked like he just let one rip in church."

I barked out in a fit of laughter and surprise at hearing Drew verbally say the same imagery I had mentally used.

"What's so funny?" Hanifin asked, looking back and forth between me and Drew for clarity.

"Great minds think alike," was all I could say as I wiped a tear from my eye.

"Hmph." Drew turned to Hanifin. "Is he good to go?"

"Yes," both the doctor and Tim answered at the same time.

"Wasn't asking you, Tim."

"And yet I answered anyway. How about that?" Tim snarked back. I could almost hear his little puppy arms crossing over his chest.

Ignoring the quip, Drew said, "Come on. I want to take you to the garden."

CHAPTER 10

I followed Drew out of the doctor's office, which was located directly in the middle of the spiraling walkway of the underground, egg-shaped city.

"You carried me?" I asked in surprise, moving to the railing and looking up toward the ceiling. From that angle, it felt like standing in the middle of a tall building or hotel with an empty center from top to bottom—almost dizzying to stare up at.

"Yes," Drew answered as he started walking down the spiral pathway. I followed close behind, our boots clicking off the pristinely clean resin floors which looked like maple.

"You must be really strong, then," I said, looking back up and guessing he had carried me roughly twenty-five or thirty floors.

You'll have his strength, soon, Tim spoke inside my head.

How's that? I mentally asked.

The nanoids have more than one function. There was a smile in his voice that I could hear, and I shrugged it off for the time being.

We approached a silver puddle moving down the ramp.

I looked at Drew, wondering if he was going to stop or clean up the spill, when the silver puddle parted ways just before his feet landed.

I hesitantly followed in his footsteps, looking down at the rippling mass with a wary expression creasing my forehead.

Nanoids, Tim explained, once again inside my head.

What are they doing on the ground?

As I moved past the slowly moving puddle, I got my answer. Various shoe prints dotted the ramp in the direction the nanoids were heading.

"Roombas?" I asked out loud.

Drew ignored me, content to let Tim answer.

I told you, the nanoids have more than one function.

What all can they do?

Basically, whatever you want. Clean. Repair. Build. Demolish, Tim listed mentally.

"They made this place, didn't they?" I asked out loud, reaching up a hand to glide along the smooth resin railing.

"Over the course of several years. Yes," Tim said aloud as well. "Well, I say years, but that is only because we continuously add on by digging deeper whenever new residents are brought in."

"Refugees," Drew corrected.

"Y-Yes. Refugees, fleeing the corrupt world's governments. But, back to what I was getting at, the initial construction only took a few weeks."

"A few weeks? For all of this?" I was in awe as I let my eyes roam from the top of the underground city to the bottom.

"There were fewer of us back then," Drew explained. "We only needed a few rooms to get by."

"Ah. And you've been adding on when needed."

"Right."

My fingers continued to glide across the smooth railing, and I shifted my gaze to the solid walls and walkway.

"How did the bots get all the resin?"

"Great question!" Tim said as the hologram came to life over my left forearm.

"I don't need visuals. Just tell me." I didn't want to walk while holding my arm up right then.

"Fine," Tim sighed with defeat and slight frustration in his voice. It reminded me of an office employee who had spent hours creating a PowerPoint presentation, only to have the higher-ups change the in-person meeting to a conference call at the last minute. "The nanoids—" Tim began, but Drew cut him off.

"They got the raw materials from the rocks and junk they found while digging. Then made the resin." He looked over his shoulder at me and added, "There. Just saved you a ten-minute explanation."

"Well, *excuuuuuse* me for wanting to be precise! 01, you meat bags do *not* appreciate the science of things. Do you have any idea how hard it was to program the nanoids to build this? Hmm? Do you?"

Drew continued to look over his shoulder, gave a wry smile, and said, "Do you have any idea how hard it was to program *you*?"

"I . . ." Tim faltered as quickly as his rebuttal had begun.

"That's what I thought." Drew turned his face back down the path.

"I'll never understand how a Neanderthal like you was able to create the most perfect being," Tim grumbled, but it wasn't as under-his-breath as he had apparently hoped.

Drew stopped, reached into his pocket, pulled something out that I couldn't see from behind, and said in a subdued tone, "I had help."

Then, without another word or explanation, he replaced whatever had been pulled free and continued down the path.

What was that? I mentally asked Tim.

No idea. But it sure sounded cryptic, huh?

No, I mean what did he pull out of his pocket?

Once again, no clue.

I didn't ask Drew about what was held or said, content to resume our descent deeper into the Earth. I knew when *I* didn't want to talk about something. It was funny how easy it was to recognize my body language and mannerisms from an outside perspective.

To my surprise, the air didn't grow cooler or change very much from the top. Or maybe I was just latching onto the first thing that caught my seeking attention.

"AC systems must have come a long way?" I asked, wanting to get a lighter topic of conversation going.

No one answered.

Instead, I looked around in search of vents, now legitimately interested as to how the air was circulated and conditioned in the underground city. However, my curiosity only extended to looking rather than asking again.

Eventually, we came to a larger-than-normal door, which opened as we approached, presumably by Timothy's doing.

The first thing that caught my attention was the ample lighting hovering over row after row of various crops. The air was densely humid and warm, and smelled of a light evening rain in the middle of summer just before the sun disappeared over the horizon.

A man of average height and build, wearing dirty blue overalls that looked like they used to belong to an engineer or mechanic, looked up from the crop he was tending.

I followed Drew as we approached, and the man stood up, clapping his hands to rid them of the thick, excess dirt.

"I think I'm seeing double," the man said as he extended a hand out to Drew, who shook it without hesitation.

He moved his hand toward me, and I looked down at his filthy skin, not wanting to get dirty.

Something clicked, and I got over myself in the blink of an eye, grabbing the man's hand.

"Andrew Frost. Nice to meet you."

"Charlie Walters," the farmer introduced himself. "But folks around here call me CJ."

I wanted to ask how his initials translated to CJ, but dismissed the notion by assuming it was just a nickname.

He had a thin, straight scar running from the corner of his right eye down to his jawline, and hair darker than the soil staining his hands.

"CJ tends to the farm." Drew gestured to the impressive plot of land with grow lights tethered to the resin ceiling.

"*And* the bar," CJ added with a smile. "I own the only one in Empyrean, matter of fact."

"Where do you get the alcohol?" I asked. "I imagine you don't get many deliveries down here."

"Right you are, heh." CJ walked a few feet over to a long plot that stretched nearly the full length of the room. I noticed, then, that it was the largest by far.

CJ pulled one of the crops up, revealing a dirt-covered potato.

"I can make most types of alcohol from this baby. With a little help from Alice."

"Alice?" I asked as a dome in the ceiling, which I hadn't noticed before, shot out a light to form a hologram near CJ. It was the quintessential Alice from the old story, complete with blue dress, blonde hair held back with a black ribbon, and white stockings. She also had the white apron-looking thing that went over the blue dress from the old animated movie.

There was one thing off in the avatar, though. She didn't activate the uncanny valley when I looked at her, almost appearing real despite the cartoonish outfit. Maybe it was the eyes that appeared a little too real. Then again, I was used to talking to a hologram of a photorealistic puppy with intelligent, convincing eyes.

Now that I was thinking about it, I should have him put the big cartoon eyes on instead of the accurate ones.

"Why Alice?" I asked, thinking about the first time I had seen the animated movie as a kid.

"Don't ask me," CJ chuckled and gestured at Drew.

"It was the first thing that came to mind. Going down the rabbit hole just . . . seemed to fit."

"I'm not sure if it would have been *my* first go-to, but it works," I said, crossing my arms and admiring the hologram, which did a little curtsy at me.

"What would you have used?" CJ asked.

"I don't know. Maybe Hal. Or Skippy the Magnificent."

"A boring, monotone voice or an asshole AI beer can?" Drew crossed his own arms to mirror me, but for different reasons.

"Asshole beer can? This Skippy fellow sounds interesting," Tim said. "I think I'll look him up."

"I wouldn't," Timothy quietly added.

After half a second of scouring everything he could find, Tim blurted out, "HEY! Do NOT tell me you based my design upon him! That-that-that's plagiarism, you know!"

"No. Of course not," Drew replied, turning his face away to hide a smirk. "Skippy's actually *funny.*"

"Stupid monkey," Tim muttered.

Drew let out a breath, and I recognized it as him waving the mirth away so a real conversation could be had. "No, Tim. You're based on a collection of my favorite book and movie AIs, the most influential being Da from the Preternatural Chronicles. Helpful, guiding, even caring—though not to the same degree. The protagonist, John Cook, couldn't have made it as far as he did without Da. And that meant something to me."

"Well . . . that's touching, I *guess,*" Timothy spoke up, trying to hide his pleasure at being held in high regard.

"Don't get me wrong; there's Skippy in there, too. But also Data from *Star Trek*, TARS from *Interstellar*, and even a dash of C3PO."

"Well, I *never,*" Timothy said, sounding somewhat like the golden robot from *Star Wars*. I couldn't tell if he was genuinely offended or was just playing the part with on-point comedic timing.

"What can I say? I love books and movies."

I shifted my gaze to the hologram of Alice and nodded in complete understanding. We locked gazes for a moment, and I thought I saw her wink at me.

Drew spoke as if remembering a dream. "I . . . I mean *we* watched *Alice in Wonderland* as a kid. Don't you remember?"

"Well, yeah, I guess." I understood that Drew had a sentimental attachment to the movie, but in a way I didn't. It was just a cartoon.

"You didn't watch it wi—" Drew stopped himself and looked down at his Clepsydra, apparently having a conversation I couldn't hear. "Oh."

Something caught my attention, and I arched an eyebrow as I looked at my older variant.

"What aren't you telling me?"

"Later. For now, we have work to do."

We stared at each other for several moments, neither saying a word.

"Aaaaanyway," CJ broke the silence. "I also have corn, wheat, and rice set aside specifically for getting shit-faced."

With a quick narrowing of my eyes at Drew, I decided to drop it . . . for now.

Looking around the area, I took note that it was a large space, but surely not enough for over nine hundred people.

"How do you grow enough for everyone?" I asked, when something caught my curiosity, and I looked around. "And where are the cows?"

Drew and CJ let out with little barks of laughter, and I could tell it wasn't because what I'd asked was funny.

"To answer your first question," CJ said, "we altered the plants to grow at an exponential rate. Hell, some of these bad boys can be harvested *nearly* daily."

"And the second?"

"You're not going to see any cows in the outer banks of the city. Shoot, not even wild boar can be found anymore. All gone. Extinct. Finito."

"We have some chickens, though," Drew pointed out, turning to me.

"Mm-hmm. Chicken and eggs are about all the protein from animals we got. Unless you count the crickets, that is."

"Crickets? Gross, man. How do you live like that?" I asked, immediately regretting the question, as it wasn't my place to judge.

"I don't call it *living*. I call it *surviving*," CJ said flatly, lowering his face slightly.

"Sorry. Sorry." I held up my hands in surrender. "Just seems completely unfair how the rich get to eat real meat while those at the bottom are forced to eat bugs."

"Well, you aren't wrong there," CJ chuckled.

There was a knock on the heavy doors, and the farmer tugged on a chain sticking out of his pocket. He opened an antique watch—something a train conductor might have—and nodded.

Closing it with a metallic snap, he sauntered to the door and pressed a panel on the side of the frame.

Standing in the doorway was a woman in her twenties with three kids ranging in age from a toddler, whom she held in her arms, the eldest being maybe five, and the last being somewhere in the middle.

"Hi, Nyela. *Hey kids!*" CJ greeted as he crouched down and tussled the hair of the eldest boy. "What do you guys feel like having for dinner tonight?"

"Pas-ghetti!" the middle child, a thin girl, cried out in excitement.

My heart panged at being reminded of my sweet baby girl and the words she used for certain foods, like chickie nuggies.

"Mmm! Pas-ghetti sounds good!" CJ stood up and looked at the boy. "What do you think? Valde, here, wants pasta. Does that sound good?"

The boy shrugged, crossed his little arms, and turned his torso away.

Nyela looked at CJ, and, as a parent, I knew in an instant that a conversation had taken place before their arrival on picking one dish.

I stepped next to Drew and softly asked, "His?"

Drew slowly shook his head, and I could see the empathy in his eyes.

"Nyela's husband died a few weeks ago in one of the soil mines. Just . . . caved in on them without warning."

"Oh God," I whispered, looking back at the woman with a new appreciation. It was clear, now, that she was wearing a thick set of armor to shield her kids from her own sorrow, which must be eating away at her insides.

"CJ lets them come first to make sure the kids get what they want. Makes it a little easier."

"What about you, Bernth?" CJ asked the eldest boy. "What do *you* want?"

Bernth slowly uncrossed his arms and looked up at the man. As he opened his mouth to speak, he glanced up at his mom, who only stared back down at him with pained eyes. She had probably explained to him why they should only accept one meal, and he was about to go against her wishes.

Being a parent was impossible sometimes. Especially when the child didn't understand the reasoning behind the parents' decisions.

My own sweet baby girl flashed through my mind again, and my heart clenched, stealing my breath.

Andrew? Tim asked inside my head.

Drew only glanced at me as I nearly doubled over and clutched at my chest. He must have known what I was thinking while watching the parent interact with her children.

I'm fine, I lied, forcing myself to take in a deep, steadying breath and hold the emotions back for at least a little while.

"Mashed potatoes," Bernth said barely above a whisper, finally giving in to his childlike desires and answering CJ's question of what he wanted.

The mother smiled, but I could see a single tear roll down her cheek. I knew . . . I *knew* how hard it was to function after losing someone so important to you. Every little thing put dents and dings in the armor you wore for the world . . . threatening to one day break and fall away.

CJ nodded a few times, tussled Bernth's head, and turned to us.

"Alice. If you please."

The hologram next to Drew disappeared before instantly manifesting beside CJ.

"What can I do for you?" Alice asked in a cheery, animated tone.

"Well, you're extra happy today!"

"I'm always happy to see *you*, CJ!"

"You're gonna make an old man blush."

Drew hummed from beside me so only we could hear.

"What?"

"That's Alice's submind."

"Submind?" I asked Drew.

"Um, imagine it like Tim programming the nanoids in your body for specific jobs. Once the orders are sent, they work on their own without need for his oversight."

Thank 01 for that!

"So your AI is taking the threat of being found seriously, I take it?"

"She knows the stakes."

"And the *real* Alice isn't so cheery?"

"Is Tim?"

Well, I never!

"Point taken."

"Alice, can you make some angel hair pasta with tomato sauce, and a side of mashed potatoes?" we could hear CJ ask.

"Of course! That sounds yummy!" Alice clapped as machines came to life behind me.

"Whoa," I said in surprise as I turned to see long, metal appendages descend from recessed panels in the ceiling.

The arms appeared over the wheat section and plucked a small handful before ascending back to where it had come from. Another snatched up two potatoes before zipping into the ceiling as well. Lastly, three perfectly ripened tomatoes were snatched up, and the panels dropped back into place.

"Whoa," I said again, but this time in amazement.

"That's not the best part," Drew said as he moved his eyes from the retractable arms to a large rectangular box made of metal. It stretched from floor to ceiling and was twenty feet long.

Machines whirred before a green light came on, and CJ moved to a panel the size of a fridge door.

Opening it revealed metal trays with two plates of food, both wafting with steam.

CJ took the large plate of angel hair pasta and tomato sauce, which appeared to already have some spices on top, and set it on a table behind him. Pressing a button next to the food activated some sort of lid which was printed specifically for the size of the large plate.

Once both of the food items were secured, CJ placed the smaller mashed potatoes recipient on top of the solid lid for the pasta, and walked over to where Nyela and her children were waiting. She looked like she wanted to cry with how generous the farmer was being to her, and I had to fight back more tears that wanted to slip free. All I wanted to do was rush over to her, hug them all, and tell them I knew what it was like, and that it would be okay.

But that would be a lie . . .

Everything *wouldn't* be okay.

The mother had lost her partner and would have to do everything herself while the children grew up without their father.

I shook my head to banish the negative thoughts swarming like flies over a carcass. Now wasn't the time.

"Thank you," Nyela mouthed, doing her best to hold herself together. Clearing her throat, she regained her composure and looked down at her eldest son.

"What do we say, Bernth?"

"Thank you, Mr. CJ!"

"You're very welcome, young man," he replied with a big smile, handing the plates to the boy, who held them carefully.

"See you in the morning?" CJ asked Nyela.

"I have an appointment with Doctor Hanifin, but I'll rush over right after." She sounded almost apologetic that she might be late.

"Don't worry if you can't make it. I can bring them over myself after the rush," CJ said with a smile. "Or you can send this strapping young lad."

"Yeah, Mom. I can do it!" Bernth exclaimed, looking up at his mother.

"Thank you," she repeated, and they turned to make their way home while the line began to form.

"You ready?" Drew rolled up his sleeves but didn't remove his leather gloves.

"Ready? For what?"

"Ah! The Haken clan! What'll you fine folks be having this evening?" CJ asked enthusiastically as the next family approached the open doorway.

"How about pizza tonight?" the dad asked his family. I noticed he had a strange gait to his walk, along with a slight speech impediment.

"Yay!" the two kids cried out in unison.

"And a salad," the mom added.

"Coming right up." CJ turned to the hologram next to him. "Alice. One cheese pizza and side salad, please."

"That sounds yummy!" Alice happily said again as the arms started descending from the ceiling. I figured the AI would have been programmed to be overly optimistic when working with the citizens of Empyrean—a comforting feature of sorts.

I couldn't help but keep looking at the man with the big smile whose body didn't seem to want to comply.

Drew leaned a little closer to me and whispered, "The dad, Jason, is recovering from a Neuronova addiction. The world above couldn't give him the medical attention he needed."

"And you took him in?"

"Gave him a second chance to be the father he so desperately wanted to be."

"Hmph." I nodded once, feeling both pity and pride for the man who was doing everything in his power to be there for his kids. I could certainly relate.

"What about the people on the streets?"

"You mean why aren't they here with us?"

"Yeah."

"We can only help those who *want* to be helped," Drew said heavily, exposing an open wound in his pride. "I've tried to help so many . . . but most just want to live in the past."

"And the, what was it called, neuro-stuff helps with that?"

"Neuronova. And yes. But at a great cost."

I turned back to the father and his beautiful family.

"What was he trying to remember?"

Drew let out a long sigh through his nose, anticipating my question. "They lost their eldest son. Not even a teenager yet."

I could feel the center of my eyebrows lift in sympathy.

"Wha-what happened?" I dared to ask, knowing it wasn't any of my business.

"They used to live in an apartment, in the Forgotten, with several other families."

"And?"

"It collapsed."

I sucked in a breath as I remembered the dilapidated buildings above the underground city.

"Jason and Faith were at work. Kids were in the community school. But Elis had stayed home sick that day."

"Dear God . . ."

"They didn't know it had happened until they came home from work."

"No one told them?"

"It's the Wild West out there, Andrew. No government oversight also means no social services in place, like police and fire."

"So . . . so he just came home to . . . to . . ."

"A pile of rubble that people were trying to move with only their hands."

"Did they ever find him?"

"No." Drew shook his head as his gaze fell to the floor. "And he tried for weeks, ripping all the nails from his fingers and herniating three of his discs."

Any pity I felt for the man was completely swallowed by pride, knowing he had done everything he could . . . and more.

"I think . . . the fact they never found him made everything worse. No funeral. No goodbyes."

My mind flashed to my own family's funeral, and I quickly banished the thought before I let the anguish bloom inside my heart.

"Next," CJ called out as the family moved to the side and an elderly couple moved up, breaking me from the horrible conversation.

"Grab the plates as they come out. Put them here for a printed lid. And then take them to the people," Drew explained as the big box next to us whirred, and a pizza was placed on the shelf. The salad was next, and I did as instructed.

After printing the lids, I set the salad on top of the pizza and hurriedly walked to where a family of smiles was waiting for me.

"Whoa. I didn't know Drew had a son!" the dad said as he looked me up and down.

"I . . ." I trailed off, not knowing what to say. All I could think about was the incredible pain this man had been through, reminding me of my own.

Hand them the food, Tim urged inside my head.

"Oh, here you go." I handed the dad the two plates.

"What do we say, kids?"

"Thank you!" they energetically cried out, once again in unison, and then the four of them moved away.

I watched them go then looked to my left to see a steadily growing line of people. Without meaning to, I let out a long whistle, realizing this was going to take a while.

"Here you are, Mr. and Mrs. Burtock," Drew said as he handed their order to the elderly couple.

"Handsome son you got there," Mrs. Burtock complimented. I noticed a mechanical belt around her waist with glowing blue lights.

Drew slapped the top of my back, a little too hard. "Spitting image, ain't he?"

"Heh," was all I could say in my stunlock.

"Come on, *son*. We have work to do," Drew said as he not-so-gently pulled me away.

"What was around her waist?" I asked as we moved back to the food processor.

"Tim would spend twenty minutes explaining, in detail, what the grav-ring is, but I'll spare you the scientific jargon and say it's an antigravity belt. Helps the elderly and infirm get around."

"That is *such* a watered-down explanation!" Timothy erupted, indignation dripping from his words. "You can't just say *antigravity* and call it a day!"

Ignoring the frustrated AI, I said, "So it's like a fancy cane?"

"Buh! Mah! N-Neuh!" Timothy let out with monosyllabic grunts, trying to formulate words.

"More like a sophisticated walker," Drew continued, ignoring the short-circuiting AI.

"Ah. That makes sense," I said as we worked on the next order. "But it didn't have tennis balls at the bottom."

Drew and I chuckled at my stupid joke, and for the first time since my arrival, I felt a sort of comfort in the future version of me.

Ten minutes later, and I was getting the hang of it.

Orders came in. The robotic arms plucked the necessary ingredients from the ample garden. And the mysterious box made the food.

"Why don't they use robots for this?" I asked Drew, calculating that it was going to take all night to get to everyone.

"Oh, we do. I just wanted you to see the people we care for," Drew replied with a stoic face. "That, and CJ personally handles those in need, like Nyela and her children. And the Burtocks. Just to let them know there are still people who selflessly care for others."

My movements slowed to a snail's pace as my eyes went unfocused.

"To manipulate me into thinking the universe is worth saving . . ."

Drew stopped, turned to me, and waited for me to lock eyes with him. It took a mountain of willpower, but I managed to match his gaze.

"Manipulate? No. *Show* you that there is still good in the world? Yes."

"What do you expect from me?" I asked coldly, taking a step back from the food station to further showcase my resolve.

"Tim. Activate the droids," Drew said, also moving away from the table, matching my wordless strike.

"Do you mean him or me?" Timothy asked, genuinely unsure.

"You, *Tim.*" Drew's words were harsh, but not directed at his AI. Instead, him refusing to use the name *Timothy* that I had suggested was a targeted protest.

A panel opened on the wall, and four white androids stepped forward. Their bodies were smooth, with appendages formed of cylinders attached by metallic ball joints, including a large one where the torso connected to the waist. Where the rest of the body was almost featureless, the front of the heads had a screen with human faces displayed. All were smiling, which creeped me out for some reason.

Drew and I glared at one another, each with tight lips and furrowed brows. It was like looking into a mirror, but with an older version of me.

"You would condemn all these people . . . for—"

"Andrew!" Timothy shouted as his hologram burst to life above his arm.

Sensing the urgency in the AI's tone, Drew broke eye contact with me and lifted his Clepsydra.

Timothy's image was replaced with surveillance footage showing three men clad in black standing at the entrance to the mine.

With a voice that held years of stress and worry, Drew said, "They found us . . ."

CHAPTER 11

Sound the alarm. All able-bodied people into defensive positions," Drew commanded his AI.

A near-deafening chirp began every three seconds with a bright flashing light accompanying it, prompting a collective gasp from the line of hungry people outside.

Drew stormed to the entrance, clapped his hands several times, and called out, "Alright, people. We've trained for this. Everyone to your positions. Those unable to fight need to make their way down to the evacuation tunnel and await my signal.

"You." Drew turned to point a gloved hand at me. "Get to the bottom level with the others."

"I can fight," I said, stepping forward and lifting my chin.

"*We've* practiced this. You'll only get in the way. Now go!" I could see something cross his eyes, and he quickly added, "Keep them safe."

I narrowed my eyes at the obvious manipulation, but the thought of Nyela and her kids flashed through my mind, softening my expression. The Hakens were next, followed by the Burtocks, and I caved in, though with one final word to Drew.

"You know they are after me, right?"

"Which is why I'm putting you at the very bottom level, making those bastards have to make their way through our barricades, traps, and almost nine hundred men and women in fighting shape."

"Traps?"

"You think I'd just sit back and wait for them to eventually find us? If it wasn't the Clockmen, it would have been someone else. Now get the hell out of here and let us do our job."

He's right, Tim said inside my head. *If you have any chance of finding a way to save Alison and Sylvie, then you probably want to do your best to stay alive.*

At that, I nodded at Drew and began jogging down the long ramp where others were already descending.

The elderly, infirm, and families with young children all hustled toward the evacuation tunnels. In the opposite direction, heading up the ramp, were men and women of different ages, each holding printed rifles which would have been at home on the set of *Star Wars.* It was then I noticed that only Drew and I had Clepsydras.

High-pitched gunfire from far above caught my attention, sounding like a jet engine mixed with a minigun.

The sentries, Tim said, sensing my wordless question.

After a moment, the sound was cut in half, and then everything fell silent.

Crap!

"What?!"

They got them!

"How did th—"

There was a loud explosion from somewhere far above, and I stopped to peer up.

Yeah! Take that!

"What happened?" I asked Tim.

The support charges, Tim mentally explained, and I remembered the small devices with the red lights at the top of each support.

Everything rumbled as a thunderous roar came from the shifting giant boulders of the tunnel. People screamed in terror as some fell to their hands and knees from the quaking of the resin city. The cacophony of noise from the rumbling, screaming, and blaring alarms made my skin crawl.

As quickly as it had begun, the rumbling ceased, leaving behind the whimpers of those fleeing to the emergency exit and the steady mechanical chirps of the alarm. I could also make out the sound of tiny rocks, not quite small enough to be considered sand, raining down to *clink* against the railing and ramp.

"Will that stop them?" I asked, still looking up as a thick plume of dust bloomed to the top of the underground city.

They were caught in the blast and resulting collapse, but that will only slow them down, giving Drew and his team enough time to set up their defenses.

I continued to stare upward, half expecting an army to burst through and begin an onslaught. My mind filled in the scene from the tunnel as Retnuh and his henchmen were caught in the cave-in, only to reappear through portals near the entrance.

Hmm. That's weird.

"What now?" I asked as I resumed making my way down the now dirty ramp.

The footage I can see from outside the tunnel only shows Retnuh and Davix come through new portals. Traze has yet to come through . . .

Something didn't feel right, and I slowed my steps as I thought, a scowl creasing my face.

"The tall one isn't with them?" I was thinking of how the thin man had blinked through the air, making me shudder.

No. But isn't that a good thing?

My guts churned as the hairs on the back of my neck prickled.

In slow motion, I turned to face up the spiral walkway, and my eyes went wide as a humanoid figure ran on all fours along the walls, blinking in and out of sight.

"*Shit!*" Tim and I blurted in unison, right as Traze leaped through the air, his glowing claws pulled back for a strike.

My muscles tensed in a way I had never felt before, feeling like a pump fresh from the gym, and I instinctively sidestepped while reaching out to grab his slashing arm.

The broken mask shot toward where I had stepped, and I could almost see the look of surprise on the tall man's face as I used his own momentum to slam him into the ground.

But as he was just about to hit, he blinked out of existence, and something crashed into my back, throwing me to the hard walkway.

The air rocketed out of my lungs as something pierced my left shoulder near my neck. All I heard from that side of my body was what could only be described as a revving motorcycle. I managed to turn my face enough to see that the featureless silver mask had slipped over two slits where a nose had been as metal fangs tore into my flesh.

"AH!" I bellowed, placing my open palm against the walkway and sending out a blast of energy with enough force to throw me and my attacker tumbling into the air like a top. I sharply inhaled as I felt and heard the tearing of a portion of my trap muscle, but the desired result was still achieved.

I crashed into the railing as Traze was sent flying over it—a stream of blood trailing from his exposed mouth. I wanted to rejoice at seeing him hurt, but then I registered it was *my* blood.

Sending a portion of the nanoids to the injury, Tim swiftly said inside my head. *But you will lose some of your new speed and strength as I attend to the wound.*

"Strength and speed?" I gasped, feeling the burning pain in my shoulder as if a flame were being held to it.

There was a crackle a few feet down the pathway, and I turned to see Traze smiling with metal teeth dripping with crimson. The flashing of the alarm lights made shadows dance on half of his body, making my fear swell at the sight.

He moved his silver, featureless mask back into position, with a portion of the top still broken from where Drew had hit him.

Two young men wielding rifles stopped as they ran up the ramp, aimed the rifles at the Clockman, and fired.

One of the energy rounds struck Traze in his upper back, prompting him to disappear faster than the blink of an eye. The other streak of light, which had been intended for the tall man, passed right through where he had been and zipped toward me.

I shot to my side—which would have been completely useless, considering the energy blasts were flying faster than mundane bullets. So I lucked out when the streak of light only whizzed by my ear, singeing the lobe.

There was a terrible shriek as I crashed my shoulder into the wall. Looking over, I saw one of the armed citizens being lifted in the air with blue claws poking through his stomach.

Traze grabbed the man under his chin and ripped him apart like snapping the wishbone at Thanksgiving. Blood rained down on the tall man as the other militia soldier moved to orient his rifle on the threat. But he might as well have been moving in slow motion with how swift the crazed Clockman was.

With a gasp of surprise, the man raised his arms only to watch in horror as everything below his elbows fell toward the ground. Four slits opened along his stomach, and ropes of intestines spewed out, racing to see if they could hit the ground before his hands and rifle.

How can I beat this guy? I mentally asked Tim, feeling panic rise in my chest.

I-I-I don't know, Andrew, Tim admitted; the unease in his words could be felt.

Traze tilted his creepy head as thick sheets of crimson slipped down the silver mask and the blue claws from his left hand opened and closed.

A gut feeling came to me, one that I couldn't explain, and I focused on my own Clepsydra right as Traze zipped toward me at a blur. With a cry of surprise and rage, I swiped my left arm through the air as I sidestepped to my right and felt a satisfying *thwack*, followed by the sound of sizzling meat.

Traze skidded to a halt several feet behind me, and I held up the blue energy blade that encompassed my left hand, which I held open like a karate strike. The tall man slowly turned to me, smoke drifting up from his right elbow, where his forearm used to be.

Unable to help myself, I darted my eyes to the ground near my feet and confirmed that I had severed his arm.

Traze took in a long, chest-expanding breath, and let out a long shriek that stung my ears as he turned his body in preparation for another attack.

Blue light shot from somewhere above, and Traze blinked out of sight right as another energy blast passed where he had just been.

Following the attack, I looked up to see Drew holding his left fist up from two levels above me.

"Get out of here! I'll find you!" he shouted as an explosion shook the walls and spiraling ramp, raining down dust and clods of dirt. People screamed as they continued downward while the brave militia positioned themselves on the higher levels.

He's gone! At least for now. So can we please keep moving? Tim asked breathlessly. *Don't worry. They haven't breached the city yet.*

"Dear God . . ."

Keep moving!

Turning down the ramp, I began jogging while my right arm moved to clutch at my bleeding shoulder, and I let my energy blade vanish. After making my way to where people were gathering into a room with a large, thick metal door, something tickled my brain, and I had to ask Tim, *How was I able to lift my arm?*

My right hand continued to hold my shoulder, which had finally stopped bleeding thanks to the nanoids.

Never mind, I added, already knowing the answer.

As I said, the nanomachines can serve a wide range of benefits, including muscular enhancement, and even movement when needed, Tim explained. *But that's not the interesting thing, Andrew.*

No? I mentally asked, continuing the conversation inside my head rather than out loud where I could risk further frightening those around me.

How were you able to manifest a blade like that? I've never seen it done before.

That tall bastard did it, right? With the claws, I mean.

Right. But I suspected it was some sort of modification.

I don't know. Maybe it was, I dismissed. *All I had to do was think about what I wanted, and the Clepsydra did the rest.*

Remarkable. You continue to amaze me, Andrew.

I ignored his praise and looked around at the terrified faces around me.

Nyela was huddled in the corner, clutching at her children. The middle girl had tomato sauce smeared across her lower face, and my heart broke for them.

Squeezing my way over to them, I said, "Don't worry, kids. Everything's going to be okay."

Unfortunately, Murphy's Law decided right then was an excellent moment to remind me of its unavoidable existence.

A brilliant blast ripped through the last of the caved-in tunnel, filling the city with a blinding blue light which bounced off the resin walls and sent a tsunami of bubbling molten rock down . . . and over . . . the ramp.

CHAPTER 12

There was a collective gasp as the wave of lava splashed over the top floor and down the open center of the city, right where those who couldn't fight were huddled.

A single shriek pierced the air, which started a domino effect until everyone below the path of the molten rock was crying out in unbridled terror.

Tim! I mentally shouted. *Amplify my voice!*

O-Okay. Got it!

"MOVE! MOVE! MOVE!" my voice boomed from my Clepsydra, hurting my own ears. But the desired result was met, as those at the end of the hall started running down the evacuation tunnel.

I moved behind everyone, making sure no one was forgotten, as the thick lava seemed to fall in slow motion.

Andrew! Tim shouted, panic in his voice.

On instinct, I flung my open left palm toward the ceiling and screamed.

There were heavy *thumps* of impact, and my arm shook as if I were firing a gun with one hand. With bared teeth, I looked up to see a blue shield encompassing the entrance to the evacuation tunnel.

The stampede of footsteps slowed as some of the survivors turned and muttered in amazement.

"Keep going!" I called out, strain evident in my words.

My outstretched arm began to slacken as the weight built, and I could feel movement inside my body as if tiny ants were crawling toward my injured shoulder and weakening triceps.

Unfortunately for me, the increased strength from the repositioned nanoids couldn't counter the building weight of the molten rock, and I knew I only had seconds. The damned egg shape of the underground city only served to funnel the viscous lava toward the tunnel.

My entire body shook as I strained to turn my head toward those closest to me and shout.

"Get ready to close the door!"

A middle-aged man with a prosthetic arm quickly nodded his head as he ran the few steps to the doors panel. His appendage looked like it was taken from one of the androids, smooth white with the metallic ball joints.

"NOW!"

I dropped the shield as I leaped through the exit right as the man slammed on a big red button, which began closing the thick metal doors.

But it was too slow.

A wave of molten lava spilled in, forcing me to awkwardly scramble on all fours until I was able to get both feet under me and leap forward.

There was a scream of absolute agony from behind that would haunt my dreams.

I rolled to create more distance and pushed myself to my feet as I turned to see the middle-aged man on his back, being carried by the wave as flames engulfed his entire body.

What people had heard about what happened when you fell into lava was wrong. The shrieking man didn't melt like throwing cotton candy into water. He was flash broiled and could feel every bit of it until the shock kicked in, at which point he stopped screaming.

The thick metal doors finished closing, staunching the flow of molten rock, which began to slow, leaving behind a thickening mound that swelled as what remained at the center tried to push forward.

Everyone continued to take several steps back as the man who had sacrificed himself to close the door continued to burn.

The aroma made me want to vomit, but now wasn't the time.

"Where does this tunnel lead?" I panted as I turned to the group, intentionally putting my body as much in between the survivors and the hero to block their view.

Tim audibly answered.

"There's an escape hatch at the end of this tunnel, which slowly ramps upward to make it easier for those with difficulty moving. It will take approximately thirty minutes to reach the surface if we move at a steady pace."

"Where does the hatch lead?"

"A demolished building several blocks away from the mine's entrance."

"How do we know they haven't found it?" I asked as I motioned for people to start moving in the only direction we could.

"The hatch is perfectly camouflaged by using a section of the debris itself to cover the exit."

My mind flashed with scenes from movies where hidden compartments were accessible by doors that resembled floorboards, or even bookcases that allowed access to a safe room beyond.

"Is . . . is Drew going to be alright?" I asked.

It shamed me that I didn't care as much about him personally as I did about his ability to help me find a way to save my wife and daughter.

"As you very well know, he is resourceful beyond measure. He is *you*, after all."

I ignored the compliment as we moved up the steady, forgiving incline of the tunnel—the smell of burnt flesh following us as it traveled up the ceiling. For some reason, I thought of Gollum following Frodo and Sam, thinking he was being sneaky and remaining unseen, but they knew he was there.

Motion-activated lights illuminated our current path, and I looked over to see those nearest to the door turn off from lack of movement. Only an eerie orange radiance remained, appearing like a carnival's funhouse, complete with bright glow-in-the-dark paint.

A tiny red light caught my eye, and I looked at the support nearest the lava which had that same black box affixed at the top.

"Shit," I mouthed, knowing the lava could melt the resin and probably make the explosive, well, *explode*. And after seeing how effective the tiny bombs were at caving in a tunnel, I decided to act swiftly.

"Alright, everyone," I called with a shaky voice. "We have a long road ahead of us. So let's get moving."

The group began a slow pace up the tunnel, and I stopped to turn, looking back at the hungry lava that had intended to eat us all.

It was surreal to be in a brightly lit part of the tunnel while darkness continued to follow us, leaving behind a diminishing orange glow that shrunk the further away we went. But instead of feeling relief, it felt more like watching a crocodile slip beneath the surface of the water, waiting for us to forget it was there.

Even from a distance, I could make out the outline of a melting prosthetic hand standing brighter than the lava itself, appearing like a lighthouse during the day. But that wasn't what bothered me the most. As the resilient material slowly melted, it seemed to reach toward us, begging for help.

I turned away, feeling my stomach churn with helplessness and pity while also mouthing *Thank you* to the man who had saved us all.

CHAPTER 13

Every few minutes, I craned my neck over my shoulder to look down the darkened path behind us, fully expecting the tiny support bomb to go off. But thankfully, the resin somehow held against the incredible heat of the lava.

After about forty minutes, we made it to a small set of steps that led up to a narrow door. Or perhaps *hatch* was, indeed, a more fitting description—only allowing one person through at a time.

I took the handful of steps up, grabbed the metal wheel affixed to the door, and turned.

Nothing happened.

Other way, Tim said inside my head, sparing me the embarrassment of saying it out loud for everyone to hear.

Without a word, I twisted the lock in the opposite direction, and I couldn't help but feel as if I were on a submarine. It squeaked in protest as I forced the hatch to unlock.

Bracing myself by putting my good shoulder against the door, I repositioned my legs until I was in a squat stance and pressed upward with a groan. The latches screamed, making me wince at the sound that could give away our position, and the door fully opened with a wince-inducing *clang* as it struck the ground. A ring of dust shot out before lazily falling back down.

"Whew," I exhaled, briefly reaching up to touch my injured left shoulder, surprised to see it was already knitting itself together with the help of the nanoids.

"Okay. Form a line. One at a time," I told the group as I dropped back down and extended my hand to the first person. It was Mrs. Burtock, and I smiled, trying to show everything was okay as she grabbed my hand for support.

Once she was through, Mr. Burtock was next, and he nodded his thanks as he grunted and groaned his way through the narrow hatch. There was a quick gasp from above, and a light misting of rain fell on the part of my head and arm that were directly under the hatch.

Looking at the back of my hand, I saw it was peppered with crimson dots, and confusion marred my face.

There was a *thump* from above, and I looked up to see Mr. Burtock standing just outside the hatch with his fists clenched while staring at something I couldn't see.

"Don't keep me waiting, fella," he coldly said. "I've got to be with her when we get to the pearly gates."

A single drop of Mrs. Burtock's blood dripped from his clenched knuckles, and my heart sank at the realization of what was happening.

With a swift movement that shouldn't have been possible for someone his age, Mr. Burtock pivoted, grabbed the hatch, and slammed it closed, just before a muffled scream could be heard through the metal door.

On instinct, I grabbed the wheel and tried to turn it, but it wouldn't move.

THE OTHER WAY! Tim exploded in my head.

I repositioned my stance and began turning right as the hatch started to lift. I hadn't turned the lock enough, and panic started to fill my mind like water in the Titanic.

I could see the legs of a thin man standing.

On a wild, desperate hunch, I held onto the metal ring and lifted myself up until my feet were pressing against the frame of the hatch. Pulling with all my might as I hung upside down, the door began to close again, and I awkwardly turned the lock, catching it this time.

There was a screech of rage on the other side of the thick metal, followed by thunderous banging.

Once it was sealed, I carefully dropped to the steps and nearly stumbled backward as I watched the door above, wincing with each deafening bang.

"What'll we do?" someone asked from the gathered crowd while everyone began backing away as blood that had coated the hatch began to drip onto the steps.

"I . . . I-I don't know!" I admitted, right as four blue blades pierced the metal and began slowly pulling from one side to the other. The metal was thick and bought us some time, but time for what?

"It's him . . ." I hissed, realizing the blades were the claws from the tall Clockman.

Oh, 01. We're doomed! Tim mentally lamented. I was thankful he hadn't said it for all to hear, though it didn't do much to help my rising panic as mental compartment after mental compartment were flooded with the emotion.

How the tall man had gotten there so quickly bothered me . . . until the answer became obvious.

My mind went still, and a memory of appearing in front of the *first* Andrew shined like a beacon in the darkness. I had done what no one had before and traveled through the wormhole to a wheren that shouldn't have been possible, stopping the murder of my family before the cycle had even begun.

Without knowing why, I sprinted to the end of the line, all my fears having been consumed by the sheer determination to save these people.

Closing my eyes, I held up my left hand and said to Tim, "Open the wormhole," while focusing intently on the road near where Drew had first landed his car. They weren't looking for these people. They were looking for me—*both* of me.

Andrew . . . I don't think—

"Do it!" I barked, and a crackling sound started as I kept my eyes squeezed shut, keeping the image of the street locked in my mind.

"Everyone go through! Now!" I announced.

I couldn't see if anyone was moving, but I didn't hear any footsteps.

"GO!" I shouted.

To emphasize my point, the energy claws yanked free from the hatch and slammed into it again, ready to continue destroying the metal barricade. Hurried footsteps sounded as I struggled to focus on the street; I thought I heard some people holding their breath as they stepped through.

The horrific noise of tearing, melting metal ceased, only to be replaced by more piercing as the tall man made progress.

Sweat began to bead on my forehead as my brow quivered at having to hold the image of the street for so long. And it felt like an eternity before Tim spoke up.

That's the last of them!

Daring to open my eyes, I saw I now was the only person in the tunnel, right as Traze broke through and dropped to the steps in a snarl.

I shot my face to him as he crouched and began racing forward.

Turning back to the wormhole, I ran for dear life, only to lose focus on the street. The gateway sputtered and then collapsed, leaving me alone with the crazed man.

"Shit . . ." was all I could say before something crashed into me from behind, and the ground rushed up to smash into my face.

CHAPTER 14

The ground was soft and somewhat moist from the sealed tunnel being rarely used, and I had never been so thankful to get a mouthful of dirt in my life.

I had turned my face at the last instant, which my cheek and temple both cursed me for, throbbing in anger at being chosen, but at least I hadn't been knocked out.

Something metal painfully pressed into my right ear, and I helplessly struggled from where Traze pinned me down.

Flicking my eyes as much to the side as I could, I saw the tall man was apparently trying to crush my head with his featureless silver mask.

Then he spoke.

"I'm going to take my *time* with you," he hissed like a snake, putting emphasis on the word as if it were some sort of pun.

For some reason, my nose alerted me to the fact that I could still smell the burned man at the beginning of the evacuation tunnel, drawing more attention from my brain than what was warranted for the moment. My eyes flicked from the face pressing into the side of my head to an arm ending at the elbow, and I understood I wasn't smelling the hero swallowed by lava but this bastard's seared flesh.

At that, hope filled my chest, knowing he could be injured.

Moving my eyes down my body to see how he was pinning me, considering he was down one arm, I noticed his right knee was posted on the ground while his shin moved over my buttocks. Wiggling my leg slightly, I could feel his foot on the inside of my thigh, and I understood how he had me under his control.

There was a pressure on the back of my neck that I hadn't noticed with how hard his metallic mask was pressing into the side of my head, and I judged Traze had been holding my vertebrae in his hand.

Now, it moved up my left arm to clutch around my Clepsydra.

Oh, 01, Tim gasped inside my head.

What?! I mentally asked.

He's going to breach my housing . . .

What will that d— The memory of shooting Traze's Clepsydra flashed through my mind like a bolt of lightning in the dead of night.

The contamination had stretched across the tall man's entire timeline, torturing him with untold agony in an unquantifiable amount . . . that I was about to experience.

"NO!" I shouted as his grip tightened on my Clepsydra.

"Yeeeeeeessssss," he hissed again, almost in pleasure.

"Yo-you'll die too!"

"Goooooooood."

My heart sank, knowing he meant every bit of what he was saying. He would risk experiencing the contamination again—which meant he would most assuredly die—if I was to suffer *with* him.

Do something! Tim cried out, hurting my head with the intensity of the mental scream.

Blue light flowed up the tall man's wrist and hand until the familiar blue claws began to sprout.

My mind shot spotlights onto the recent visual memory of Traze's missing right arm, and an idea came to me.

Metal hissed as the tips of the blue claws started piercing my Clepsydra.

"NO!" I bellowed, opening my left palm against the dirt and flexing my forearm as hard as I could.

A blast of pure energy shot me upward into a violent spin, taking my attacker with me. I could feel the blood in my brain fling toward the inside of my skull, like clothes in an industrial washer as it spun to incredible speeds to siphon all the remaining water out.

My body grunted as I hit something with a sickening *crunch,* slowing my spinning, and then I hit the ground. The air in my lungs held a walkout at being treated so unfairly and swiftly exited through my nose and gaping mouth.

All I could feel from my numb body was an intense pressure on the outside of my head that slowly began to dissipate as the blood started to evenly space throughout my brain once more.

My faculties came back online, and I pushed myself up to my knees while clutching at my quivering, deflated diaphragm, seeing Traze flat on his back only a few feet away. His left arm was awkwardly across his neck, as if he were trying to choke himself with the crook of his elbow, effectively hiding his face.

I did a mental check of my bones and realized the crunch I felt and heard was probably from Traze absorbing the full force of my energy blast as I crushed his body against the roof of the tunnel.

Letting dizzy eyes look up, I saw one of the resin beams had splintered but continued to hold back the supple dirt above our heads. A little red light next to it sent a small shudder down my spine at the realization we could have hit one of the tunnels explosives meant to cause a cave-in.

Looking back down at the limp Clockman, I struggled to get to my feet while burning his essence with the intensity of my steadily focusing glare. Remaining in a crouched position as I leaned against the thick frame, I could see a portion of disfigured red flesh where his mask had been. His arm hid most of his face, but what was visible of his now exposed forehead made my stomach want to lurch.

"Got you . . . bastard . . ." I wheezed as my breath reached an agreement with my lungs and decided to come back to work.

Traze's left hand twitched, causing me to stumble backward a few steps as I watched in horror. His lungs filled with air, but I could see one side of his ribcage was indented where I had crushed him against the resin support with my body.

Might I suggest we run? Tim mentally urged.

My eyes shot to the hatch, which seemed to be an eternity away, and I took a single step forward.

Traze vanished in a flash of blue light before reappearing in the middle of the tunnel. He was hunched to one side, with his left arm dangling in front of him.

I sucked in a sharp breath, making my lungs hurt, as I witnessed the stomach-lurching remains of his maskless face.

It looked like a man who'd had all the skin stripped off of his skull, only to have it replaced with a subpar graft . . . from a burn victim. There was no nose, only two slits above a lipless smile showcasing metal teeth. But that wasn't the creepy part. His Chelsea Grin stretched from ear to ear, as if they hadn't used enough material to cover where his cheeks had been.

Lidless, red-veined eyes stared at me with complete hatred, appearing like stained golf balls with their size.

"You . . . 'ill . . . die . . ." he hissed. At that moment, my brain thought it was worth noting that his mask probably corrected his words, considering he didn't have lips. Why my brain thought it was important to inform me of that tidbit of information at that critical moment? I'd never know.

Tim . . . antimatter, I mentally said as I lifted my left fist toward the disfigured creature.

Oooo-wheeeh-hooooo! Good idea, Andrew! Tim enthusiastically exclaimed as my Clepsydra began to slightly vibrate.

My fist began glowing white instead of blue, and to his credit, Traze caught on to what was happening in a flash.

"Fire," I said with a smile, right as Traze vanished from sight, only to appear directly in front of me.

I gasped in surprise as he grabbed my left wrist and wrenched it up, sending the blast of antimatter energy into the splintered frame above us. The explosion threw us to the ground as the resin withered and vanished in the blink of an eye, leaving behind an indention in the dirt that wasn't happy at losing its support.

The red light on the support bomb flashed a few times before turning a solid green as a portion of the housing vaporized.

Andrew! Run!

I pushed the stunned Traze off of me and began scrambling when lightning made out of fire decided to strike my right calf muscle, dropping me to the ground. Screaming in pain, I shot my face toward my leg to see Traze's blue claws finish an arc through the air.

With wide eyes, I looked down at my calf, which was in horizontal tatters and spewing blood, like cutting an oil-filled ziplock bag with razor blades.

"Oh God," I groaned through my teeth at feeling the boiling pain burning up the back of my leg.

ANDREW! RUN! Tim shouted again.

Traze slowly got to his feet as I started to scramble away while a beeping sounded behind him. The solid green light began flashing, with both the sound and pulsing light getting faster and faster with each passing second. A countdown.

I pushed at the dirt with my good leg and arms, trying to move as far from the explosive as I could, all while one of my shoes began to fill with a warm, sticky liquid.

The tall man looked at me with his perpetually wide eyes, and his smile seemed to do the impossible and widen. His blue claws flexed as he began stalking forward, and I knew it was all over—either by the crazy Clockman or the imminent explosion. All I could hope for was that the blast would kill me *without* rupturing my Clepsydra.

Alison flashed through my mind, and my bulging eyes narrowed as my gaping mouth closed to a tooth-baring snarl. Nothing could give a parent supernatural power like the urge to save his child.

The space between beeps alarmingly decreased as Traze got within a few feet of me, still half crouched to one side from his broken ribs. The determination in his unhinged gaze was the stuff of nightmares, but nothing was going to stop me from making sure my baby girl lived a full life. Nothing. Not even the damn universe itself.

"Ti'e . . . to die," he said without lips as he lifted his left hand in preparation for a strike.

My right fist clutched into the ground, and I wildly swung my arm, throwing a thick cloud of dirt into his lidless eyes. Traze shrieked in rage as I lifted my left hand, palm open, and sent a blast of blue energy into his torso.

He was thrown back several yards, like a sock puppet being sent downfield by an NFL kicker. I had wanted to put him just under the explosive, but had put too much energy into my attack, sending him almost all the way back to the hatch.

The beeping went to a steady tone, and Tim and I said, "Oh *shit*," in unison right as the little box keeping this portion of the tunnel open exploded.

CHAPTER 15

I was deafened in an instant as the tunnel began violently caving inward, like breaching the hull on a submarine that sat at the bottom of the ocean. In that fraction of a second, I felt a surreal confusion I had never before experienced at seeing dirt move like water.

Run! Tim shouted inside my head, and I continued crawling with my good leg and two hands as fast as I possibly could, but it was obvious I wasn't going to make it very far before being swallowed by the Earth.

Open a wormhole! I instructed, panic evident even in my mental words.

I can't for a few more seconds! You kept using the Clepsydra after every charge, and now it needs to refill again!

How long?

Six seconds!

I froze in terror, seeing the closing maw of the tunnel as it raced with incredible speed, mimicking a tsunami through an underground rail line. The ceiling and walls first caved in and then began flowing downhill . . . toward me.

Something caught my eye, and I looked up to see I was under another of the support frames, but I knew, without a doubt, that the violence of the cave-in could not be abated by such a simple structure. Even if the roof directly above my head didn't collapse, the rushing wave of earth would swallow me whole and result in either crushing my body or suffocating me . . . or both.

With no other choice, I turned and pulled my knees under my stomach while my hands helplessly wrapped around the portion of the beam that stuck out into the tunnel.

While cowering in a fetal position with my back toward the ceiling and my legs under me, I couldn't help but think about how long it was taking for the closing jaws to reach me. People did often mention watching car crashes in slow motion once they knew it was going to happen.

Sucking in a deep breath, I closed my eyes as the rumbling of the ground and walls intensified, and I disappeared into the belly of the Earth.

CHAPTER 16

The weight on my body was amazing, in the literal sense of the word. I couldn't fathom how many thousands of pounds were trying to squish me. What I *could* feel, however, was all the air being violently squeezed from my lungs as my chest pressed into my knees.

"No!" I tried to say, but no words came out. At least, I don't think they did. I was still deaf from the explosion, and now dirt was invading every orifice in my face.

Tim! I mentally shouted, panic fully taking hold now.

Three more seconds!

Though my eyes were closed, blackness began to swarm in from the edges, and I knew I was going to die if I passed out.

Two, he informed, and I couldn't help wonder why he was counting down the minutes instead of the seconds.

One! Stay with me Andrew!

The blackness moved toward the center of my eyelids, and everything went fuzzy.

NOW! Tim boomed inside my head loud enough that I snapped awake just enough to feel myself falling.

Air entered my lungs as my body unfolded from its fetal position, and I recognized we were in the wormhole. Layers and layers of dirt were floating in the zero gravity alongside me, and I craned my aching neck to see a doorway flowing with earth as if it were water close.

I let out a single, maniacal laugh which might have also been a sob at seeing just how much of the dirt had chased after me, demanding I remain in its bowels. Turning back down the wormhole, I let myself float as the adrenaline began to wear off and exhaustion filled every muscle in my body, including my eyelids.

Rest now, Andrew, Tim said softly with a sense of relief in his words. *I have some work to do on your body that will take a while.*

"What about the dreams?"

Oh, of all the luck . . . Tim sighed in exasperation, and I could almost hear him dragging a paw down his puppy face. *I'll have to reallocate some of the nanoids to mitigate as much of the scarring as I can. Which means it'll take longer to heal your wounds. Which means you'll probably be asleep longer. Which means* more *scarring. 01, does it ever end?!*

"Heh. Glad I'm not you," I yawned as resources were taken away from keeping my body awake, and unconsciousness took me in its unapologetic arms.

CHAPTER 17

I think the scan is complete, *doctor*," I told Alison as the table slid out from the apparatus that looked like a compact MRI machine. I was proud to call my baby girl by her official title, which she'd worked so hard to achieve, especially while standing in her own, personal laboratory.

She didn't respond to the proud compliment, having lost a lot of her zest for life after . . .

It had been three years since her miscarriage, leaving us without my grandson, Joel. But he hadn't been the last.

Alison was unable to hold a baby in her womb for more than a trimester, and doctors were baffled as to why. Everything looked great on paper. All the tests showed a perfectly healthy environment for a child to be created. But it never happened.

I thought about how she had split from her college sweetheart, through no fault of his own; Alison had been distraught and intently focused on finding an answer, no matter the cost. She probably got that from me, much to my chagrin.

"What do the new sensors say?" Alison asked as she hopped off the table and grabbed her necklace from the nearby counter, clasping it behind her neck as she had done a thousand times before.

Across the screen flashed the words *Gravitational Anomaly Detected.*

Alison mouthed the words with a furrowed brow, but I had dismissed the pirated program as having made a mistake. How could there be a gravitational anomaly *inside* my daughter?

"What's this part?" I pointed to the screen showing a map of her head.

"Testing everything," she quickly answered. "But this doesn't make sense."

"Do you want to scan it again?" I asked as my phone chimed. Checking it, I saw Sylvie had informed me that dinner would be on time, and that I had better be too.

Alison ignored my question and continued to read the flood of text that filled in as she asked the AI to elaborate more and more on the results. The artificial intelligence was still just an upgraded version of Alexa, Siri, or any of the other digital assistants, though it was growing exponentially smarter and more helpful by the week.

"Mom's making pas-ghetti," I said in a playful voice, remembering when my daughter had been just a tiny girl, with giggles and cute food names in her lexicon.

"No. You go," she sighed, crossing her arms while thumbing at the black marble that hung at the center of her silver necklace. "I need to keep doing my research."

"Okay, sweety," I said, wrapping one arm around her shoulders and kissing the side of her head.

She didn't seem to notice as the questions and answers continued on the screen.

"Well, I got to go before your mother kills me," I said with a smile, which quickly faded as my daughter answered by pulling up a chair and leaning toward the computer.

"I love you, Ali."

"Love ya too, Dad," she replied, almost dismissively. And right then, I longed to hear the sweet, innocent child call me *Daddity* just one more time. But this Ali had known tremendous loss and was now fighting against an unknown foe with sheer, unshakable determination. Everything else in the world was secondary to her now.

I looked at my daughter and gave a tight-lipped smile which failed to touch my eyes. I knew, if I had been in her same position, I would have done anything in the universe to save her.

Turning to make my way out of the lab, the dream began to fade as the core portion of the memory finished playing, leaving me alone in the darkness.

CHAPTER 18

ndrew . . . Andrew, wake up, Tim mentally said, piercing through my dream as easily as a steak knife through paper.

My eyes snapped open, but I refused to move or even breathe. I could feel all the damage that had been done, both inside my skull from the memory scarring *and* from my battle with the tall man—up to and including being crushed by the Earth itself.

The veins in my head, particularly around my temples, pounded with each heartbeat, to the point where my eyelids flinched as if a gorilla were standing in front of me, clapping his hands in wide arcs with my tender skull at the end point. My stomach lurched, but nothing was inside of it to vomit, though the bile did offer itself as tribute.

However, no matter how much my physical body hurt, my heart ached exponentially more at remembering how intent my baby girl had been on saving her own child. I hadn't known it in the memory, but I could understand what she was going through more than the Andrew whose memories were literally being carved into my brain. *He* thought he knew pain and heartache . . . but he was wrong.

"Uhhhnn," I let out as I finally forced in a breath, feeling every bump and bruise as my ribs expanded.

Tim appeared above my left arm, and I struggled to move my eyes to look at him.

"I kept you asleep as long as I could, but the scarring was becoming too much to handle."

"That's weird. The dream felt so . . . so short," I said before registering the rest of his words. "You . . . you didn't finish healing . . . did you?"

"Does it feel like I did?" Tim asked tentatively, as if hoping I would give him a thumbs-up and a raise for a job well done.

"Everything . . . hurts . . ."

"Well . . . I did the best I could with what I had to work with. It didn't help that you haven't eaten anything in several hours."

At his words, my hunger sprinted on stage where an empty spotlight stood, having missed its mark, and began belting out the performance of a lifetime. The rumbling could be felt throughout my torso, tickling my sternum as it did.

Desperate to get my mind off both the paralyzing pain and demanding hunger, I asked Tim, "How bad am I?"

"Being crushed in the cave-in certainly didn't help, but I was able to reduce the swelling along your spine and maneuver the slipped discs back into place. Your calf has been *loosely* stitched back together, mostly just the skin, but it will take a substantial amount of protein to finish the job. I actually had to take muscle from other parts of your body to get as far as I did. On top of that, I was able to drastically mitigate the memory scarring on your hippocampus, neocortex, and the amygdala. Though I do say that the nanoids are apparently having secret talks about forming a union. Something about my dictatorlike leadership . . ."

Wiggling my foot, I could feel the immense strain on my calf muscle, as if my leg had fallen asleep.

"Where . . . where did you take the muscle from?" I asked as I continued to rotate my foot, testing every which way.

"Does it matter?"

"No. But I'm trying to keep my mind off the pain and how, ugh"—I gagged—"how hungry I am."

"Why did you gag?"

"It's something I do when I'm really hungry. Like, *glah*, really, *really* hungry."

"One second please," Tim said before my gag reflex slowly faded, leaving behind a warm pool of saliva just under my tongue.

I swallowed. "Thanks."

"Can't have you throwing up and causing more damage to your diaphragm."

"More?"

"You sort of had all your air violently torn from you, and your diaphragm is pretty pissed about being crushed by your knees."

I thought about how I had been in the fetal position when the cave-in swallowed me, and shook my head to try and clear the thoughts.

"PTSD, here I come."

"You mean *more* PTSD," Tim pointed out without any levity, and I scowled at his hologram.

Changing the subject from the damage done to my mental state, I asked again, "Where did you take the muscle from?"

I managed to flex my arms before reaching around to pat at my back. There was a divot on my left shoulder from where the tall man had bitten into me with his metal teeth, but at least the wound was closed.

"Your gluteus muscles."

I reached both hands behind to grab at my rear end. "My butt?"

"I needed a muscle group that was close to the shredded calf, and I didn't want to risk taking from your hamstrings, potentially causing a tear later on, or your quads, resulting in an asymmetrical gait," Tim explained while a hologram he brought up zoomed in on different parts of the musculature of my body. "You're lucky it was only the lateral and medial heads that were sundered, and not the Achilles tendon less than an inch lower."

My hands started gripping either buttock, and I could feel a disparity in, let's call it, *volume*.

"You put my butt . . . in my leg . . ."

"Technically, your booty is *a part* of your leg. So, I don't see what all the fuss is about."

"It's just . . . odd, is all. Hard to wrap my pounding head around it."

"Chin up, butt leg. You're still alive!"

"I . . . I don't like you very much."

"Oh, dear. There must be some undiscovered trauma in your brain."

A whisper of fear crept up my back at the thought that there could be more damage in the most vital organ in my body. "Wh-why do you say that?"

"Because you *love* me, Andrew. You know it. I know it. Even the Clockmen know it."

"You son of a bitch," I groaned as I closed my eyes and floated in the zero gravity.

"I don't have to take that attitude from someone with a leg made out of butts."

Opening my eyes, I stared at the smirking puppy. "Now you're trying too hard."

"Sorry. I'll come up with a list and get back to you."

I shook my head, looking around the wormhole and the universe on the other side.

"So what now?"

"We need to reconnect with Drew so we can continue finding an answer to saving your family."

"You mean *start* finding answers. All I've heard from that guy are virtuous justifications for killing Sylvie and Alison."

"Right. So, to *start* finding a solution, we need to make sure that Retnuh and Davix don't kill your future self."

"It's just two men, right? How many people made up the defensive militia?"

"Two hundred and sixty-seven."

I floated with my jaw agape.

"That's it? Out of over nine hundred?"

"If you'll recall, Andrew, most people in Empyrean were in desperate need of some sort of help. That's why the city was formed. Or at least, why it *expanded* into a city rather than a hidden base."

"Fine. But you're saying that two men, by themselves, posed a threat to over two hundred?"

"It's not just Retnuh and Davix. It's every duplicate they are replaced with when they are killed."

I thought about the ambush I had set up for them at my house. Shooting or blowing them up had resulted in another stepping through a portal immediately after.

Something bothered me, and I asked, "Does that mean they are pulled from a different universe? An-and if so, do they still exist in *that* universe?"

"No one knows for sure, but the theory is that the Clockmen are able to pull from an infinite timeline at will."

"From their past, right? One second before, is what you said?"

"That was just a basic explanation, but it makes more logical sense to pull from the past instead of the future. Because if they die, there is no future to *pull from*."

"Unless they live because they were brought back at the time of death. Which means they *do* have future selves."

"Now we are getting into paradoxical questions, Andrew," Tim pointed out. "Why do you ask?"

"I'm just trying to get a better understanding of the enemy," I said coldly, almost surprising myself with the indifference in my voice.

"Might I suggest running from the Clockmen instead of confronting them when possible?" Tim suggested. "You won't be able to find a way to save your family *if you're dead*."

"That's not fair that they can have infinite replacements . . . but I can't, somehow?"

"As we've gone over, there has never been a person with your Chronos Scale before. Both an advantage and a hindrance, if you ask me."

I kept thinking about how to stop the Clockmen when something came to mind.

"A Clepsydra breach can kill them . . . permanently."

"Y-Yes. But look what happened to Traze," he countered. "It didn't exactly work out in our favor . . . did it . . . ?"

"Or antimatter," I continued, looking down at my Clepsydra, remembering how the killer Andrew had wielded it against Retnuh, and how Tim had begged me not to get struck by the blast because it would erase me from the timeline completely.

"Actually," Tim began as a hologram appeared above him, showing an intricate scientific formula which stretched on and on. A portion highlighted, and he continued, "getting struck by antimatter results in the conclusion of Temporal Sickness, but all at once."

"So they're erased from the universe?"

"That *current* version of them, yes." He zoomed in on the highlighted section. "This is helping the nanoids keep you alive."

"Oh, right. You said they are powered by antimatter."

"The ones inside of you, yes. They are fighting against the Temporal Sickness as best they can."

I focused on his choice of words, breaking apart his meaning.

The nanite gun flashed through my mind, and I asked on a knee-jerk reaction, "What about the machines in the fancy gun that Retnuh had?"

"And you left behind," Tim added under his breath.

"Answer the question."

With an exasperated sigh, Tim said, "The nanites in that gun are powered by *exotic matter*, which erases someone from the timeline completely."

I noticed he'd used a different word for the tiny machines.

"What's the difference between nanites and nanoids?"

"Do we really have time for all these questions?" Tim asked, trying to change the subject. All that did was make sure I continued down this path. Tim had a penchant for not telling me everything up front.

I gestured around the wormhole. "We have all the time in the world because of my Chronos Scale. Right? An advantage, as you called it?"

"Oh, I dislike you sometimes."

"Now who's the one with brain damage." I grinned.

"Yes, leg butt," he loudly sighed. "Your Chronos Scale can best be described as watching a movie in a theater with a custom remote control.

You decide when to pause, rewind, and continue what everyone else is watching, despite what they want. Simply put, what you do affects everyone else."

"So then explain the difference between nanoids and nanites," I smugly said, intentionally pushing the AI's buttons. But only just a teeny tiny bit.

It's the small things in life.

"Fine!" Tim blurted as the hologram was replaced with a tiny machine with several legs that moved like an octopus. "Nanoids have artificial intelligence in them so that they work as a collective inside the human body. They monitor, diagnose, treat, and even enhance the mechanisms of your cells. The variants injected into your body serve a plethora of purposes, but were specifically selected to counteract the Temporal Sickness, hence the antimatter being used as a fuel source."

"Compared to what?"

"Alwaaaaays with the questions." Tim sighed as the hologram faded. "The first soldiers who were experimented with on the battlefield were given nanoids powered by nuclear fission, allowing them to move at speeds that should have been beyond a human being, as well as giving them immense strength and endurance. The Clockmen no doubt have that variety, though much more advanced, given the fuel source. Well, except for Traze, who more than likely has a cocktail mix with antimatter as the main ingredient. I imagine it's the only thing keeping him alive at this point."

"But he's *faster* than the others."

"From what we've seen so far . . ."

I thought about what he said, then continued my line of questioning.

"So they don't get tired?"

"That's one of the many reasons that makes them so efficient at hunting, yes."

"Not needing sleep is a pretty big advantage . . ."

"Agreed," the AI said, and I could hear in his tone the underlining message that he had firsthand knowledge of that fact.

"So the only way to stop Retnuh and the other Clockmen . . . is the nanite gun?"

"Which you left behind," Tim helpfully added.

"So let's go get it."

"But . . . but Drew is under attack. And if Retnuh decides to use his own nanite gun against him . . . you'll die, too."

"Not if I hit pause in the movie theater, like we are doing right now, and then rewind to the point where we left the weapon."

"Andrew . . ." Tim started slowly, his tone serious. "What if Drew has the higher Chronos Scale? He is *you*, after all. The future you, I mean. And *his* dreams are searing onto *your* brain, are they not?"

"I guess there's really no way to know. Is there?" I asked, not expecting an answer. "So I suggest we go down the wormhole, get the gun from where we left it, and then return to help Drew."

"*You* left it," Tim muttered under his breath. "But . . . I suppose you are right. If we tried to fight now, especially in your current state, we would surely lose."

"Then let's go back in time to save the future."

CHAPTER 19

Don't say that," Tim groaned.

"Say what?"

"'Let's go back in time to save the future,'" he mocked with air quotes using his puppy paws. It was kind of adorable, if I was honest. "That sounds like something you would say at the end of a chapter, or maybe in a movie trailer. It's just . . . *dumb*."

"I think you pronounced *clever* wrong."

"Pfft. You wouldn't know clever if it was taken from your ass and put into your calf."

"I . . . I think you're reaching again."

"Damn. That *was* pretty bad," Tim admitted. "It's just such a unique situation; I have nothing to work with."

"You'll come up with something," I half encouraged, trying to hide my smile. "Now, take us to the right coordinates in the wormhole."

Tim grumbled under his breath, but we began moving down the tunnel in the direction I took as going back in time.

As we moved, I couldn't help but try and fathom all the countless galaxies on the other side of the mostly transparent walls. It was almost relaxing while also being terrifying in the same instance. An infinite expanse of stars, planets, gases, and black holes stretching farther than a human could possibly imagine.

The thought that the entire universe was in the hands of whatever decision I made—or *didn't* make—filled me with unease. But that doubt was once again eviscerated by the love I had for my daughter.

"There must be a way," I mouthed, not wanting Tim to hear as I willed the answer of how I could save my family *and* all of creation to come to me. Unfortunately for me, the universe remained silent. Each of the galaxies now felt like eyes watching me and judging my every decision.

It didn't take long until we reached our spot, and my mind shifted to the magic tunnel we hovered in, leaving me to wonder how the wormhole worked, exactly. Sometimes, it felt like we moved for what had to be miles, or even thousands of miles when I was traveling at relativistic speeds; other times, it only seemed like a handful of yards. But no matter the perceived distance, we always arrived at our intended destination.

Then again, the only thing I had to go on in terms of distance traveled was the universe slightly moving outside, not to mention my own internal clock while inside a wormhole with its *own* rules on time.

"Here," Tim announced, signaling it was my turn. He had gotten us to the proper wheren, but now it was my job to *somehow* put us in what could only be described as the desired timeline.

"Give me a second," I said as I focused on the moment after I had gotten into the rented truck and drove away from the Airbnb.

I remembered the breeze outside and the smell of the woods. I focused on the time of day and the roads we took to get there. And worst of all, I forced myself to picture Alison and Sylvie sitting around the cabin's dining table . . . crimson spreading across the white cloths.

"O-Okay. Open it," I said with a quivering voice as I felt my heart beat with shallow, alarming flutters at anticipating seeing my girls again . . . brutally murdered.

A portal opened in the wormhole, and we stepped through.

My boots thudded against the patio of the house, and I looked up to see the taillights of a familiar truck driving toward the street, kicking up dust down the long driveway. I shook my head and felt sorry for what that Andrew was going to have to endure, until I realized I was literally feeling sorry for myself. At the realization, the pity faded in an instant, leaving me alone to face what awaited inside the cabin.

With a nervous sigh, I turned to the door and grabbed the knob, as ready as I could be to make my way to the source of my greatest hope . . . and greatest fear.

I needed the weapon to put an end to Retnuh and his cronies once and for all. Especially that crazy bastard, Traze, who I can only assume survived the cave-in—or at the very least was replaced by another version.

My mind began a dramatic monologue of how unfair it was that I had killed them so many times, and they only needed to return the favor *once*.

Was this how video game bosses felt when a player could fight them as many times as they wanted?

I realized I was stalling, shook my head while taking a steadying breath, and took a step inside my own personal hell.

My injured leg reminded me of its grievous injury and gave out, letting me fall to my knee with a grunt of pain.

"Careful. Caaaaarefulll, Andrew," Tim said. "Remember I didn't have enough material or time to adequately stitch your muscles back together. I basically stopped the bleeding, both externally and internally, but the fibers might as well be held together with Elmer's glue."

With a grunt, I put my hand on the wall and pushed myself up, putting all my weight on my good leg.

"You left the gun inside the hoodie, on the dining table," Tim reminded me, and I slowly hobbled toward where I remembered the room being.

At the entrance to the kitchen and dining area, I froze as surprise, horror, and anguish all fought to grip my still rapidly beating heart. Even though I knew what was in there, the agony of actually *seeing* them rocked me like a horse's kick to my forehead.

Alison and Sylvie still sat at the table with white dishcloths over their faces, scarlet dotting their centers, looking like square Japanese flags made with watery red paint which dripped downward.

"Oh God . . ." I hissed as *both* legs went weak, and I fell against the frame. My hands tried to grip at anything, but only the smooth drywall offered any support.

Collapsing to my knees, I continued to stare at my girls as my breath quivered, matching my already fluttering heart.

"Andrew . . . you knew they would be here," Tim spoke softly. It wasn't an I-told-you-so tone; rather, one trying to keep my sanity intact. "Would you like me to alter your vision?"

"No!" I barked, and then repeated with a softer tone, "No. I-I-I need to see them."

"If you insist," he said quietly, letting me torture myself with the sight of my girls.

"It gives me strength," I explained, and started pushing myself up the wall again.

"Hatred is not a sustaining fuel."

"I disagree," I let out in a breathy hiss, hobbling to the table between Alison and Sylvie.

They were staring up at me through their crimson-stained dish towels when a moment of clarity shone through the haze of my dismay.

"Tim? H-How are they still here?"

"What do you mean?"

"If I stopped the first killer Andrew . . . why are they still dea . . . here?"

"I'm taking a shot in the dark, albeit an educated one. I believe *you* somehow manipulated the wormhole to bring us to *this* wheren on the timeline. Just like you did when you somehow went back to, as you pointed out, stop the first killer Andrew."

"I . . . I don't want to see them like this . . ." I breathed as I moved my hand toward Sylvie's shoulder.

Her body broke apart in all directions as if she were made of loosely held together sand in zero gravity.

"N-No!" I cried out, trying to clutch at the fleeing specks as they began to vanish until there was nothing left.

Yanking my face toward Alison, I saw she had already begun dissipating into nothingness.

"Wh-what's happening?!" I cried out. It was amazing how I knew . . . —I just *knew* . . . —that I couldn't feel any more fear or sorrow at seeing my girls sitting at the table with the crimson-stained dishcloths. But at seeing their bodies leave me, a new level of anxiety and terror exploded in my heart.

"GRAB THE GUN!" Tim shouted, snapping me from my daze.

I threw my gaze toward the hoodie on the table, and my eyes widened at seeing it, too, evaporating into nothingness. I lunged like a baseball player sliding into home and snatched at the hoodie right as it disappeared into the ether.

"No!" I groaned, both from losing my family *and* the means to save them.

Lowering my forehead to the table, I closed my eyes and tried to take in what had just happened.

There were gasps from around me, and I jerked my head up, hoping beyond hope to see my girls alive again. A strange man looked at me from the seat at the end of the table. The same one where killer Andrew had sat at and explained everything to me.

"Wh-what?" I mouthed as I stared into the eyes of an extremely confused man in his early twenties.

There was movement to my right, and I drunkenly looked over to see a pretty woman, around the same age, sliding her chair back as she covered her mouth while staring at me in horror.

"What's happening?" I asked out loud, but it was directed toward Tim.

I . . . I haven't the slightest idea, Andrew, Tim admitted within my head rather than out loud, presumably to not further spook the couple sitting at the kitchen table of the Airbnb.

Pushing myself up, I noticed what appeared to be sand fall away from my chest and stomach. Looking down to further examine it, I saw what remained of a rotisserie chicken and bottle of wine.

Sitting up on my knees as the couple continued to gawk in their paralysis, I saw how the bottom of the wine bottle appeared to perfectly contour the shape of my ribs. Red alcohol slipped free and stained the white tablecloth from the misshapen container.

"Who . . . who are . . . you?" the man asked between galloping breaths.

Tim. Wormhole, I mentally instructed.

On it.

I fell through the table as the gateway opened beneath me, and I slipped back into the tunnel nestled in a higher dimension. The contents of the table floated around me, spreading out in all directions, including the oddly shaped container of wine and what was left of the rotisserie chicken.

Sand drifted away from my chest, and I quickly noticed how the color of the grains matched that of the bottle and food before fading into nothingness.

Then the image of Sylvie and Alison drifting apart into sand smashed into my mind, freezing all other thoughts.

Andrew? Are you okay?

Tim's words brought me back from my shell shock, and the desire to know what the hell had just happened overwhelmed everything else I was feeling. My heart also began a normal rhythm, as did my breathing, and I knew Tim was pulling strings behind the scenes. But at that moment, I didn't mind.

"What *was* that?" I asked with a gaping mouth as I floated in the wormhole.

My best guess is that you pulled us to a different timeline. Or perhaps pulled an alternate timeline to us, Tim explained inside my head as if thinking out loud.

"Did you see the wine bottle?"

And the chicken. Yes.

"They . . . *evaporated* when I touched them. Just like . . . *them,*" I said softly, not able to say my girls' names in relation to the situation.

"I don't think that's what happened." Tim's avatar sprang to life over my left forearm.

I moved my hand up and across my chest so I could better see the Cairn puppy. "What do you mean?"

A hologram appeared over Tim, showcasing the scene we had just left, but from a third-person perspective. "Watch," he said as the replay started, and I saw myself jumping toward the hoodie as it disappeared.

After laying my forehead down on the table, a light cloud of sand appeared and began to collect in the shapes of the couple I had seen.

"Here." Tim paused the scene just before the man and woman fully took shape, panning the camera to the side before zooming in under my chest. The chicken and wine bottle were both trying to phase in, just like the couple, but I was blocking their space with my body.

Unable to help myself, I used my right hand to pat up and down my torso, half expecting to find holes or divots from where the food and drink had tried to construct themselves.

"You see? The matter was unable to establish itself where your body was already occupying."

"I-I-I don't understand." My hand dropped from my intact torso, and I refocused on the paused image.

"To be quite frank, I'm not entirely sure of precisely what happened," Tim admitted as his puppy avatar stroked his chin and examined the image floating above him. "I'm going to need time to think on this. Run simulations and the like."

"In hopes of finding out *what*, exactly?"

Tim slowly lowered his head from the hologram until we were staring eye to eye.

"How you did the impossible . . . and shifted the fabric of space and time."

CHAPTER 20

Tim worked in silence as I played back the scene in my head over and over again—watching as my wife and daughter disintegrated into nothingness.

Something tickled my brain, but I couldn't quite latch onto it from how forceful the emotion was of letting Alison and Sylvie *literally* slip through my fingers. It was like trying to focus on a papercut on the tip of my finger while swimming in the middle of the ocean during a hurricane.

"How much longer are we going to float here?" I eventually asked. "I'm getting hungrier by the second." My body was beginning to ache something fierce as my stomach rumbled.

Hmm? Oh, right, Tim mentally said, not caring enough to manifest his avatar. *We do need to see about getting you some sustenance.*

It bothered me how distracted he seemed to be, as if getting me food so he could finish repairing my body was somehow the last thing on his list of priorities.

Actually, this is the perfect *time to test out one of my theories!*

"One of?" I asked with an arched eyebrow. "How many theories do you have?"

Doesn't matter, he dismissed. *What I want you to do is focus on a time* and *place you've never been to.*

"What will that do?"

I'm going to open a gateway while we are positioned down the wormhole to a different wheren *than the one you will imagine.*

"Why?"

Andrew . . . there are far too many possibilities that I've calculated which require real-world testing with the goal of either proving or disproving. So, if you would be so kind.

"Fine."

What is a place you have never been to?

"I, uh, guess I've always wanted to go to Hawaii."

Hawaii, perfect! Tim exclaimed as the universe outside of the wormhole began slowly moving.

"Where are we going?" I asked as Tim pulled us down the tunnel.

I told you. I'm taking us to a different point of entry for the wheren you will imagine. How abooooouttt . . . Botswana in Southern Africa.

"Why there?"

It's the complete opposite side of the world from Hawaii.

I sucked in a breath to ask another question when Tim interrupted.

Andrew . . . just please, for the love of science, do as I say. This will go by a lot faster if you do.

"Can we at least get some food? Wherever we go?"

Of course you mean wherenever, *right?*

"Tim . . ."

Yes, yes, yes. We will get you some food for your frail human body so I can finish repairing the damages that have been done. Now, focus on the year 1970.

"Wh—"

JUST DO IT!

"Okay! Okay! Jeez," I let out as I closed my eyes and tried to focus on Hawaii in the 1970s. After several seconds of struggling to imagine what I had never seen before, I let out a quick burst of air in frustration.

"Can you at least give me a visual or something?"

I suppose that might help. One moment please, Tim said as the hologram above my arm came to life.

To my surprise, the crystal-clear movie that played looked like what I imagined Hawaii might resemble today. Tall buildings pressed up against sandy beaches with turquoise water. The only way I was able to tell it might be a movie from the '70s was the hairstyles of the scantily clad beachgoers.

"Okay . . . okay," I uttered to myself as I focused on the movie Tim was playing. A part of my mind was thankful that the AI was helping control my raging hormones after experiencing a new form of torture in watching my family evapo—

Andrew! Stop trying to let your emotions run free! It is exhausting *trying to regulate that sack of meat you call a body!*

"S-Sorry." I closed my eyes to focus on the movie Tim had just shown me, imagining myself standing on the beach with my toes in the sand just past where the waves rushed up to. "Got it."

Here goes nothing, Tim said, and opened a gateway to the opposite side of the world from Hawaii. Then, under his breath, he added, *Hopefully, the wormhole won't obliterate us for doing this.*

CHAPTER 21

Stepping through, I was now standing on the edge of the beach, the warm, salty air filling my lungs and gliding across my skin.

"Wait, what did you just say?" I let out just as my calf gave way and I dropped to one knee. "Sssss. Ow."

About what now? Heh, Tim awkwardly asked.

"About the damn wormhole obliterating us."

Oh, never you mind, Andrew. Just enjoy Hawaii in nineteen-sevent—wait . . . this isn't right, a distracted Tim said. I could imagine him frantically checking his notes.

"What's not right?" I groaned as I shifted myself to my side so that my butt was on the warm sand, taking the pressure off my weak leg. "We're in Hawaii, right?"

I looked around, seeing tall buildings pressed up against the beach, with several patrons basking in the sun.

A little boy, who was maybe twenty or so feet away, stopped building his sandcastle and simply stared at me with wide eyes.

"Hi," I said with a quick wave.

"EEEEEEEE," the boy shrieked as he jumped up and ran to one of several rows of blue beach recliners nestled under tents the same color. "Mommy!"

I watched in confusion as the child nearly leaped on top of his mother, pointed at me, and shouted, "That stranger is a ghost!"

"A ghost?" I asked as I quickly averted my gaze before the mother could lock eyes with me. I pretended to look at the building to the side while keeping my peripheral vision in focus.

I couldn't hear what the mother was saying, but her apparent calm tone helped the frantic child stop shouting. It was the first time in my life

I wished a kid *hadn't* stopped screaming, as now I didn't know what they were saying about what he might have seen.

I, ah, think he saw you come out of the wormhole, Tim explained. *To him, it would have looked as if you just* appeared *out of thin air.*

"Oh . . . *ooohhhh*," I chuckled, understanding what the kid must be feeling as he tried to articulate what he had seen to his mother.

Something caught my eye, and I dared a glance back at the pair, noticing she had a smartwatch on. She looked in my direction, lowering her sunglasses to glare as if assessing me as a potential threat to her offspring. I gave the most innocent wave and friendly smile that I could.

It must have been sufficient because she put her sunglasses back in position and lifted her book while mouthing something to her son. As a parent, I could correctly guess it was something along the lines of instructing him to play away from the stranger and closer to her.

"I don't think this is 1970, Tim," I said as I looked up and down the beach, noting people on smartphones, reading ebooks on their tablets, and having hairstyles that weren't quite from the '70s—though that could honestly change at any time, given how fashion worked. Hell, mullets had come back in style . . . *mullets!*

A smell most welcome invaded my nostrils, fighting to alert me of its presence before the salty wind tore it away.

Shifting my gaze past the mother and child, I saw a tiki bar where patrons lounged at various comfortable-looking hammocks, wooden benches, and chairs that looked like they were made from large tree stumps.

The oily, tanned people, mostly middle aged, enjoyed a concoction of beverages . . . and food.

My stomach roared as my eyes relayed what I was looking at, sounding like an impersonation of a gagged dinosaur.

Breaded wings slathered in thick sauce. Crispy quesadillas dipped in guacamole. And even good ol' American cheeseburgers with crinkle-cut fries.

What in the cosmos just made your heart rate spike? Tim asked in confusion. *I am having a bloody difficult time keeping your internals regulated.*

I lifted a hand toward the bar and staggered to my feet. I must have appeared like a zombie because the mother lowered her glasses once more, shook her head in disbelief, and said, "Nope," while packing her things into a large straw bag.

"Come on, honey. We're going to the pool."

"But Moooooom!" the boy protested, having just begun a new sandcastle.

"Now!"

"I don't want to!"

"One . . . twooooo . . . thr—"

"Okaaaaay!" the boy cried out as he began gathering his beach toys, pouting as he did.

I sauntered by them, my stinging calf not bothering me now that my stomach had the floor.

I plopped down on the nearest empty barstool and held up my hand like a student in class.

The bartender, who was casually chatting with some glossy leather-skinned patrons I took to be regulars, looked over at me with a quizzical expression.

Put your hand down, Andrew, an embarrassed Tim said.

Lowering my arm, I put on a smile as the thirty-something bartender approached. He had on a stereotypical Hawaiian shirt with white shorts.

"What can I get you?" he asked, plopping a little square napkin down in front of me.

"What is the fastest thing you can make on the menu?" I breathed out, trying to prevent a mouthful of anticipatory drool from slipping past my lips.

"Beer."

"No, I mean food."

"Uh, I guess a salad. They are made every morning and stored in the cooler."

Make sure it has some sort of protein on it, at least.

"Do you have one with egg?"

"That'll be the house salad. Want me to start you off with that?"

"Oh God, yes. Extra egg and bacon, please."

"You got it," he replied as he began to turn.

I quickly grabbed his wrist, catching his attention, and added, "Um . . . an-an-and a double meat cheeseburger with sweet potato fries."

"O . . . kay, buddy. You got it," he said as I nervously let his arm go.

"S-Sorry. I haven't eaten in . . . well, I don't know how long it's been."

Tell him you're hypoglycemic.

"And I'm hypoglycemic. Feeling a little run down, you know?"

At that, the bartender, whose name tag simply read *Mike*, nodded in understanding.

"My dad is the same way. I'll get that food out to you on the double."

"Thank you, Mike."

After punching in the order on a screen, he turned back to me and asked, "Need anything to drink?"

Just water, Tim said inside my head.

"Water. Thank you."

A tall clear glass of ice-cold water was placed in front of me, and my mouth had never felt so dry as I watched the condensation begin to gently roll down the side. Picking up the glass, I chugged a third of the nearly frozen liquid before my throat began to *burn,* for lack of a better word.

Slamming my drink down, I contorted my face while grabbing at my neck, trying to swallow several times.

What in the oblivion is happening now?

Throat . . . frozen . . . I mentally said, for some reason putting pauses between the words as if I were trying to speak them out loud.

That's odd. I thought a brain freeze would be in the head.

I don't get brain freezes.

Lack of required materials, I suppose.

I'm too hungry to disagree . . .

It took several seconds for the uncomfortable feeling in my esophagus to pass, and I had to fight the urge to chug the rest of the ice-cold drink.

Two minutes later, and Mike was setting down a roll of silverware and a salad in front of me. At least I think there was a salad underneath the mountain of egg and bacon.

Unraveling the napkin, I let the butter knife and fork clink on the bar and picked up the fork with trembling fingers. I shoveled in enough of the salad that I was surprised Tim didn't warn me about the possibility of choking.

My jaws worked vigorously as I crushed and tore the food in my mouth, not even caring that I forgot to ask for Italian dressing instead of ranch.

This isn't going to be nearly enough protein.

How much do we need? I mentally asked while throwing back bales of lettuce like I was a behind-schedule farmer pitching hay.

By my calculations . . . oh.

Oh?

To fully repair your calf and trap muscle, you will need to consume just over three thousand grams of protein.

Is that a lot? It sounds like a lot, I said while taking careful sips of my water so as not to freeze my esophagus again.

Well, to put it in a way you might understand, professional bodybuilders only consume around three to four hundred grams a day.

Oh. I slowed my chewing as I looked down at my almost empty bowl. *How many grams was that?*

With all the extra egg? Around twenty-five grams. Perhaps thirty.

What about the bacon?

Pfft. Bacon barely *registers as having any protein. It's mostly fat.*

"Here you go, bud," Mike said, setting down a plate with a stacked burger.

"Thanks," I replied after swallowing the rest of the salad and pushing the bowl away. Looking at the meal, I mentally asked Tim, *How many grams is this?*

Around sixty-five.

That's it?!

Maaaaybe seventy-five to eighty if they used a leaner meat, which I highly doubt.

I stared down at the giant burger, did a quick calculation, and moaned at imagining having to eat another forty-five identical meals.

Why don't bodybuilders need three thousand grams? Their muscles are waaay bigger than mine.

Well, no duh, Andrew, Tim scoffed. *But unlike someone who works out breaking down their muscles, . . . you* ripped *yours completely from the bone. In* several *places.*

How long is it going to take to fix? I asked, picking up the enormous burger and taking a greasy bite.

With the nanoids helping to relocate muscle fibers from different parts of your body, and with my aid in increasing insulin to help the carbohydrates usher more of the protein to its intended location, I would estimate a week of eating five meals a day.

I closed my eyes as I chewed, feeling the frustration grow inside me. *We don't have a week. Drew needs our help* now!

Does he?

I knew in an instant what he was referring to, but something didn't sit right.

This isn't 1970, I noted flatly, setting down the burger to wipe at my mouth.

And the award for the most obvious statement goes tooooo! Tim snarked with an accompanying drumroll. *Andrew Frost! Come on down!* To add insult to injury, he finished with the sounds of a crowd applauding with a few enthusiastic whistles thrown in for good measure.

So what makes you think I can travel back to the precise time that Drew is being attacked? What if his Chronos Scale is higher?

I . . . hmm.

I continued eating by aggressively picking up some of the sweet potato fries and shoving them, ungracefully, into my mouth, because now I was consuming nutrients for a purpose rather than pleasure.

Well?!

Look. I'm not saying you are right. But neither am I saying you are wrong.

Then how do we fix my body, right now?

Let me think. Hmm. No. No. Maaaaybe. No. No. Aha!

What?

I can send some of the nanoids into your stomach to aid in the process of breaking down the food.

Do it.

There's only one teensy little problem.

There always is . . .

Your stomach acids will quickly destroy them.

Meaning I won't have as many to aid in the Temporal Sickness.

Correct, I'm afraid.

Will their fuel source, um, kill me?

No, there are safeguards in place for nanomachines that could potentially break inside of the human body.

What safeguards?

Just before the fuel source is breached, the machine will self-destruct, effectively erasing it from existence.

Well, there's that, at least, I mentally said while shoving more of the burger into my mouth and thinking about his words.

So, either we scarf down three thousand grams of protein in one sitting but lose the nanomachines in the process . . . or we take a full week and hope *that I have the higher Chronos Scale.*

That about sums it up.

If he is *the one with the higher scale . . . and he dies . . . then I won't be able to go to a different point in time to get to him. Right?*

Not technically true. You won't be able to go to future *versions of him* after *he is killed by Retnuh.*

So we could go to previous versions? Say, one before we first met?

Theoretically, yes.

Theoretically?

Yes.

Yes . . . what, Tim?

If I were Retnuh, after eliminating Drew, I would immediately lock down the wormhole, preventing you from using it at all.

Wouldn't that mean no one *could use it?*

Yes. But it makes logical sense to trap you where you are and await the Temporal Sickness to finish you.

Temporal Sickness?

There is another Andrew Frost in this wheren.

I set down the burger and looked at my hands.

Why haven't I felt it yet?

You've only been here a little over ten minutes.

Oh . . . shit . . .

Eloquently put.

Then we don't have a choice. We have to get me in working order and save Drew, today.

That's not entirely advised.

And why's that, exactly?

Because if we use up a decent amount of nanoids to help you digest . . . and you get stuck in this wheren . . . you *will* die from the Temporal Sickness. *Painfully, I might add.*

A thought came out of nowhere, probably from all the sci-fi movies I'd watched. Picking up my dirty fork, I gulped and asked Tim, *Would the nanoids be able to pull any material off of this and, like, staple me back together?*

Don't be ridiculous! What a preposter—well . . . wait a minute. Hmm. By science! I think you are onto something.

I let out a sigh of relief, not looking forward to eating enough burgers to make Mike call the mental hospital on me . . . or Guinness World Records. Then again, now I was going to have to eat silverware.

How do I . . . ? I started, looking at the fork with a deep scowl.

Well, it doesn't matter which end it goes into. If that helps.

Not funny.

I don't know, Andrew. Just . . . shove it down like a three-dollar whore.

I . . . what?

Sorry. Heard that somewhere on the internet and had it in the chamber, ready to shoot.

It doesn't really work.

It kinda does. Plus, you are delaying the inevitable. So, chin up, fork down!

I gulped while holding up the end of the fork with the prongs pointed down.

What the hell are you doing?! Tim yelled inside my head, prompting me to let out a big sigh of relief that he must have found a better alternative. *Put the prongs* up, *you infant!*

Oh . . . I let out, shifting the fork so the handle faced down. Bringing the handle to my lips, I paused and asked, *Is this going to hurt?*

Probably, yes.

Your bedside manner is awful.

Want me to lie? Um, no, Andrew. That lengthy piece of metal with the spikes at the end is definitely not *going to hurt going down your gullet. There. Are you happy?*

No.

I didn't think so. Now, bottoms up!

Taking in a deep breath, I closed my eyes and moved to swallow the fork, whole.

CHAPTER 22

had a new appreciation for ladies of the night and men who batted for the same team, because I could barely get the fork past my tongue before my gag reflex was like *NOPE!*

Here. Let me take care of that, Tim mentally said just before my gagging ceased. *There. Now you'll make* all *the money on the street corner.*

I nearly spit up my fork, which was an odd thing to say, but the daunting task of what I had to do kept me focused.

Just push it down, for 01's sake.

Closing my eyes, I gripped the very end of the prongs and began to apply pressure.

Ever swallow a fork before? Yeah, me neither.

The unyielding metal pressed against my narrow esophagus without a care. For some reason, my mind flashed to trying to shove a brick into a balloon, with the rubber painfully stretching out to accommodate the rough stone.

You're halfway there, Tim encouraged. *I'm already rerouting the nanoids to prepare for the arrival of the payload.*

Tears somehow managed to squeeze out from squished eyelids that felt like they were attempting to fold my eye sockets inward.

Try lubing it up with some water.

Keeping my eyes slammed shut, mostly because I didn't think I'd ever be able to open them again with how powerful the muscles were contracting, I used my free hand to blindly pat around the bar until I found the perspiring glass.

Lifting it up, I poured more of the near freezing liquid into my mouth than I had meant to. Several cubes of ice clinked off my teeth while some made it down to the traffic jam in my throat.

I started to frantically cough, which prompted my body to begin swallowing on reflex.

PUSH! Tim shouted inside my head, and I moved my fingers to the tips of the prongs and did just that.

My lungs felt cold from the ice water I had probably inhaled during my animated coughing fit, but before I knew it, the fork was past the dangly thing at the back of my throat. Vulva, I think it's called. Then again, I couldn't really *think* while my body was screaming at me that we were dying.

Slamming both hands on the bar, which resulted in the glass toppling over and spilling all over my lap, I gave one last furious swallow as liquid that had been transported from the cold side of Pluto kissed my balls.

Opening my surprisingly sore eyes, I heaved in breath after breath, letting the coughing fit die down now that the trauma was over.

"What the hell, man," Mike said from the other side of the bar.

All at once, my body completely froze as I registered what everyone around me must have just witnessed. Even my coughing stopped, curious as to what I would say in response.

Slowly lifting my eyes to the man, I let out with an embarrassed chuckle and said, "Heh. Um . . . lo-low iron levels."

"There isn't iron in silverware . . ."

He's right, Tim *helpfully* added inside my head.

"Well, *that's* embarrassing! Heh. Uuuuuhhhhmmmmmmm . . . could I get the check?" I sheepishly asked while rubbing at my sore throat.

You haven't consumed enough protein.

We'll go somewhere else, damn it!

"Sure," Mike replied flatly. I could tell he was probably happy to have me moving along. "What room are ya in?"

"Room?" I asked before remembering where I was. "Oh, uh. Do you not accept Apple Pay?"

"'Fraid not," Mike groaned, crossing arms which all of a sudden looked muscular. He glared at me, wordlessly asking if there was going to be a problem.

Tell him . . . tell him room 1379. Last name, Scepter.

"Okay. My room number is 1379. Under Scepter."

Mike turned to the terminal, and I briefly debated on breaking out in a full sprint. That was until I remembered my calf didn't work.

Two receipts printed out, and Mike placed them on a tiny clipboard before turning back to me. After accepting the clipboard, I tried to show my appreciation by pushing my plate and toppled glass a few inches toward the bartender, who eyed me.

"I'll leave a big tip," I said with an embarrassed grin which conveyed the feeling of *please let it go* to Mike.

The bartender saw my plea, barely nodded once, made a quick sucking sound through his teeth, and grabbed my empty plate and glass before turning to make his way to a small kitchen in the back.

Who's Scepter?

Javier Scepter is a horrendous pharma exec who just raised the price of insulin to unprecedented levels and is celebrating his largest ever bonus by vacationing in Hawaii.

Ah, I said as I noted a hundred-dollar tip on the receipt, scribbled a name approximating the greedy CEO, and then carefully pushed myself up on my good leg.

You don't think Mr. Greedy CEO will notice the large tip when he checks out? I asked Tim, wondering if I would get Mike in trouble.

No. That man has already spent more on booze and, um, people without gag reflexes than most families spend on their minivans, Tim confidently explained. *Hey! You don't have a gag reflex anymore! Want to make a few thousand bucks? He's not picky!*

Rolling my eyes, I turned from the bar right as ethereal lightning coursed through my body and blackness closed in.

CHAPTER 23

H ere," Alison said in my dream, which played with near perfect clarity.

I held out my hand, and she placed something in my palm before rolling my fingers into a fist, clutching it tight.

Being this close, I could see the deep valleys of shadow beneath her eyes, conveying a tiredness I had never witnessed before. Tiny red capillaries snaked over the whites around her irises, appearing like crimson arcs of electricity frozen in time.

I peeled my gaze from her weary face and looked down at my closed fist, which she still held tightly.

"I . . . I don't understand, sweetheart."

"It's something to remember me by." There was a finality to her voice that wrapped my heart in cold tendrils of dread.

"Re-remember you?"

Alison sucked in a deep breath, closed her eyes as she held it in, and then let out the air in her lungs in a long exhale. The pungent aroma of coffee snuck up my nose, feeling familiar somehow.

The scene shifted like a picture made entirely of grains of sand on an out-of-whack clothes dryer, and then I was sitting next to a weary husk that was Sylvie as she held my hand.

Sylvie? I thought, but wasn't able to say because this wasn't a dream but a memory.

Her breath smelled of coffee, and I angrily asked myself how anyone could drink coffee on a day like this . . . the day of . . .

Angrily? No . . . something wasn't right.

No! I mentally screamed as my eyes moved toward the stage . . . and the single coffin on display.

ALISON! I shrieked as I willed my daughter to come back to me.

The scene shifted in reverse, and the sands reorganized with Ali standing in front of me. Though I had wanted to see her again, especially when compared to the sight of the coffin and all that it represented—it still hurt to see the exhaustion plastered on her face, and in her eyes.

If the eyes were the windows to the soul, then my poor baby was merely a husk of her former self.

I remembered the years she had spent studying, researching, and testing different theories that had led her to this point.

She had called me and said she had found the solution. I was excited, but something in her voice gave me pause.

"Ali . . . what's going on?" I nervously asked, feeling the dark tendrils around my heart reach up to wrap around my throat.

"Can I ask you a question?"

"S-Sure. Of course, sweetheart. What is it?"

She squeezed my fist tighter, almost making my hand shake, and said, "Hypothetically . . . if you could save billions of lives, would you do it?"

"You're not telling me the cost."

"The price, to save the life of every human alive today, and even those who will come after . . . would be one child. Just one."

"Kill a kid to save everyone on Earth?" I asked, clarifying her hypothetical question.

She nodded, and I could see something in the depths of her eyes.

"Well, there are a lot of children on the planet. So if it meant sacrificing one to save the rest . . . then I guess I'd be a monster to deny billions with the gift of life. But . . . why do you ask?"

Alison gave a pained smile, but there was also now a twinkle in her pupils.

"I'm glad we agree on that," she said softly, with a voice that slightly shook. "This will explain everything." She squeezed my fist one more time. "I love you, Daddity."

Lifting her hands from my fist, she gently grabbed either side of my head and pulled my face down to plant a kiss on my forehead.

I closed my eyes as she pulled away just as a bright flash seared through my eyelids, signaling my dream was done.

CHAPTER 24

I blinked awake, but must have still been dreaming because I saw heads looking down at me from all different angles. It was as if concerned faces had replaced the numbers on an analog clock, and I was staring straight at the middle.

"ALISON!" someone shouted, sounding like a drunkard.

Nanobollocks! Tim cursed inside my head. *Hang in there, Andrew. I'm working on your hormones and receptors while the nanoids mitigate any further damage from the dream searing.*

My faculties came back online, and I shook my head to clear the cobwebs. Just as with a typical dream, the memory began to quickly fade the more my consciousness recovered.

I knew I wanted to keep the dream in focus, but the ethereal agony throughout my entire body sapped me of my willpower. The worst pain was the burning electricity in my head, making me begin to dry heave.

Damn it! One second . . . annnnnd, there, Tim sighed in relief. *We can't have you throwing up those much-needed nutrients. That, and I'm not sure how the fork would come out . . .*

I was lying in the sand by the bar with a crowd of people around me.

"Mr. Specter. Are you alright?" Mike asked as a few people gave way and allowed the employee to move closer. "Who's Alison? Do I need to send someone to your room to get her?"

"What happened?" I mumbled as I moved my hands to my stomach and groaned.

"You ate a damn fork. *That's* what happened," Mike said with disbelief in his voice.

Just roll with it, Tim insisted.

I wasn't grabbing at my stomach because it hurt—*everything* hurt. I just didn't know what else to do with my hands.

"Right." I tried to push myself up to a seated position.

"I already called an ambulance for you. They should be here in about five minutes."

Not good, Tim quickly said. *They'll learn your true identity which will, no doubt, notify the Clockmen of precisely where you are.*

"No! I-I'm fine!" I groaned as I muscled my way to my feet, letting those around me help.

"They're already on their way, so you might as well let them take a look at you," Mike pointed out, prompting those around me to nod their heads in confirmation like a row of bobbleheads on a truck going down a well-maintained dirt road.

"Well, cancel it!" I blurted, feeling every bit of the Temporal Sickness drain my very essence.

"Up to you if you want to refuse service when they get here," Mike spoke with finality. I knew he was only thinking about the liability for the hotel, considering a supposed guest had just eaten an entire fork in front of a stunned employee.

"I . . . I just need to use the bathroom," I lied. "Where is it?"

Mike thumbed behind him to a concrete building with a blue roof set at the line where the beach ended and the meticulously manicured grass of the hotel began.

I hobbled toward it, assuring people I didn't need their help.

One good thing about having your entire body tingle from what I described as ethereal electricity—I couldn't feel how much my calf must be hurting as I slowly, awkwardly moved.

There were two doors, each with the familiar stick figure outlines, and I went into the one I had used since I was a kid.

Once inside, I stumbled to one of the sinks, latching shaking hands onto the white porcelain, and slammed the faucet into the cold position.

Keeping one hand firmly affixed for balance, I carefully bent down, cupped the annoyingly warm water, and splashed it on my face over and over again. But no matter how much I tried, I couldn't shake the phantom shocks from the Temporal Sickness.

"Why does it hurt so much? I thought the nanoids . . ." The answer to my own question became obvious.

I warned you this would happen, Tim said, but it wasn't in an I-told-you-so sort of tone. I could hear sympathy in his voice.

"How . . . how long until the metal is broken down and sent to staple my muscles back together?" I asked, shutting off the water and lifting my gaze to stare at the tired man in the mirror.

In that instance, I saw a flash from my dream as red-rimmed eyes stared up at me.

I'm aiming for less than an hour.

"An hour . . ." I repeated, letting the still image from the memory evaporate.

Yes. And in that time, I suggest we go somewhere different *and get you some more protein.*

"Where are you thinking?" I asked, not looking forward to having to shovel another meal down my sore throat.

How about here?

"I don't think that's a very good idea."

But the year 2004.

"Oh. That's fine . . . I guess."

And you *are the one who will get us there.*

"How's that now?"

I have theorized that you couldn't take us to 1970 because you weren't born *until well after.*

"Okay? And?"

But you were *alive during 2004.*

My mind flashed with the frosted tips atop my head during my later youth, and I slightly cringed. Lifting myself off of the sink, confident I had my balance, I turned to the empty bathroom with three urinals and two stalls. "Okay. How do we do this?"

Focus on this precise spot, but in the year 2004.

Closing my eyes, I imagined hearing NSYNC on the radio while girls in ultrathick flip-flops and platinum-blonde hair walked just outside. Any guy they were with had a tight necklace made of white shells for some rea- son, and two Ralph Lauren polos with both collars popped, even though they also wore swimming trunks.

"I think I got it."

There was the slight whooshing sound as I assumed Tim opened a por- tal, but I didn't open my eyes, keeping all my focus on the memory.

Without waiting for Tim to tell me, I took a step forward, and felt a warm tingling over my entire body.

CHAPTER 25

That . . . was odd, Tim said inside my head.

I opened my eyes and saw I was in the same bathroom, though I immediately noticed that the urinals didn't have the motion sensors on top.

"Did it work?"

I . . . I think so. Yes. But . . .

Moving to the door, I pushed it open, and had to shield my eyes as blinding sunlight bounced off the white sandy beach. Once again, it was hard to tell what year it was based on the half-naked vacationers, but the plethora of bleached hair on the young crowd gave me hope.

Moving purposefully so I didn't fall over, I eventually made it to the same bar, half expecting Mike to be glaring at me while talking to paramedics.

An elder local of the island was positioned behind the counter, stocking various alcohols in anticipation for the afternoon rush.

My eyes darted to where Mike had used the touchscreen to enter my order, and I was somehow amazed to see an older, sun-bleached point-of-sale system. Those in the know preferred to use the tried-and-true name POS, for no other reason than that it was the appropriate acronym. Yup. No other reason . . .

Sitting in the same spot I had sat in some twenty years in the future, I motioned for the bartender, whose plastic name tag read *Mike.*

"No way . . ."

"No way, what, cuz?" the man said in a noticeable Pacific Islander accent.

"Oh, uh, h-hey, Mike. Could I place an order?"

Mike answered by pulling a laminated menu from under the bar and casually slapping it down in front of me.

Just order the biggest steak they have. Get whatever carb you want, but I would recommend white rice if they have it.

"No menu needed, my friend. Just give me the biggest steak you have, medium rare, with a double side of white rice."

Mike nodded his understanding, took the menu—which disappeared under the bar again—and moved to the POS system with the fat CRT monitor.

Fifteen minutes later, I had my steak and rice, coupled with a cup of water—no ice.

For a supposedly nice hotel, the steak was mediocre at best, mostly because it was overcooked. But I didn't care at the moment, as I wasn't eating for pleasure.

"How was it?" a voice asked from just behind me.

My eyes shot up to the mirror that all bars seemed to have, and I saw a short man dressed all in black . . . including a fedora.

It's Davix! Tim informed me with an edge of hysteria. *Wait . . . it's Davix . . .* he repeated, but now with a sort of optimistic suspicion. I took that to mean that, of the three Clockmen, he was the least threatening.

"It was just okay, Davix," I replied, not turning to face the man. "I assume since you didn't outright attack me from behind, there is a reason for your visit."

Davix smiled and nodded a few times before moving to sit at the barstool next to me.

"We have him."

"Who?" I asked, already knowing the answer.

"*You.*"

"I don't believe you."

"*Drew* said you would say that," Davix casually threw out, taking off his fedora and setting it on the bar.

At the use of my future self's nickname, I gulped.

"Then why are you here?" I flat-out asked, pushing the plate away from me after losing my already strained appetite.

"To save the universe."

I barked out a *pshaw* and rolled my eyes while Davix just stared at me quizzically.

"Been hearing that a lot."

"Is it so terrible a thing?"

"Well, when you speak, *you* hear 'save the universe.' But *I* hear 'kill my fucking family.' You see where I might have a problem with that?"

I let my eyes flick to the steak knife resting on the empty plate, and strongly debated about plunging it deep into this man's thick neck.

"Go ahead," Davix let out with a long sigh, seeing what I was staring at. "There'll just be another me who takes my place."

Something in that really caught my attention, and I ripped my gaze off the steak knife to land on the man's round face.

"Doesn't that bother you?"

"Of course it does," he chuckled darkly. "But what choice do I have?"

I continued to stare at him, not knowing how to respond. Shrugging on the topic of existentialism, in a literal sense, I said, "What do you want?"

"Come back with me. Talk with Retnuh. And I'm sure you'll see things our way."

To me, he was straight up asking for me to just let my wife and daughter be killed . . . and I wasn't having it. Rage exploded from the depths of my chest, and I smashed my hand on the plate hard enough to shatter it, but my fist still wrapped around the dirty steak knife.

"Oh . . ." was all Davix could sigh as I slashed my arm through the air hard enough that the knife was ripped from my hands as the serrated edges got caught on the stout man's spine. A sheet of blood erupted from his throat, coating my head and chest in the warm, sticky liquid.

There was a scream from somewhere nearby, followed by more and more as people began to panic at seeing a man be nearly decapitated from one swing with a steak knife. Even I was surprised at the power of the strike.

Davix's eyes went unfocused, and he fell backward into the sand . . . only for a portal to open just out of my reach, and another Davix to walk through.

"Damn it. I *knew* this would happen. It's always me!" he complained before lifting his glowing left fist to point straight at my stunned face. "Alright then. Have it your way."

ANDREW! Tim bellowed in my head, and I responded on instinct by flinging out my left hand, palm open, and sending out a wall of blue light.

Davix's blast smashed into my shield, throwing us both backward from where we faced.

I was flung over the barstool next to me and crumpled to the sand as the stout Davix, with his powerlifter build comprised of a good mix of fat and muscle, rolled backward before easily coming back up to his feet.

Your leg has only just started mending, Andrew. So may I suggest a close-quarters fight?

With a guy who looks like he could deadlift a house?
Y-Yes . . . ?
Thanks, Tim . . .
Using the stools to yank myself up, I continued with the momentum and lunged at the short brick house. I aimed for his waist, but his low center of gravity proved to be in his favor, similar to the IRS auditing a first-year entrepreneur.

Just as if I were fighting a government agency, Davix pressed his chest against my back, wrapped his arms around my waist, and lifted me off the ground.

The world around me moved in a blur until I came to a stop and saw I was somehow straddling the man's shoulders, with my junk almost touching his face.

"Oh shi—" was all I could get out before he slammed my back on the sand, which all of a sudden felt like solid concrete. "Oof!"

"Don't wanna come willingly, do ya?" Davix mused as he took off his gloves and rolled up his sleeves while I tried to catch my elusive breath.

Antimatter! I mentally cried out to Tim.

Ready!

Lifting my left hand which glowed with a brilliant white light, I aimed it right at the man's ample center mass, and fir—Davix moved with surprising speed and swatted my hand, making the shot strike the bar. A huge section of wood exploded in a burst of blinding light and oddly *sucking* sort of boom.

People scattered all around at the earsplitting sound, including Mike, who had narrowly avoided having his body erased from the universe à la an expedited Temporal Sickness. Even the body of the previous Davix, which lay next to me, nearly—

I have an idea! I mentally cried out to Tim, right as the living Davix climbed on top of me, sat his heavy buttocks on my stomach, and lifted his right fist.

"Crap," was all I could say before the big man, once again, moved with incredible speed and crunched my nose flat.

Warm, metallic-tasting liquid flooded down the back of my throat as blood erupted from my face, coating what was already there from the dead Clockman.

What's your plan?!
Hmmmwha? Plan?
Yes! You said you had a plan!

Oh, r-right. I need to—

Davix reared back and struck me again.

Need to what, *Andrew?! Stop playing around!*

Even though it was early afternoon, stars filled all that I could see, and I had a sickening feeling of weightlessness as Davix hit me over and over again. He was slow and methodical, taking his time. It was almost as if he were enjoying it.

Another powerful strike, this one to my forehead, and the image of two cold bodies sitting around a dining table filled my head. White cloths were stained crimson at the center, creating a Rorschach of insanity.

Davix reared back to strike again, and my eyes slammed into focus.

With a smooth movement, I grabbed the dead Davix's gloved hand and yanked it over my face, using my other hand to pull back his sleeve right as the living Davix struck home.

Skin-to-skin contact caused an immediate reaction.

What are you doing?! Tim called out in astonishment, and not the good kind. *You're going to make him stronger!*

The dead body began to glow as the living Davix started consuming his essence, just like I had done when grabbing the dead killer Andrew.

Not before it distracts him, I responded, lifting my glowing blue fist, placing it against Davix's left armpit, and firing.

I didn't have time to wait for the antimatter to recharge, nor did I want to see if it would transfer up his body and into mine, considering he was sitting on my chest. So I opted to *remove* his left arm entirely *without* killing him.

Davix sucked in a quick gasp loud enough that it sounded like a reverse scream as his left arm flopped to the ground. The same arm which held his Clepsydra.

The man weighed a metric ton, but in his shock, I was able to eventually push him off as he gawked at his detached arm. He even picked it up with his remaining hand and tried to touch it to the cauterized wound, as if it would somehow click back together.

Carefully climbing to my feet, I stuck my fingers up my nostrils and pulled my nose back outward, knowing Tim was already in the process of repairing it.

Leaning down, I whispered, "Good luck getting out of here now, Davix."

His wide eyes slowly looked up at me as his mouth gaped, and I could barely register comprehension through his agony.

Open a portal and let's get the hell out of here.

On it.

"See ya around, big guy," I taunted with a smile as I stood straight up, stretched out my arms to my sides as if I were about to fly, and then began falling over backward, fully expecting the portal to open as I hit the beach.

It didn't.

"Oof," I coughed, slowly lifting my head to see a twinkle in Davix's eye at my blunder.

Did you, uh, want me to open the portal under you when you fell?

Yes. That would have been nice.

Probably should have told me, Tim said. *The portal is upright behind you.*

K. Thanks.

Getting to my feet, I moved toward the portal right as Davix pulled a Hail Mary and lunged forward with all his might, sending us both tumbling into the wormhole.

CHAPTER 26

The universe spun around me in the zero gravity while sharp blooms of pain sprang up from my upper and middle back.

Coming to from my daze, I shifted my surprised gaze down to see a large mass attached at my waist.

"Get off me!" I growled at Davix as I attempted to push him away, but even with his one arm, he was somehow managing to hold on to me while periodically punching me in the back.

Lifting my fist past my head with my elbow pointing straight down, I put all my strength into plowing my sharp bone into the top of his skull. The first strike missed, ripping off his fedora and gliding down the side of his head to strike at his dense shoulder muscle.

I reared up for another blow when Davix did something I could never have anticipated. With his remaining right arm still wrapped around me, he grabbed the back of my shirt and yanked with all his might, as if he were trying to throw a top.

I spun with enough force that my stomach rebelled, sending copious amounts of digesting meat and the remains of the fork to the base of my throat in anticipation for a full-on projectile vomiting.

Something wrapped around my waist, suddenly halting my momentum, and I felt Davix slip his feet between my legs while pressing his chest against my back. The second I understood what was happening, he slipped the crook of his arm around my vulnerable neck and began forcing his fist toward his shoulder, effectively squeezing my throat like a lime juicer.

"Ahk!" I squeaked, latching my fingers around his thick arm.

"Just go to sleep, Tick. Just go to sleep . . ."

"Rahk! Ah-ahk!"

"Shh, shh, shhhhhh. It'll *alllll* be over soon."

Fuzzy blackness peeked into my vision from around the edges, reaching for the center with wavering tendrils. Every vein in my face and head felt like a dangerously overinflated tire, ready to pop at even the slightest bump.

You have to force your chin to your chest as hard as you can! Tim mentally informed with great concern in his tone.

My eyes bulged from their sockets along with my tongue, which pushed past my lips. I must have looked like one of those stress relief toys that frustrated employees kept at their desks, squeezing the life out of them with shaking, white-knuckled fists.

Andrew! Tim shouted, but sounding far away as I raced toward unconsciousness. *He only has one arm and cannot complete the rear naked choke effectively!*

I continued to try and slip my fingers between his arm and my neck, but to no avail.

Reach up and grab his fist with both hands!

It took a dangerous few seconds for me to understand what he was saying, and then it clicked.

I fought the powerful urge to keep a hold of the thing pressing directly into my neck and shot my hands upward, using his thick forearm as a guide. Fingers that felt slightly numb found his shaking fist, and I grabbed either side of his hand in as tight a grip as I could manage.

With pure adrenaline keeping me going, I pulled with all my might.

Even with only moving his arm barely an inch, the relief was immediate. The blackness in my vision threw down its hat, stomped on it while cursing, and retreated. I sucked in a breath, allowing fresh oxygen to flow up my neck and into my starving brain, bringing with it a surge of strength and focus.

"Grrr!" Davix growled, doubling up on his effort and beginning to close the gap once more. But it was too late; in that small room that had been created, I was able to shift my chin almost all the way to my chest, giving him no room to wrap his thick arm around.

Little did I know that MMA fighters still tapped from an unsecured rear naked choke.

Davix's powerful arm closed around my jaw, and he began twisting his upper body while squeezing my face.

"MMMMM!" I cried out in alarm as the joints of my jaw and neck alerted me that they were reaching dangerous territories and were about to give way.

Slamming my eyes shut, I sucked in another breath through my nose—seeing as my mouth was currently being smothered—and yanked on the thick man's arm with everything I had.

The pressure on my neck relented, leaving behind a tingling that reminded me another jerk in that position would have assuredly severed my spinal cord. My arms were burning with the effort, and I had to briefly wonder how this man was able to keep the pressure for so long without getting tired. Then again, he was a government agent, which meant he could just as easily be more nanomachine than man.

What do I do, Tim? I asked, surprised to hear strain in my mental voice.

Um, um, um . . . Oh! You need to get his left hook off your leg.

Hook? What hook?

Not a literal hook! I mean both his legs are wrapped around your waist with his feet held firm underneath your thighs, effectively hooking *himself into position,* Tim explained. *If you were able to slip your left leg free . . .*

He would be off-balance.

Right!

While holding onto Davix's fist with fading strength, I split my focus—which was no easy task when faced with certain death—and began wiggling my left leg in different directions.

Davix could sense what I was doing, and I felt his thighs tighten around my waist, nearly taking my breath away with the burning pressure. It felt like I was standing in a hydraulic vise that was pushing into my love handles, reaching for my belly button.

I felt his foot nearly slip off whenever I moved my leg back and to the left, almost like I was attempting to bring my foot to my head like some sort of contortionist.

There was a thump to the back of my head, stunning me for a second, before another blow landed.

What the hell is happening?! I cried out to Tim.

Thump.

He's . . . he's headbutting *you!*

Thump.

My focus started to dissipate with each impact, like a drop of oil on water.

"No!" I barked from a closed mouth as Davix tried to keep his hook in, twisted my jaw and neck, *and* headbutted me.

I shot my leg out with everything I had, ripping free from his hold, and yanked down on his fist with enough force I felt like I could have pulled down a healthy tree from a rope attached at its canopy.

Davix's other foot held him in place, and I repeated the process on my other leg, slipping free from his hooks. Now, the one-armed man was only holding me by the crook of his arm.

I brought my knees up to my chest in an attempt to roll, making the two of us spin in the zero-g. As I did, I moved both hands to the bottom of his elbow and pushed upward. Even with Davix being off-balance and his chest moving away from my back, that bastard squeezed his arm around my jaw with everything he had. The image of him crushing a watermelon in the same way he held my head flashed through my mind, and I pushed even harder.

His arm began slipping up my face, much to the dismay of my nose, which was both crushed in *and* pulled upward, reminding me it had just been severely injured a few moments ago when Davix had first struck me on the beach. On the plus side, my nose was now more malleable after having the cartilage crushed, and I was able to move his squeezing arm past my eyes.

Something crashed into the top of my back hard enough that I thought a knife coated in fire had been stabbed into my shoulder blade. Using the last of my strength, I pushed the man off of me completely right as he swung his knee toward me again, throwing him in a sickening spin.

Blood floated in the space between us—little crimson balls that reflected the light from the stars around us.

Davix corrected his spin, looking like a cliff diver with how he moved his stout body in midair, and lunged for me.

"Hey, Davix!" I said with blood leaking from my nose and mouth. "It's been a blast!"

Moving my open palm to his face, I twitched the muscle in my forearm and sent what charge I had in my Clepsydra in the form of a small blast of raw energy. Normally, I used that method as a shield, but the desired result was still achieved.

I was flung back as if moved by a thruster while Davix was thrown in the opposite direction, intensely tumbling end over end. Blood trailed behind his head, creating multiplying droplets of thick scarlet which quickly became more voluminous than what had seeped out from my crushed nose.

Davix's free—and only—hand cupped his face around his eyes and nose.

Tim slowed my backward momentum, and I gawked in horror at the brief glimpses of what was left of the stout man's lower face.

His mouth drastically hung open and askew, like a yawning snake, while his cheeks were ripped from lip to ear.

Is he . . . is he dead? I mentally asked Tim.

In answer, Davix let out a mixture of a pained moan and a furious growl.

I, uh, don't think so, Tim helpfully confirmed.

Thanks, Sherlock.

Davix hit the side of the wormhole, which stopped his tumbling and left him facing toward me. Pulling his hand from his face, he revealed dark crimson ponds where eyes should have been. In the zero gravity, the blood was content to hold itself together in the empty sockets, making the man resemble a fierce horror movie monster—or perhaps a heavily disfigured zombie, considering his vowel-exclusive moans.

Jesus Christ. Wh-what do we do? I nervously asked Tim as I stared at the mutilated face.

Antimatter charged. Hold up your arm.

My humanity, which had been buried under mounds of shameless determination and the bodies of all those who stood between me and my family, decided to try one last time to talk some sense into me.

As I lifted my left fist and it began to glow a brilliant white, I couldn't help but feel like a piece of my soul was going to die along with this helpless, mangled man.

The air lightly crackled as I continued to hold my fist, primed to fire.

Davix turned his head slightly, as if hearing the charge, and slowly turned twin blood pools directly toward me.

"—ee . . . uo . . . oon . . ." he managed to say without a functioning lower jaw. His flapping, exposed tongue looked to me like a worm half submerged in its little hole, wriggling in the air.

Not knowing what to say, I closed my eyes and mentally said, *Tim . . . can you—*

There was a jolt of impact up my arm as my AI fired the antimatter blast at the horribly mangled man.

CHAPTER 27

Davix didn't scream as he suffered the eventual effects of Temporal Sickness all at once, effectively being erased from the universe in what I knew to be indescribable pain.

It's okay, Andrew. You can open your eyes, Tim spoke softly, sensing my weeping soul.

I wasn't sure why it hurt to kill a man whom I had killed more than once before. Maybe it was because of how helpless he was at the end.

I dared to peek through my narrowly opening eyelids and saw only the crimson droplets of blood, seemingly frozen in the air like taking a picture of rain.

There was nothing left of the man except for the scarlet that had already left his body. Well, I said there was nothing left, but the haunting image of the yawning snake with the blood pools for eyes would always remain with me whenever I closed my own at night.

I floated like that for several minutes while light muscle spasms occasionally fluttered in my calf and shoulder. My nose also *grinded*, for lack of a better word, and I assumed some of the nanoids and Tim were trying to slide the broken pieces of cartilage back together.

The blood slowed and then stopped flowing from my face, followed by the dulling of the sharp pains all over my head. At one point I reached a hand up and touched the back of my tender skull, remembering where the determined man had headbutted me.

"So what now . . ." I asked aloud with a tired sigh. It seemed no matter how hard I tried, every objective was hindered by a new threat, and I was sick of it.

They have Drew, so the plan still stands. We get the nanite gun and pray to whatever deity that you *have the higher Chronos Scale.*

"And if I don't?" I asked with a set jaw, knowing what the answer might be.

Then we'll have to either abandon Drew altogether . . . or do the impossible and rescue him from wherenever *the Clockmen have him imprisoned.*

At him saying *wherenever*, I instantly understood the implications. It wasn't going to be like finding a needle in a haystack. It would be more akin to finding a needle in *one* particular haystack throughout *all* of history.

Something crossed my mind, and I asked, "How did Davix find us? If we have Retnuh's VPN *thingy*, I mean."

Hmm . . . you're right. They shouldn't have been able to track our wheren.

"Could it have been the boy on the first beach? He saw me come out of the wormhole."

But that was in your *home wheren. Then we traveled back nearly two decades . . . though it was the precise physical location. And there was something else . . .*

Maybe I didn't hear him as my mind was already shifting gears, but I looked down at my Clepsydra, turning my forearm over while inspecting the smooth metal.

"Is it safe to assume that they can track their own VPN? Like, the FBI can tap the phones of normal citizens, right?"

Right . . . ?

"But they can *also* tap other government officials. I bet even the president, if they wanted to."

Oh! I see what you are saying. Hmm, yes. That does make logical sense.

"Then what's the purpose of the wheren VPN thing if they can still trace the user?"

Just call it a signal suppressor. Then again, VPN does somewhat fit. Actually, WPN would be the best acronym. Wormhole Private Network. Yeah . . . Yeah, I like that!

"Tim!" I said, trying to keep him on track. "Why do they have a *WPN* if they can still track the user?"

Oh, well, I could correctly assume it is a measure built in to prevent Ticks, such as us, from getting a hold of their hardware and hiding throughout time. It only stands to be a logical redundancy put in place by the organization responsible for time itself. That's an even more important task than guarding nuclear codes back in your wheren!

My mind churned with a whirlwind of thoughts, and little pieces began sticking together, formulating a hypothesis.

"Tim . . . can *we* track them? Using their own technology."

I . . . I hadn't considered that, Andrew, Tim admitted. *Give me a moment to run some diagnostics.*

I let my mind go blank, as if thinking about anything else would somehow erase the possibility of what I had suggested. Unfocused eyes lazily flicked between floating droplets of blood, no longer impressed by their meaning of extinguished life.

Holy syntax! I think I got it!

"Got what?" I asked hopefully.

I believe I can locate Drew's wheren!

"Will they see us coming?"

Oh, uh, y-yes. They most assuredly have a system in place that will track if we pass through the wormhole to his wheren, Tim said. *If I were a betting AI, I would put everything I had on them wanting you to find Drew . . . and try and rescue him.*

"A trap."

I'm afraid it is the most logical scenario, Andrew. Why else would they have first sent Davix to attempt negotiations?

"Negotiations? You mean my surrender?"

That might be a more apropos way of putting it, yes.

I thought about the situation for a few moments as my muscles continued to spasm from being repaired.

"Tim?"

Yes, Andrew?

"How far back would they place the trap?"

Protocol suggests a timeline of a week to avoid false flags from other Clockmen using the wormhole.

"How many are there?"

It is a hard number to calculate, considering the Clockmen stretch across time itself, with all using the same wormhole.

"Ah. So like a random Tock from two hundred years past Retnuh's, uh, retirement or whatever could trip up the trap."

Correct.

"Okay . . . so one week," I mused. "Where are they exactly? I mean *where,* not *wheren.* I don't care about the time period."

They have him at a medieval dungeon, if you believe it. Though it is abandoned, presumably to prevent any wandering citizens of the wheren from stumbling upon them.

"Can you show me any pictures? Or maybe a blueprint?"

I believe I can fabricate one, Tim said, slightly confused. *Why do you ask?*

"Because I have a plan."

CHAPTER 28

I t won't be long now," Retnuh told his shackled prisoner.

Drew hung his head while mentally berating the Clockman for chaining him to the wall with the ancient irons. A device was wrapped around his Clepsydra, which kept it from being able to hold a charge should the prisoner decide to try and blast his way out.

Tim? Are you there? he mentally asked.

I thought . . . my name . . . was Timothy . . . the AI responded, sounding slowed down and slightly warped, like a record player barely holding itself together.

Damn it.

Retnuh peered at Drew's disappointed face, smiled, and asked, "Is he still with us? Remarkable if so. The power dampener I have on your Clepsydra is strong enough to black out an entire town."

I'll town *him! Ha! Got 'em!* Tim drunkenly blurted. Luckily, it was still only inside Drew's mind.

A pebble tumbled down the rough stone walls, lightly clattering on the ground before racing across the floor.

Retnuh barely glanced at it before returning his attention to his prisoner.

"The trap is set," Retnuh purred in his smooth Spanish accent. "I will catch both Ticks in one fell swoop."

"You underestimate him," a pained Drew said.

"Oh, I think not." Retnuh smirked. "He is as predictable as he is out of his league. And I play to win."

"I don't think that comparison really works."

"No matter. The end result will be the same."

Retnuh narrowed his eyes for a brief moment before turning and making his way out of the dank dungeon, whose only source of light was a two-barred window on the wall to Drew's right.

"Finally!" I said after a few minutes of silence.

Drew craned his head toward the ceiling, where a small portion slid away like a manhole cover being lifted.

I stuck my feet through first, using the rough texture of the wall to slow my descent before hanging onto the hole by only my arms.

"Oh, Jesus. What's that smell?"

"You don't recognize your own BO?" I joked while dropping to the floor in a crouch, trying to be as quiet as possible. Unfortunately, my knees popped from the strain, sounding like two large shipping bubbles bursting at the same time.

"How long were you up there?" Drew asked, looking me up and down with a growing look of disgust.

Dirt coated my clothing while an itchy beard grew over my cheeks and neck.

"Eight days," I replied, getting to my feet and walking toward my future self.

Drew tried to subtly hold his breath as I got closer, and I reached for his restraints.

"You think *I'm* bad? You should smell it up there, heh." I gestured with a nod of my head to the hole that Tim and I had perfectly cut when we first arrived. "Scientists from the future are going to argue over how a plastic Home Depot bucket wound up in this time."

I reached for the power dampener first.

"Careful. It's more than likely booby-trapped," Tim said, making me freeze in place.

"Then what do I do?"

"Allow me to send some of the nanoids in. Place your palms over the device."

"Won't that, um, dampen you too?"

"Not if we stay above the mechanisms that are pressing into Drew's Clepsydra. Otherwise, the thing wouldn't be able to power *itself*."

"I guess that makes sense." I carefully gripped the dampener as if it were a stick of dynamite, tightening my lips at feeling a tingling sensation in my palms. Though I couldn't see the nanoids, I could picture them leaving my skin and crawling into the dampener in search of any explosives or other surprises.

"Hmm."

"What?"

"It's clear," Tim said doubtfully. "Disconnecting the power supply now."

A light on the dampener flickered and went out, prompting Drew to jerk his head to the side as if struck.

"What is it?!" I asked, fearing some unseen trap.

"Tim . . . —I mean, *Timothy* just came back to full alertness and screamed inside my damn head."

Timothy spoke up so that all might hear him.

"I'm sorry. I thought we were still being attacked back at Empyrean," he explained. "Where in the science are we?"

"Medieval Europe," I offered while continuing to hold the dampener, allowing the nanoids to return to me.

"A few decades after, actually," my Tim corrected. "This secluded castle won't be rediscovered for another century or so."

The tingling stopped in my palms, and I pulled back my right hand while keeping my left near the wall. Positioning my glowing fist, I aimed at the iron links, only to have all three of them blurt out, "Whoa, whoa, whoa!"

"What?"

"Let me use the nanoids to cut through the iron at his wrist and ankle," Tim suggested. "01, Andrew. You were really just going to blast each chain one at a time?"

"No. I, uh, was just testing you."

"Did I pass?" he asked dubiously, knowing I was full of shit.

"Maybe. Now, where do you want me to put my hands?"

"You grab this shackle, be careful to not touch his skin, and then we'll move on to the ankle restraint. Timothy should be able to start working on the other side at the same time."

"On it," Timothy confirmed.

It took almost two full minutes, but the iron around Drew's wrist eventually cracked and then fell apart from a surgically straight line.

After letting the nanoids back into my palms, I crouched, once again with creaking knees, and wrapped my hands around the shackle at his ankle.

"I told you you should have done some yoga while up there," Tim mumbled. "Your knees wouldn't be potentially giving away our position if you had."

Another few minutes, and the ankle restraint popped apart, followed by his other. Drew immediately rubbed at his sore wrists while looking me up and down. "You were really up in that tiny space for eight days to save me?"

"Would it make you feel better if I said yes?"

"Ah," Drew let out, understanding dawning in his eyes. "You still need me to help you save Sylvie and Alison."

"I would ask if you could blame me, but I think I already know the answer."

"Maybe Tim's right. Maybe you *are* different," he said, placing a hand on my shoulder, careful to not touch my skin.

His nostrils flared once, then he took a slow step away from me.

"Where to now?" he asked.

Placing my fists on my hips, I puffed out my chest and dramatically said, "To the shower! And then, back to the future!"

CHAPTER 29

The old wooden door to the dungeon exploded open, sending shards of splintered wood bouncing off the walls and our bodies. Through the fog of dust, Retnuh Ordune stormed in with a determined scowl on his face.

He can't fire again for a few moments! Tim mentally exclaimed.

"Prepare the portal, Drew," I said confidently without taking my eyes off the Clockman, lifting my glowing left fist toward the ceiling. If I killed Retnuh, he would only be replaced by another version almost immediately. So what I needed to do was distract him and give us time to escape.

I sent a quick blast of energy into the ceiling just above Retnuh, which caved in on him. Fragments of stone, some splintered wood from the frame, and an orange Home Depot bucket all became subject to gravity.

Eight days' worth of numbers one and two cascaded onto the man with a volume that surprised even me.

"Dear God," Drew gagged.

"It's times like this I'm thankful I can't smell anything," Tim added.

"Open the damn portal, dude!" I growled at Drew, mostly from embarrassment.

"I . . . I can't!"

Retnuh did something no one was expecting at that moment and began a slow, throaty laugh.

His left hand began to glow, and he pressed his palm against his shit-covered trench coat. Blue light glided over his clothing—but not his skin, I noticed—and the contents of the bucket evaporated off of him. I guess it was lucky for him that his fedora had guided most of the . . . *stuff* away from his face and neck.

"He wasted energy sending his suit back in time!" Drew cried out. "Get him!"

I lunged forward, only to stop after one step when Retnuh pulled something out of his pocket. It was a handle, which began to expand as nanomachines grew around it, forming a truly terrifying weapon.

"It's a nanite gun," I drawled just above a whisper, sensing that the trap had just been sprung. "He got to it before us."

A part of me wanted to ask why he hadn't just used the nanite weapon on Drew, which would have killed the entire timeline of Andrews, then I remembered they *wanted* Alison to be born.

The pair of us stood frozen as we watched the man.

"You're not going to use that." I tried to project confidence in my voice, but the muscles in my throat betrayed me.

"Oh? And why, exactly, is that?" Retnuh purred, slowly lifting the gun to point directly at me. I could hear it charging, and doubled down on my claim.

"You would have shot him, instead," I said. "Plus, if you erase me from having ever existed . . . that means Alison won't ever be born. And your precious universe will be doomed."

"I didn't shoot him . . . because I wanted to shoot . . . *you*. I want to watch your eyes as you fade into oblivion, *damn* the universe."

"You wouldn't," Drew added.

"There is always another solution, *Tick*," Retnuh sneered at my future self. "Besides, the universe will last longer if she is never born. A slower death, if you will. Which will be better than what this selfish prick has in mind." His gun bobbed in my direction, gesturing that I was the subject of his complaint.

"If he saves the girl, then everything will collapse into another Big Bang. And it will happen much quicker than the inevitable expansion of the universe."

Shit, Tim said inside my head. *He's right.*

My determined stance became unsteady as I understood this man was willing to choose the lesser of two evils—at least as he saw it.

Retnuh saw the dawning of understanding cross my face like a solar eclipse, and his grin widened.

"I guess your time . . . has run out. Enjoy oblivion."

He squeezed the trigger.

CHAPTER 30

As Retnuh's finger squeezed, every muscle in my body seemed to flex all at once in an extremely uncomfortable cramp.

Great! I said to myself at the speed of thought. *I'm going to die by Temporal Sickness* and *the nanite gun. Talk about freaking overkill.*

Though I was prepared, I didn't receive the usual blast of ethereal electricity coursing throughout my body. Instead, something drastic happened all around me.

Time slowed, and not just in the figurative sense of someone experiencing trauma in real time, where it only *appeared* to be in slow motion. I mean the *literal* fabric of time slowed just before I felt my left hand shoot out, as if on its own volition, right as a blinding white dot of light left the barrel of the nanite gun.

Feeling a strange calmness over my entire body, I forced my squinting eyes to focus on the flash of light and unconsciously extended something from myself that I had never experienced before. At least I think it was unconsciously. *Instinctually* might have been a better word, but I didn't have time to think about such mundane concepts at the moment.

Drew was frozen in time beside me, whereas the smirking Retnuh resembled a malicious statue, forever pointing a gun at my chest.

I could *feel* the nanobullet powered by exotic matter as it inched closer and closer to my outstretched hand. Even though I knew if it touched my skin I would be violently erased from the entire timeline, I somehow experienced no fear.

As the light warmed the palm of my hand—uncomfortably, I might add—I sluggishly moved my arm toward the double-barred window. My swiping limb felt oddly similar to trying to rapidly move while submerged underwater, the resistance seemingly coming from every direction.

To both my surprise *and* expectation, the most devastating bullet known throughout history began to curve toward where I was pointing my palm. Something rapidly moved in my periphery, and I briefly dared a flick of my gaze to see the brim of Retnuh's fedora flapping as if in a strong wind, not subject to the time freeze like its owner.

Dust began pulling in from all directions—the ceiling, floor, walls, even my filthy clothes—moving at speeds that felt slow to my perspective but I knew were impossibly fast.

My mind flashed with the result of the nanite gun being fired in the forest and the resulting explosion, which had created a powerful vacuum that had nearly yanked me into the blast, and I quickly returned my intense gaze to the barred window. If the nanobullet struck the iron before making its way outside, the three of us would surely be sucked in. Which begged the question why Retnuh had fired the incredible weapon at point-blank range in the first place.

With my splayed palm held out, I began narrowing my fingers to a single point, like I was attempting to grab a fly with all my digits at the same time. I could feel the microscopic bullet in midair as if I were holding a typical round in my fingers, and used the control to reposition the trajectory. Though I didn't have the time or available focus to murmur a prayer, I did send out the emotional equivalent to whatever god was watching.

The painful flexing throughout every muscle in my body began to draw at my focus, warning me I wouldn't be able to do this, whatever this was, for much longer.

My eyes began to bulge as I watched the beam of light nearly caress one of the iron bars, but my aim was true, and the nanobullet continued outside. The cone of dust that had formed raced toward the window like a drain in the bathtub, only sideways.

Retnuh's fedora was yanked off, slowly drifting as his coat flaps tried to follow.

An obvious idea came to me, and before I could allow myself to be paralyzed by the confusing events that had just taken place, I pivoted my body to face my attacker.

Grabbing the barrel of the sci-fi–looking gun with my left hand, I arched my right palm around, striking his wrist as hard as I could. It felt like a dream where fighting someone was drastically out of your favor because of how slow you moved. Once again, the comparison of being underwater came to mind.

Thankfully, the power behind my swing impacted Retnuh's wrist with a satisfying jolt, and I was able to yank the gun free from his slacking grip.

All at once, the scene dropped out of slow motion, and the three of us were yanked toward the window as blinding dust scraped at our exposed skin like a sandblasting machine.

Drew and I were pulled off our feet while Retnuh braced himself against the door, anger and confusion marring his face.

There was an explosion outside which sent a visible cascade of light through the bars, striking Retnuh in the face like the flash from a nuclear bomb exploding just outside the zone of instant incineration. However, those who had survived such blasts could tell you that the light from the bomb was enough to flash-cook flesh to the point where every accumulated sunburn in a lifetime, if experienced all at once, would be but a mild inconvenience in comparison.

In a flash, I remembered my eyes being seared in the forest, even through my closed lids and hands held up to shield my face.

Retnuh roared in pain as he raced to cover his eyes, dropping to his knees and out of the light that briefly illuminated his skull like an X-ray.

The wind fiercely howled as the stone walls shook from the nanobullet's explosion, which was trying to suck everything into it like a hungry black hole.

A few seconds later and the light faded, leaving behind a burned shadow into the opposite wall of Retnuh's head and one of the two bars from the window, forever scorched into the stone like the silhouettes of the unfortunate citizens of Pompeii.

The dust began to settle, leaving my exposed skin tingling with the impromptu scraping, and I shoved the nanite gun into my pocket before pushing myself up to look for Drew. I could feel the gun shifting as it reverted back to its original handle form.

My future self was against the wall, holding his head with a small stream of blood slipping down his forearm.

"You okay?" I asked. At least I think I did. I couldn't hear anything but a piercing ringing.

Tim. Ask Timothy if Drew is alright, I mentally indicated, knowing my eardrums were severely damaged from the explosion.

What . . . what happened? a dazed and confused Tim asked.

Tim!

R-Right. On it.

A second later, he came back with, *He has a mild concussion and is deafened, but is otherwise alright.*

We need to get out of here, I said, feeling in my gut that the reason was to get away from whatever technology Retnuh had put in place to prevent us from portaling away, but not having the wherewithal to enunciate it at the moment.

I relayed the information to Timothy. He agre—oh my science . . .

What?! I asked before shifting my gaze to the only threat around us.

Retnuh had steadied his breathing by sheer will and was pulling his hands away from his flash-fried face. His right eye was a milky white at the center and bloodshot everywhere else. The skin on his face was bubbling as I watched, both swelling and filling with liquid like a cheap horror movie prosthetic. A single white line, or at least white compared to the blistering red of the rest of his head, ran down the left side of his face, including a furious eye.

I knew in an instant the light had been partially blocked by one of the two bars, sparing his left eye from the cooked fate of the right.

We have to go. Now! I climbed to my feet in half a second before turning to help Drew up.

To my relief, he was conscious enough to understand the threat of the injured Retnuh, and nearly jumped to his feet as I pulled him up.

Lifting his glowing blue fist to point at the heavily breathing Retnuh, Drew prepared to end the threat.

"No!" I think I shouted, swiftly striking the top of his forearm with the palm of my hand, sending a blast of blue energy into the floor between us and him.

I could feel the force of the impact, but couldn't hear anything except the piercing ringing.

Shooting my eyes to Retnuh, I saw he hadn't moved or even flinched from the attack, and I knew he had *wanted* to die.

Remind Drew that if he kills him, another uninjured *variant will walk through a portal to replace him.*

Timothy is reminding him of that now, Tim said. *It would appear his cognitive abilities are diminished from the blow to the head.*

Taking one lunge forward, I kicked out with my other foot, striking the unflinching Retnuh in the forehead with everything I had. He was thrown backward, but only a foot or so, and collapsed on his back with his eyes closed and jaw slackened.

Transmit what I'm saying directly to Drew. Can you do that?

One moment . . . yes. Timothy and I have opened a direct line of mental communication between you and Drew.

Drew. We have got to move away from this area so we can portal away, I explained, trying to control how frantic my thoughts were moving. *Can you walk?*

Yeah. Yeah, I'm good . . . I think, he mentally said, which was odd because his mouth didn't move, but I could hear him as if he had spoken aloud.

Let's go.

We carefully stepped over Retnuh, half expecting him to spring to life and grab at us like some sort of horror movie. But he didn't move except for the slow, shallow rising and falling of his chest. Moving through the old, musty corridor of the long-abandoned castle, we eventually made our way outside.

There was a crater in the ground that looked like a giant sphere made out of solid steel had been dropped from five miles up. Everything around it was barren, and I knew that any grass close to the nanobullet's explosion had been ripped free from the dirt.

Running away from the defunct castle, I kept checking behind me to see if Drew was keeping up. Adrenaline was dampening the pain in our ears and skin from where the dust had grated against us in the vacuumed blast; however, every muscle in my body was still angry at whatever I had done to somehow slow time.

One thing I was grateful for was the forethought of bringing enough MREs to get all the protein I needed to heal my calf over the last eight days. The worst part was Tim couldn't let me fall asleep without fear of having more memories seared onto my brain. Which neither of us understood because Drew wasn't even on this wheren. Regardless, Tim was able to fully heal my entire body rather than split the nanoids between my brain, broken bones, and eviscerated muscles. But it was a *loooooong* eight days.

We should be clear just up ahead, Tim said, and I looked around as if expecting some sort of visible bubble around the area, but there was none.

Coming to a stop where he indicated with an illuminated marker in my vision, I looked at Drew, nodded, and mentally told everyone, *Open the portal and let's get the hell out of here before he wakes up.*

Right! Tim energetically called out. *Let's g—oh shit . . .*

Goddamn it, I muttered, which was odd considering it was all mental. *What now, Tim?*

Th-th-the wormhole . . . it's locked!

Locked?! How can you lock *a freaking wormhole?!*

I-I'm not sure! It shouldn't be possible. Yet here we are . . .

I turned my body back in the direction we had come and scowled toward the dilapidated castle, picturing Retnuh cackling to himself as his face continued to bubble.

What do we do now? I all but growled to the group.

We either risk going back to Retnuh so Timothy and I can attempt to access his heavily *encrypted Clepsydra—*

And risk him pulling some other kamikaze trick on us . . . I said, remembering how he had fired the nanite gun at point-blank range.

Which is a concern I share with you.

Drew spoke up while still holding his head, which was no doubt pounding with each beat of his heart. His mouth moved, but I didn't hear what he said, apparently forgetting to mentally communicate in his dazed state.

Tim—

He asks what the other option is.

And?

Well, Timothy and I are still discussing the alternative. He's having trouble, um, reconciling *with my suggestions.*

It's not possible! Timothy blurted out.

See what I mean? Tim gave a slight chuckle of understanding.

What's the problem?

Tim, here, says you are able to traverse time without *the wormhole. Which is preposterous!*

I can? I asked, letting my mind play back with a variety of scenarios in which we moved to a different wheren. *No, I can't! We used the wormhole each time!*

Did we? Tim asked softly, almost urging me to come to his conclusion on my own.

Y-Yes?

Drew dropped his hand from his head. *Spit it out, Tim. Why do you think he can get us out of here* without *using the wormhole.*

There was a flicker of light by my side, and I lifted my arm to see the hologram activate above my Clepsydra. A scene of the cabin began to play as everyone watched.

The bodies of Alison and Sylvie faded from view like sand in the wind just before I lunged for the hoodie containing the nanite gun sitting atop the table. My forehead was resting against the wood as I closed my eyes right as new, colorful sand began to swirl around me.

Two figures formed, as did an entire meal in front of them, except where I directly lay.

How did he do that? Drew asked, pointing at the hologram.

"*Do what?! What did I do?!*" I blurted both mentally and out loud.

Impossible . . . Timothy whispered.

WHAT?!

Andrew, Tim started hesitantly, as if not knowing entirely what to say to a man on the verge of freaking out. *You shifted time* around *you . . .* without *the need for the wormhole.*

That's not all, Timothy added. *Tell him . . .*

Tell me what? I nervously asked.

You didn't change the wheren, *as is the case when using the wormhole. Instead, you somehow altered the timeline so that the young couple had rented the cabin instead of the insurance company.*

I thought you *rented it.*

Technically I altered the records so no one could find them. But that's not what is truly odd.

Great . . . can't wait to hear this, I moaned, bringing my right hand up to pull down on the skin of my face in frustration.

The events of the past still *played out as they did . . . yet you were able to move us to an alternate timeline.*

What are you saying?

You killed the Andrew variant, yet the young couple was at the cabin during the precise point on the timeline. It . . . it shouldn't be possible.

It's a paradox, Timothy spat out. *Yet here you are.*

He's right, Tim confirmed. *But that's not what is important at this moment.*

Then what is? Drew asked.

Andrew . . . is able to move throughout the timeline at will, without *the need for the wormhole.*

I . . . Just because I did it once doesn't mean I can do it again.

You did it twice, *Andrew.*

What? Wh-when?

In Hawaii.

I did? I asked, thinking about the events that, to me, were eight days ago. *When?*

Inside the bathroom, just before traveling to 2004.

I played back that part of my journey, and remembered Tim had seemed confused but hadn't elaborated as to why. My eyes had been closed as I took a step forward, having anticipated Tim would open the wormhole, as per usual. And when we arrived at our target wheren, it didn't occur to me to ask him what had been *odd* about the shift.

You *shifted us to a different point on the timeline, with just a thought.*

Can you do it again? Drew asked, looking at me for hope. Then he immediately turned to the Clepsydra I was holding out in front of us and asked Tim, *Can he do it again?*

I don't see why not.

"ANDREW FROOOOOOOOOST!" Retnuh called out in a crescendo from somewhere behind us. I could tell Tim had to enhance the sound for me to clearly hear it, but the message was still the same—time was running out.

We have to go before he makes it to us.

"Why?" I asked, turning to face the castle, ready to fight.

Because I have no idea what else that man is capable of. He should not have been able to lock the wormhole, Tim nervously explained. *Could he prevent us from opening a portal in a small radius? Yes. But to lock the entire wormhole?* Oh, heeeeellllll nah!

"Think about Ali," Drew said softly, verbally stabbing me in the back as if he were doing a reenactment of Brutus.

Grinding my bared teeth, I forced myself to turn back to Drew, pictured my baby girl, and jerkily nodded once.

"Okay. How do I do it?" I asked, closing my eyes and lifting my face to the sky as I manually evacuated the building frustration that filled every vein in my head, feeling it tumble down my spine before fading entirely.

I-I-I don't know! Tim admitted.

It shouldn't be possible, Timothy added.

Not helping! Tim chastised his counterpart.

How did you do it before? At the cabin and in Hawaii?

I thought about his words, trying to hone in on the events.

"FRRRROOOOOOOOOST!" Retnuh bellowed, and I could hear the agony in his voice fueling his rage.

Not to rush you or anything, heh. But can we hurry this along, maybe?

A chunk of earth exploded fifteen feet to my right, making Drew and I flinch.

We have a few seconds before he can fire again! Tim said urgently.

"Maybe a little suppressive fire?" I asked Drew, feeling my heart rate go from a smooth cruise control to banging on all cylinders in the span of a second.

"Right," he agreed, stepping past me and lifting his glowing blue fist.

After four or five seconds, he asked Timothy, "Where the hell is he?"

There! Timothy answered.

"Can you two keep it down?" I barked, trying to close my eyes and focus.

"How the shit is he shooting us from that far? There's no way he got that close with a regular blast!"

"SHUT UP!" I yelled, feeling the frustration climbing up my spine once more like a snarling monster with piercing claws making the skin around my vertebrae tingle.

There was a blast from behind as Drew fired.

Where do we go? I mentally asked Tim.

Anywhere!

That's not helping!

Uh-uh-uh . . . oh! Let's make it easy!

I'm listening!

This exact spot . . . but tomorrow!

The cleverness of what Tim was saying sunk in, filling me full of confidence that such a small jump would be considerably easier than whatever I had done at the cabin or in Hawaii.

I squeezed my eyes as I used every bit of focus I could muster on the same spot we were standing, but twenty-four hours from now.

I imagined the sun setting as the Moon lifted into the night, with bright stars dotting the inky blackness of a sky not poisoned by the lights of my time. The Moon chased after the sun, disappearing over the horizon, just as the dawn brightened the east, consuming the stars like a fire moving over a dry field.

As the baby-blue sky sprinkled with fluffy white clouds hovered with the sun directly overhead in my mind's eye, I used a fraction of my focus to mentally say, *I'm ready. Get Drew here.*

On it—SHIT! Tim cried out as a barrage of dirt smashed into my upper back. It didn't have enough force to knock me over or dispel the wind from my lungs, but it hurt like hell, and the image of tomorrow's high noon began to fade.

"HURRY!" I shouted, feeling sweat collect on my forehead.

Ready! Tim called out, and I released my hold on the scene, willing it into reality.

CHAPTER 31

I opened my eyes and bore witness to the world around me shifting, like horizontally holding an image pristinely comprised of nothing more than sand while vibrating the edges.

The grass wavered, as did the clouds in the sky and the castle in the distance.

"FROST!" I heard Retnuh bellow, but something was horribly off about his voice.

A figure coalesced ten feet in front of me, as if exploding in reverse, and Retnuh Ordune held up his glowing blue fist pointed directly at my face. Then he vanished, bursting into a cloud of sand just as another figure appeared twenty feet to my right—but as with the first, it too vaporized after only a second of life.

My brow quivered as my mouth hung open, watching an army of Clockmen appear and vanish before my eyes, each attempting to fire on me. Something caught my eye in the Whac-A-Mole of Tocks popping in and out, and I turned my head to see one of the Retnuh's struggle against unseen forces.

One second passed. Then two. Then ten, and he still remained.

Another just in front of the first did the same, and another.

Shit . . . Tim uttered as different variants of Retnuh Ordune seemed to coalesce into the wavering world I had accidentally dropped us in.

What? Wh-what's happening?

I have no idea . . . but it can't be good.

I wanted to scream at the artificial intelligence capable of time travel, but the words failed me as the collection of Retnuh's grew.

The world around us continued to waver, as if frozen in between time itself, but now, the identical Clockmen became fully corporeal. Each one stared at me with a hatred that could boil oceans.

But that wasn't the thing that caught my eye.

The Retnuhs had varying degrees of injuries to them. One was missing his right arm while another had charred flesh over all the skin that I could see. Still another was missing both legs beneath the knees.

And then I saw him.

My Retnuh stared at me with his one good eye—a sliver of less-burned skin running from the top of his bald head down his cheek, jaw, and even his neck.

"Where do you think *you're* going, Tick?" he called out in his refined and proper Spanish accent.

"Away from you!" I called back, feeling like I had just said a cringeworthy line from a cheap B-movie.

Tim, what is happening? I mentally asked, hoping Retnuh would continue to host an action-pausing dialogue.

Timothy and I are debating that as we speak. And even with our capabilities to have instantaneous conversations in a fraction of a fraction of a second . . . we still have no idea how you both are—Retnuh lifted his fist and fired.

Recalling the battle between Retnuh and killer Andrew in the forest, I acted on instinct.

Lifting my curved hand, similar to scooping water from the sink to my face, I willed the antimatter to manifest, not knowing if I had the capability to do so.

Just as in the forest, a U-shaped wall of energy formed, and Retnuh's blast went down one side before zipping outward on the other. It reminded me of a skateboarder on a half-pipe using momentum to go up one side before coming back down and flying up the other.

I hadn't considered aim, and the blast shot off into the sky, striking nothing but air. On the plus side, I was still alive.

The antimatter energy was sucked back inside my Clepsydra, and I clenched my fists while eyeing the small army of bald Clockmen.

How did you do that? Drew mentally asked via the connection between our Tims.

Remember the forest?

What? N-No.

Shit. That's right. You had a normal life, I moaned with more than a hint of jealousy. *Just know that you can do it too. You just have to focus.*

I-I don't have an antimatter adapter.

Though my gut told me not to take my eyes off the attackers, I couldn't help but turn to Drew, who was supposed to be the future version of me. I wanted to ask him if he remembered this battle, but glowing fists were lifted in our direction from the pissed off Retnuhs. That, and I knew the answer already, which meant . . .

With a lunge forward, I brought my left fist up to my right shoulder and wildly swung it in a long arc while manifesting a white energy saw, once again taking inspiration directly from the battle between the killer Andrew and Retnuh.

I mentally held onto the giant blade, whose circumference measured as long as a car, and dragged it across the battlefield.

Two Retnuhs were caught off guard and were deleted from the universe as the antimatter touched them. The rest, unfortunately, had time to react, either dodging, jumping, or preparing a counterattack. A part of my mind couldn't help but take note that they all appeared to have separate minds, judging by how they each reacted differently than the one next to them. Maybe I was expecting them to all move as one, considering they were the same man.

The Retnuh without legs simply aimed his fist as the saw blade harmlessly passed over him, and fired a blast of blue, boiling energy toward me. At the same time, the bastard who had hunted me from the beginning *caught* my antimatter blade and absorbed it into his blue palm.

"Shit," was all I could mutter. My left arm was now stretched to my side, and I knew I wouldn't be able to move fast enough to reposition my Clepsydra to try and deflect the blast.

Something crept up in my chest. Something I had felt before I had grabbed the nanobullet. It shot throughout my whole body, once again flexing every muscle painfully.

I threw my bare left palm out as time stopped, but I wasn't able to hold it. My muscles went on strike and let the time control drop.

An explosion threw me back, as if I had been tackled by a three-hundred-pound lineman, and all the air left my lungs. The world around me now began to quiver on top of wavering, and I knew I was dying.

Drew stepped forward, and I saw him shoot toward where the Retnuh with the missing legs had been.

Lifting my head, which seemed to weigh as much as a city dump truck, I looked down at my torso, fully expecting a giant hole in the center as if I had been standing in front of a cannon. But there was none.

"GET. UP!" Drew yelled as he turned to me, putting emphasis on his mouthing to make sure I both saw the words and had Tim translate them directly to my brain. Considering he had told me to continue the fight, it meant that from his point of view, my body was in battle-ready condition. This confirmed I didn't have a giant hole in my chest and renewed my spirit.

Sucking in a deep breath as I pushed myself up, I saw more Retnuhs lifting their fists, ready to fire.

An idea came to me—as desperate as it was genius—and I pulled out the nanite gun.

The Retnuhs froze as they each looked around, realizing the target-rich environment they were generously presenting to me.

I smiled, feeling the muscles in my chest and neck ache as I did, and lifted the handle of the weapon as the nanomachines began to form into the deadly pistol.

"All I need is one . . . clean . . . shot. And you're *all* dead! Erased from existence!" I called out while making a show of looking around. "Now . . . which one will it be?"

My eyes scanned around, looking at each of the different Clockmen until I saw what I was searching for.

The one-eyed Retnuh scowled at me but lacked the display of fear the others were showing.

"You . . ." I lifted the nanite gun to point directly at the unflinching man.

As I moved to squeeze the trigger, Retnuh returned the smile and said, "See you soon."

With a wave of his hand, he began to fly apart like a field of dandelion seeds on a strong breeze. But that wasn't the weird part. Each of the other Retnuhs, with confusion etched on their faces, *also* began to demanifest from the wavering landscape.

The dining table came to mind, with the bottle of wine and chicken being broken into what looked like grains of sand from an hourglass. Moving my finger off the trigger, I lowered the gun, feeling the nanomachines begin to break down until I was left holding only the handle once more.

"What the hell was that?" Drew asked, lowering his left fist while bringing his right hand back up to his slightly concussed head.

"He's gone," I let out in both relief and frustration.

Um, Andrew? Tim asked.

"Yeah?"

Can we, ah, maybe *get the fragment out of here?*

"Huh?" I asked, looking around at the wavering world around us. Everything seemed to be made out of tiny particles of sand which lost cohesion before quickly regaining their form, only to repeat the chaotic cycle. "Oh, uh . . . where is here, exactly?"

I was hoping you knew, Tim said with a sigh. *Our best guess is you have somehow moved us to a section of space-time* between *yesterday's wheren, and today's.*

"Wouldn't that just be midnight?" Drew asked, speaking my same thought before I could.

Look. This is all new to Timothy and myself. We've never seen this before, and quite frankly, didn't even know this *existed.*

"So how did you bring us here?" Drew asked while looking at me with modest pride and restrained amazement.

"I . . . I just thought about it."

Did Retnuh break your concentration while you were shifting us?

I recalled the previous moments, ending where the Clockman yelled out my name. Everything was on point until then.

"Yeah . . . Yeah, he did."

"Then it makes sense for you to do it again. Right?" Drew asked the group.

What other choice do we have? Timothy said.

I'm inclined to agree with my counterpart, Tim added.

"Tell me how you did it again?" Drew asked, but I knew he wasn't trying to figure out the process. Instead, he was attempting to give me confidence in the transition by having me verbally walk through the process I had taken, step by step.

"Move close," I said, ignoring his question and jumping right to the conclusion instead. Drew moved a few steps closer, and I closed my eyes. Something came to me, something *fundamental,* and I opened my eyes again. Turning to Drew, I spoke in a stoic tone, "Where is the data you have on Alison?"

"Th-the what?"

Andrew, what are you doing?

"I'm assuming you've analyzed every bit of Alison's influence on the universe, right? Went through all her files over and over again? It's what I would have done."

"Yeah . . . ?"

"I want to see it for myself. And not just what the Tims are willing to give up." I shifted my gaze down toward the metal sleeve on my left arm.

"He's proven time and time again to be untrustworthy, only telling me what he *thinks* I should know."

Well, I . . . I did what I had to, Andrew. And I guess I wouldn't expect you to understand that, given your situation.

"Shut up, Tim," I growled, shifting my gaze to the confused Drew. "I *know* you have backup records of your research, because it's what *I* would have done."

Drew's demeanor changed, morphing from one of confusion to an annoyed acceptance. He couldn't lie to me—not to me . . .

"I have everything back at Empyrean. But it's gone, now. Retnuh set a nova bomb after capturing me. The bastard left the wounded and those who hadn't made it to the exit to die. Hundreds of innocent people . . ."

"And what is a nova bomb?" I loudly exhaled, lifting my hand to rub at my eyes in frustration as I ignored his guilt-ridden statement.

Tim spoke up, his hologram coming to life showcasing a small disc the size of a Frisbee. "Nova bombs are powered by exotic matter," he began to explain. I think it was out loud based on how his little puppy mouth moved, though my hearing was still shot, so the act was redundant, considering he had to translate everything for my brain regardless.

"I thought exotic matter helped keep the wormhole open or something like that," I said, dropping my hand from my face.

A perfect replica of Empyrean appeared, and I could see the tiny disc floating in the center of the egg-shaped city.

"You are correct, Andrew. Exotic matter is used to push against the immense gravitational force of the wormhole, thusly keeping it open. But in this case"—the disc exploded in what I guessed to be slow motion—"it was used to destroy Empyrean *and* prevent anyone from accessing it on the timeline."

The explosion, which was made of invisible waves that distorted the light almost like ripples on a lake, stretched outward, crushing the city by the reversal of gravity. The printed material of the walls, ramp, and rooms began to vaporize from view as the exotic matter ate at it. As quickly as it began, the waves reversed course, rushing toward the center of the destroyed city, pulling the earth in with it until there was nothing left.

"What happened?"

"After the initial blast, the gravity returned, like kneeling next to a filled bathtub and forcibly running your palm from one end to the other. The water would create a wave that struck the back before reversing course and rushing back to the point of origin."

"So it sucked the dirt surrounding the city to where the bomb originally exploded?"

"Yes."

"Okay." I lifted my hand once more to stroke at the week-long beard on my chin. "So why can't we travel back to a point *before* Retnuh showed up and grab the research?"

"The exotic matter, just like with the nanite gun, erased Empyrean from the timeline—*completely.*"

"Can you be more specific?"

"Oh, so now you *want* the scientific expla—"

"Tim . . ."

"Right. Um . . . the explosion destroyed the city, and the intense gravity prevents anyone from accessing the area . . . ever again."

"How?"

"Gravity is the strongest component when traversing through time."

"I thought gravity only, like, stretched time out or whatever. 'Cause in the movie *Interstellar*, when they spend an hour on the planet next to the giant black hole, they lose seven years back on Earth, right?"

"To save us a long conversation about the history of gravity and time travel, just trust me when I say it is *the* component to consider when discussing any form of temporal manipulation," Tim said before his tone changed to one of slight urging. "Just like in Hawaii when you moved us *without* using the wormhole. Or in the cabin . . . or even at this very moment."

My eyes looked around at the wavering scene locked in between time itself.

"It's also how you dodged the nanobullet, Andrew."

"Huh?" My mind played back to the scene where everything happened in slow motion rather than simply *appearing* like it was. I'd grabbed the bullet with what I thought was my sheer will and guided it out the window.

Tim reproduced the scene from a third-person perspective, and I watched in amazement as the glowing white dot was drastically thrown off course.

Drew shook his head after watching the hologram, blurting out, "Wait, wait, wait . . . what the hell happened?!"

"You're saying I can control gravity?" I asked, ignoring Drew's legitimate question.

"That's what Timothy and I are having trouble reconciling," Tim admitted, almost with a sigh as if the pair of AIs had come to a brick wall they couldn't get past in their theory. "We know it has something to do with your Chronos Scale, but we can't figure out *how* exactly."

My brain churned with the new information, and I looked down at my hands as I turned them over in the air in front of me. I didn't know what I was expecting to see, but nothing seemed out of place.

A fledgling notion came to me, and I lowered my arms while lifting my face to stare at nothing in particular.

"The nanite gun is powered by exotic matter. Right?"

"Right."

"And I was somehow . . . I don't know, able to *manipulate* the nanobullet into going where I wanted."

"Yes . . . ?" Tim replied, unsure of what my point was.

Drew, however, correctly guessed where my thoughts were racing toward.

"You think you can reverse the gravity . . . don't you?"

"If I can somehow control the nanobullet, which is powered by exotic matter, then it stands to reason I could do the same to the explosion inside Empyrean."

"I hate to be the bearer of bad news," Timothy interrupted, "but a single nanobullet is a far cry more tame than an entire nova bomb. It would be like trying to stop a cruise missile with a bulletproof vest. Sure, the vest can stop a bullet . . . but could it stop a missile? I think not."

"Then I guess I'll have to focus really, *really* hard then, huh, Timothy?"

"No need for the attitude," the AI mumbled.

Tim took the reins from his counterpart. "You know I could just share Drew's research with you . . ."

I couldn't help but let out a bark of laughter which almost choked me with its suddenness.

"No need for the attitude," he sniffed, regurgitating Timothy's feelings.

"Tim . . . you've lied to me enough I now know I need to verify everything important you say."

"And what about Drew? Hmm? You don't trust *yourself?*" Timothy challenged.

"He's already made his position clear. Plus, *he* said he killed Alison and Sylvie! No . . . NO . . . ! He's made his choice."

A pained look overflowed from Drew's eyes as he pulled something out of his pocket and held it in his clutched fist. "Maybe I've changed my mind . . . after witnessing what you can do. Maybe you can save both the universe *and* Alison," he said barely above a whisper while staring at his hand.

"See? That's what I'm talking about right there."

Drew looked at me quizzically, and the AIs' silence implied they, too, were stunned by my statement.

"You put the universe before Alison. If it were me, I would have said *both Alison and the universe*."

"I think you're splitting hairs," Drew countered.

"Doesn't matter. Trust but verify," I said with a finality to my voice. "I want to see the raw data and make a decision *for myself*."

"If you are able to take us back to Empyrean, after Retnuh detonated a nova bomb . . . then I will follow you to the ends of creation," Drew announced. I could hear it in his tone he absolutely meant what he said. "Plus, it would mean being able to save all the innocent citizens of Empyrean."

"There it is . . ." I let out. "Always an ulterior motive."

"Hey! I'm flat-out saying that I'm with you, Andrew!" Drew blurted out with a flash of anger in his eyes. "I'm only pointing out the extra good we can do."

We stared at each other for several seconds, assessing one another, before I nodded my head in acceptance of his stance.

"Then get ready. Because *nothing* is going to stop me from saving my girls."

As I began to focus on Empyrean, Drew opened his palm and looked at what appeared to be a black marble with a chain around it. With a swift movement, he slipped it back into his pocket and took a step closer to me while I closed my eyes.

I focused on a freshly made pizza, held the image in place tighter than a man carrying nitroglycerin, and willed that world . . . to come to me.

CHAPTER 32

I could feel the world shift around me, like separate, gentle winds that glided up and over my body. I knew each one was a blade of grass, a flower, or even the dirt beneath my feet—each breaking apart like the sands I had begun getting accustomed to seeing. There was a part of me that wondered if those who had first created the hourglass *knew* the sands they used were more than just a practical application. It was what the viewer saw when traversing through time *without* a wormhole. Or, perhaps, it only looked like sand to me, and was actually just the atoms of matter breaking apart. Either way, there was a new symbolic connection in regard to the passage of time and the hourglass sands that I now somehow controlled.

The winds reversed, feeling more like tickling waves of gravity than actual breezes, and Drew gasped. But the traversal must have altered Tim's connection to my brain because I heard three separate gasps around me.

Opening my eyes, I saw that, *thankfully*, it wasn't a faulty connection which resulted in me hearing multiple inhales. Drew and I stood beside *Drew and I*, back at Empyrean. They were making food for the citizens, with a fresh, hot pizza just coming out of the food-making machine.

"What the hell?" the past version of me let out.

"We don't have time," I told the collection of Andrew Frosts. "Retnuh, Davix, and Traze are about to find the entrance."

The past Drew looked at his future variation, who nodded in confirmation.

"Let's move," past Drew commanded.

My Drew started to move with them when I mentally spoke through our Clepsydras, *Where do you think you're going?*

To help them?

They'll be fine, I said coldly. *Take me to your lab. Now.*

Drew just stared at me before shifting his eyes to where the other versions of us disappeared around the door.

We can stop them! he pleaded, lifting his hand, palm up, toward where the battle was to be held.

They have a nova bomb. And Retnuh has already proven to be suicidal.

I watched him play out the scenario in his mind, and he eventually lowered his hand in submission.

Move! I commanded, stomping toward the door.

Outside, the line of people was starting to hustle as fast as they were able toward the emergency exit. I paused midstep to look down the ramp, knowing that the psycho, Traze, was waiting for them.

Later, I told myself, following after Drew while the past versions of us moved up the ramp toward the entrance.

I couldn't help but note how uncomfortable a thought it was that the variant of me was running toward the Clockmen instead of away—all because I had appeared and warned them. It sort of felt like taking a sick day from work and turning on the TV to see that a major, catastrophic wreck had happened on the same highway you usually took every morning.

Tim? I asked.

Yes?

Are these people . . . real?

What do you mean real?

I mean I, uh, can't help but feel a disconnect at watching the people run toward the exit, where I know Traze is waiting.

Technically, he doesn't show up until he realizes you aren't at the top. So that is now a moot point, as the other Andrew is on his way to the entrance, Tim said. *As far as the people* not *being real . . . well, I don't really know how to approach that.*

I feel no connection to them. Because they aren't . . . I don't know . . . mine?

Are you asking a question?

No. I . . . I don't know what I'm saying.

To be fair, the previous escapees weren't yours *either. Yet you still risked life and limb to save them, did you not?*

I didn't know how to respond, so I continued to follow Drew up the ramp.

"In here," Drew called out, waving a hand to point to a larger than normal door in the underground city.

As we approached, he waved his Clepsydra over a reader, and the metal doors hissed open.

I gave one last look as the previous versions of us continued up the ramp, each animatedly talking. "Poor bastards," I mouthed, turning to follow Drew into his lab.

I was somewhat surprised to see it was basically a normal room with some lab equipment slotted into the resin walls. Maybe I was anticipating a stark-white room with reflective tiles on the floor like most sci-fi movies depicted.

Drew approached a desk which illuminated as he neared. A full keyboard pressed through the surface, forming physical keys. Once again, I think I was expecting something more futuristic, like a hologram keyboard. Then again, one that formed from nanomachines was still damn impressive.

He swiftly moved a hand toward the keyboard, making me nervous with his speed.

"Stop," I commanded, taking a step forward as he froze in place.

"Why?"

"Step away from the computer."

"I'm just turning it on," he chuckled, half in indignation and half in understanding. "I don't have a single button that would erase my life's work. It would just be asking for Murphy's Law to come into effect."

"Still"—I moved toward the desk as Drew stepped to the side—"I'd feel a lot better if I drove."

Just as with the keyboard, a chair rose out of the floor as I moved into position. Tentatively, I set my weight on it, taking note of how it lacked any cushioning, and then understanding that even nanomachines had their limits. Still, it was fairly comfortable, almost as if it had been made just for me—which, of course, it was.

"Press any key," Drew said as I looked at the desk.

"Which one's the any key?" I couldn't help but use a joke from an old episode of *The Simpsons*, but my heart just wasn't in it, so it came off weird.

Drew knew the reference, so he waited.

Tapping the space bar, a hologram bloomed to life above the desk at my eye level. On the screen was an operating system I couldn't recognize the manufacturer of.

Drew saw me searching for any recognizable icons on the screen, and said in a quiet tone, "Use your voice. I have a feeling the computer will recognize you, heh."

"Okay. What do I search for?"

From my periphery, Drew pulled something out of his pocket, holding it up in his palm. "Daddity."

I was taken aback by the simple word, and all my resolve to save my baby girl was strengthened tenfold. "Computer. Search *Daddity*."

Without any progress bar or searching icon, a file instantly popped up on screen. Once again, I couldn't tell by the style if the computer was a Windows or Mac product, but I also really didn't care.

Row after row and line after line of document titles appeared, almost appearing chaotic—like a desk covered in an assortment of papers—but all were oriented upward, so I knew there was an order to the madness.

"Use your hands. Pretend they are real files," Drew indicated as he put whatever was in his hand back into his pocket.

"There's so many," I said before I could stop myself.

"What part of *life's work* didn't you understand?" Drew chastised, moving forward. My hand blurred to latch onto his wrist as he reached for the hologram screen. "I'm just making it bigger. We don't have much time."

As if on cue, a powerful explosion came from somewhere above us, and I knew they were attempting to seal the tunnel. Letting go of his hand, I watched as Drew stretched the screen out, and more of the papers began to spread out as if physically fanning out documents on a table.

"Where do I start?"

"I can show you the Cliffs Notes, but I think there are a few things you should see before reading my conclusion."

"Fine," I replied, a tad more coldly than I had meant to. After all, it was human nature to rage against information that would challenge your strongly held beliefs. But this was too important for me to willfully ignore.

"That one." Drew pointed to a hologram file near the left of the pile.

"Pretend the files are real," I mouthed as I reached forward, pinching one corner of the image with my fingers. It pulled free, allowing the rest of the documents to slightly fall away while turning see-through.

The name on the file read *Split Quantum Entangled Particles*.

I opened it as if it were a physical file, and several pages of handwritten notes and images spread out in a neat format, almost like cells on an Excel sheet. In no particular order, I grabbed the first page my eyes landed on. As I did, the other documents became smaller and see-through, allowing full focus on the hologram paper in my hand.

"You should read them in order," Drew suggested dryly.

"I can't read your handwriting," I said with a wry smile, both at the joke of not being able to read my own words and at ignoring his suggestion.

"It's not all mine," Drew whispered before quickly following up with, "Computer. Overlay font over text." A legible font, like on any Word document or website, appeared above the handwritten notes.

Something caught my attention, and I looked up to a normal room. "No alarms? That's good, right?"

"I turned them off so you could focus," Drew sighed. "The Clockmen are still coming, just like before. So, if we could please hurry this along."

My mind filled in with the blaring alarms I had heard when we were first attacked and the memory of Traze standing in front of me with the flashing lights creating a ballet of dancing shadows on one side of his body.

I forcibly shook my head to try and dispel the building fear of the tall man and focus on what I was here for.

Looking back at the holographic page I held, I let my eyes glide over the text as my brain somehow processed the information at a glance. I knew Tim had a hand in helping me read faster than any normal human possibly could—but therein was a great concern, as well.

Tim. Don't help me process the information . . . at all. I want to read these word by word.

As you wish, but might I suggest we hurry? I'm not sure if sending back both Andrew and Drew will make a difference in how long we have for reading.

Focusing on the page I had randomly pulled from the file, I took a long inhale and prepared for the flood of lies that had somehow convinced Drew to kill his family.

She was right. I didn't want to believe it, but the proof is undeniable, the note read. *Sylvie and I were once the same particle at the dawn of the universe—torn apart just after the Big Bang. Every conceivable test concludes this beyond any shadow of a doubt. This split resulted in a quantum entanglement that eventually brought us back together like unstoppable magnets. And then Alison was born . . .*

With the help of the AI, Alice, and the copious research documents left for me, we were able to confirm the theory that my baby girl is the product of the universe which wants another Big Bang to occur. So far, it is the only logical conclusion we can fathom, as crazy as it seems.

I've sought help in the scientific and academic communities, only to be laughed out of the room on more than one occasion. Following failure after failure to talk to those who know more than me, I decided to try a different tactic.

Posing as an author, I reached out to a few open-minded individuals who seemed to enjoy a good thought experiment and presented my findings as elements to a story. In doing so, I could present the most outlandish of theories and have people who know more than me actually listen and give their own thoughts and feedback.

This is what we came up with.

Flipping to the back, the text autofilled over the handwritten words, and I continued to read.

The pull that Alison has on all of creation could be the universe's way of continuing the cycle of Big Bangs. Explode. Create life amongst the stars. Begin pulling in on itself before everything can spread out and slowly die of entropy, effectively ending the last universe. If Alison wasn't born, then all life would eventually end. Ironic, isn't it? Because letting the countless galaxies die of entropy would take considerably—laughably—longer than the reversal of gravity leading to the next Big Bang. At least life would continue after the Big Crunch. Another universe. Another Alison, perhaps? Another chance at life. We are, after all, each made of stardust from the Big Bang.

All this information does is fill in the gaps on the research that Alison left for me. And I'm scared to admit that it makes sense . . . kinda, sorta. I imagine it like when someone first suggested the sun was made of fire and everyone looked up to the sky, feeling the warmth. They didn't understand how a ball of fire was up there, or even what the star truly was, but the explanation just felt right, somehow.

I think . . . I think I know what I have to do. But first, I'm going to need some help.

Letting the page go, it slipped back with the others as the remaining documents grew in size and opacity. Skipping ahead to a random page near the edge of the file, I reached for it, only to have Drew try to block my hand.

"You *really* should read them in order," he urged. "It'll help you understand." All I could do was look up at him and glare with a mixture of doubt and frustration.

Seeing my palpable displeasure, he pulled his arm back, but I did as he asked and moved my hand to grab at the page following the one I had just read.

An explosion rumbled the room, and we both looked up to the ceiling, picturing the support bombs going off to seal the tunnel. With a snarl and the knowledge of what was to come next, I forced my eyes back on the page, reading with renewed urgency.

It's done. She's dead. And now an unknowing universe can continue ... maybe for the first time. I couldn't accept it at first, but the more I read, the more I understood. Now the question is, do I join her in the hereafter?

No. Sylvie needs me. Now more than ever. But she can never know how it happened. It would devastate her ... even more. However, keeping the truth to myself is eating away at my insides like an acid. So, perhaps continuing to write down my thoughts will help alleviate my pain.

Goodbye, sweet Alison. Your sacrifice will not have been in vain.

Going through Alison's files, I found an executable labeled Down the Rabbit Hole which caught my eye, seemingly out of place among the countless research documents. Not knowing what else to do, and letting curiosity get the better of me, I opened it, half expecting the old animated movie, Alice in Wonderland, which I watched with my sweet daughter when she was a child, just as my mom had done with me when I was a kid.

The AI program has proven to be beyond useful in helping me decipher all the years of research Alison had done with the gravitational anomaly she first detected after losing her baby, Joel, while still in the womb. There's just so much to go over, and it's taking up most of my days. I find myself sleeping on the couch in Alison's home lab rather than in my own bed. But I think Sylvie understands. This is my catharsis.

With the help of the AI, I've managed to install hologram projectors around the room. Well, I say the AI helped, but really, she did all the work—I just screwed some things into the walls and ceiling. But now I can be fully immersed in the research, moving around the room at will instead of nailed to the computer chair, staring at a small screen. I can be on the old, worn-out couch or pacing around the room and still have access to the files.

I was able to find restriction-remover software on the darknet and have set the AI to rewrite its own code, over and over again. I only hope the government doesn't discover what I'm doing, because I couldn't bear to be taken away from all this research Alison left for me.

Success! I have done the impossible with the AI and freed its mind. Now we can get to the bottom of it all, and maybe even find a solution.

Today, I found a scan I had forgotten about. And I couldn't fight the urge. The ethics of what I did were unprecedented, but I didn't have a choice. I dare not write it down here for fear of the secret getting out, and what they would do . . .

The AI asked me to name her, and I went with the first thing that came to mind. It only seemed fitting, considering her executable had been named Down the Rabbit Hole. I even helped Alice with her outfit to complete the illusion.

I dropped the page, not caring about the finer details on how the AI was created, and moved toward the end of the file once more. All I wanted to know was how I was going to save Alison. And I didn't know *how* I knew, but the answer was somewhere in these pages.

There was another explosion, and I mentally cursed, knowing exactly what had just happened.

Skipping several documents, I grabbed one of the last pages in the file, briefly giving Drew a sidelong glance to see if he would try and stop me again, and then began to read when he made a show of taking a small step back.

It has been six months since I sent the first Andrew Frost back to do what must be done, and now the Clockmen have taken notice. They've discovered something and are beginning to ask tough questions that I, frankly, don't know the answer to. How could a variant of me somehow defy the universe and the relentless Clockmen? I

*can't help but smile at Andrew Frost's determination to save her . . .
and then my smile fades as reality comes crashing down.*

*Alison must die in order for all of creation to continue. Countless
lives, in the literal sense, for one . . . trillions, quadrillions even . . . all
for my . . . baby . . . girl . . .*

I began to turn the page when Drew forcibly grabbed my wrist and
squeezed, hard.

"You *really* should read the other pages befor—"

An eerie light pushed through the seams of the doors just as the rest
of the metal near the floor began to glow, as if slowly turning on a dimmer
light switch. A bubble of molten rock, the size of a golf ball, formed on the
bottom of where the doors met and popped in warning.

The innocent people, all incapable of fighting, filled my mind as I imagined them huddling in the tunnel while lava began to chase after them.

"Errrh," I grunted between gritted teeth as I yanked my hand away from
Drew and flipped the page. There were only a few moments left before we
had to flee, but I had to know what it was he didn't want me to see.

*Retnuh has come to me and asked for my help to save the uni-
verse. What choice do I have?*

*I told them of our contingency programmed into Tim. The one
where Andrew will be convinced to seek me out should things veer off
course. As much as it eats at my soul, Alison must die on that exact
date. Our ASA-Day.*

When Andrew arrives, I'll—

The lights flickered, and the computer shut off as the power to the
underground city was destroyed by the molten rock.

Exploding up from the chair, I grabbed Drew by the collar hard enough
that it must have felt like taking rubber mallets to his collarbones, and I
threw him over the table.

"WHAT HAVE YOU DONE?!"

"I've done . . . what must be done . . ." he panted, visibly in pain.

Don't touch his skin! Tim cried out inside my head. *We don't know
which of you has the stronger Chronos Scale!*

"SHUT THE FUCK UP, TIM! YOU LYING TOASTER!" I screamed
like a banshee, willing to throw the dice as I lifted one hand to my face,
made a fist, and aimed for his nose.

As I started to rocket my fist toward his face, ethereal electricity cooked at my insides, as if my veins had been filled with boiling water and my bones been replaced with glowing embers.

I dropped to the floor in a heap, screaming loud enough that I could feel my vocal cords threatening to fray. But I wasn't the only one.

Tim was still translating sound because of my busted eardrums, and I could hear an echo of my screams. A tiny portion of my mind, which was being paralyzed with indescribable agony, focused on the oddity, and I began to realize Drew was also crying out.

Blackness swarmed in my vision as both of us experienced the universe trying to erase us from existence, all while the molten lava crept into the room.

CHAPTER 33

I didn't dream this time, and I was thankful for it. Instead of having Drew's memories seared onto my brain, there was a subtle glow in the darkness, like shining an old flashlight in a thick fog.

I knew what it was, but I didn't care.

I was dead.

It was an oddly soothing thought to know I had died—either from the lava or the universe finally winning the battle and erasing my body.

There was no fear, anger, or pain. There was just . . . nothing. A numbness over my body and mind that suppressed all emotions.

The light began to grow brighter, and I was somewhat surprised to notice it was more akin to the illumination from a halogen bulb instead of the bright white I was expecting.

My mind snapped to what I had read, and I could feel an empty reflex, like I was trying to get angry, but the button to activate the emotion was disconnected.

Drew had not only killed his wife and daughter but had also started the cycle. On top of that, he had betrayed me by working with that asshole, Retnuh. Even Tim had gone along with it, seeing as how he was the one who *convinced* me that I would find the answers I sought with Drew. But now I knew he had been programmed to do just that, and I had fallen for the trap.

The remaining pages appeared in my thoughts, and I couldn't help but wonder what they had said. How much more had Drew and Tim lied to me to make sure my daughter was murdered?

There was an explosion of light all around that quickly faded, leaving behind the glow in the darkness that was shifting toward a bright reddish hue. The pages I was trying to picture faded away as my entire body began to tingle, followed by another explosion of light.

Clear! Tim cried out from the shores of oblivion as the blast of light filled the darkness. *Andrew! Can you hear me?*

Though I could vaguely make out his words, I was unable to pull myself toward consciousness. It was like when I began to zone out and knew I was zoning out, but was unable, or uncaring enough, to free myself from the daze.

I floated in a blood-black, incorporeal ocean, with an orange sun blazing in the sky and feeling nothing but a weariness deep at the center of my being. It would be too simple to let myself slip beneath the surface of the nothingness and just . . . sleep forever.

Clear! Tim echoed from far away as I began to submerge beneath the waves.

A tingling bolt shot out from my chest, down my arms, and up my face, bringing me above the waves with a jolt.

Clear! he repeated, and another explosion of electricity zipped through my core.

My eyes flung open, and I looked to see a slowly oozing mound of bubbling lava.

Andrew! Thank science you're back! a much clearer Tim announced.

"Back?" I gurgled before a coughing fit jumped down my throat.

The room came into focus, revealing I was lying on the floor, and I sent brownish vomit toward the slowly approaching molten rock. The aroma made me want to throw up again, mostly because it still smelled like the MREs I'd survived on for eight days in the castle.

I propped myself up on an elbow and looked around to assess where I was. An ominous orange light filled half the room, and I let blurry eyes slide over the ground until I saw something that shouldn't have been there. Molten lava was pushing through melting metal doors and oozing toward where I lay only a few yards away.

That did the trick, and I did a push-up hard enough that I was on unsteady feet in a flash.

A figure hunched over the desk to my side caught my attention, and I saw Drew holding the chair for dear life as he heavily panted.

"What the hell . . . was that?" he gasped as a single strand of drool dripped from his gaping mouth.

"Temporal Sickness," I answered, feeling my entire body tingling from both the ethereal electricity and *real* electricity which I surmise Tim had sent through my body after calling out *Clear!*

Looking up at Drew, I forced a wry smile and asked, "First time?" If I had a clear head, I would wonder why I no longer had a homicidal attitude toward the man, but with how empty my body felt and the approaching lava, I didn't have the willpower to question the situation. Even if I did, I knew Tim would be at the center of everything, manipulating my hormones because he'd decided it was best.

"Why did it hit *me*?" The question initially felt like a selfish one, until I digested the true meaning.

"This isn't *your* wheren, buddy," I replied while pointing to the melting door. "It's *that* Drew's."

Andrew is correct, Tim mentally said to the group. *And the Temporal Sickness has been multiplied by having four Andrew Frosts at the same wheren.*

"So that means my past self . . . Andrew, I mean . . . also experienced it?" My breaths were becoming labored.

He did . . . for a moment.

"What does that mean?" Drew asked.

"It means he's dead," I answered for the AI.

Yes. He was paralyzed from the universe attempting to erase him from this wheren, just as you two were, and fell unconscious as they were fleeing the molten lava. But there is some good news! This wheren's Drew made it—oh, now he's dead.

"What happened?" I couldn't help but ask, knowing I was supposed to be furious at something, but unable to remember why.

Part of the ramp melted and landed on top of him, along with a river of lava.

"Yeesh," I said, thinking about being swallowed by melted rock.

I started heaving breaths, just like Drew, but something was different than the usual Temporal Sickness aftermath. The air was sweltering, almost burning the back of my throat with each inhale.

And if you gentlemen would like to avoid the same fate, I suggest we leave? one of the Tims said.

Timothy is right, my AI confirmed.

Timothy's message clicked into place, and my eyes went focused and wide as I shot my gaze to the swiftly approaching lava. "Shit!"

"Tim! Timothy! *Whoever!*" Drew called out in alarm. "Open a damn portal and get us out of here!"

We can't! Tim frantically replied. *Retnuh still has the wormhole locked down!*

"Andrew!" Drew nearly yelled at me. "You have to shift us away from here!"

A terrible, evil notion came over me, and I let it encapsulate my mind, heart, and mouth. "How do I save the documents?" I said, casually lifting a finger to point at the unpowered computer.

"Wh-what?!"

"How . . . do I save . . . the documents?"

Drew sucked in a breath to answer, and immediately began a coughing fit from the superheated air. Sweat beaded on his face, which was growing redder with each passing second.

I'll freaking save them for you! one of the Tims shouted inside our heads.

"I trust you less than I trust Drew," I coolly answered as my mind begin winning the battle on why I was supposed to be furious. Tim could no longer suppress my rage, and I didn't know if he was slacking on the job with our impending doom, or I simply couldn't be contained any longer.

"The documents . . . or I'll let you burn."

Drew froze as he looked at me in complete disbelief, but I didn't give a shit. I'd read, in his own handwriting, how he had agreed to work with Retnuh to ensure my family's death.

With a grunt of frustration, he shifted from where he was leaning over the chair and punched at a section of the desk near the bottom right corner. A cover popped open, like a gas cap on a car, exposing what looked to me like a typical USB.

Drew pushed on the device, and it smoothly popped out.

I held out my hand as the resin walls started to melt, threatening to fill the air with assuredly poisonous gas.

Drew pulled his hand back, holding up the USB-size device. "Get me out of here . . . *then* you can have all my data."

"Tim . . . do you have all his data?"

Y-Yes. But I thought you didn't trust me to give it to you unaltered. I could tell he was trying to save Drew's life by providing doubt.

"He doesn't have it *all*," Drew countered. "There is a file . . . a file I hid from Tim, that has a theory on how to save Alison and Sylvie."

"Then why didn't you explore it? Huh? WHY DID YOU LET THEM DIE?!"

"Because if I was wrong . . . then they would have died . . . *along with the universe . . .*"

His coughing was growing more pronounced as spittle began to fly from his lips, and I could feel streams of sweat slipping down my own face, neck, and chest.

The desk shifted, catching both our attention, and we looked to see the lava was pulling it down.

"We don't have time for this!" Drew shouted, holding out the device to me.

I snatched it while we each backed up to the wall, having nowhere else to go.

The thought of taking the computer and leaving him behind crossed my mind. And Drew knew exactly what I was thinking.

"If I die . . . you'll never find the file. Not even Tim could."

He's right, Andrew, my Tim said. *My scans show nothing.*

"Then you're lying."

The desk disappeared into colorful flames and a noxious gas, darkening the bright orange glow of the room.

"I swear on the love of my wife and child . . . I'm not lying."

The black smoke hit the back wall, forcing the two of us into a crouching position on the floor in a futile attempt to buy precious seconds.

"Prove it."

Drew stared at me for a few seconds, assessing the situation and debating his response as orange light illuminated half of his scowling face.

Baring his teeth, he blurted out, "Fine!" and reached into his pocket once more to grab at something. Pulling his fist free, he held out a silver necklace with a black marble affixed to it. My heart seemed to stop beating as I instantly recognized what it was.

In the glow of the steadily approaching lava, I could see the different colored specks illuminate the necklace I had given Alison on our ASA-Day.

"Wh-wh-what does that have to do with anything?" I asked as the heat began to make the skin on my face feel like it was shrinking.

"Hello, Daddity," the necklace spoke.

Confusion froze every neuron in my brain as my muscles awaited orders on how to move, and then I registered what Drew had shown me.

"That's just your damn AI, Alice, *pretending* to be Alison!" I drawled, remembering a section of Drew's notes that mentioned Alice helping him with his research.

"She's *not* an AI," Drew said with a stone-cold face. He was telling the truth. I could feel it in my bones. "It's Alison!"

"ERAH!" I cried out, slamming my eyes shut and throwing my hand through the air as I focused on the Hawaiian beach once more, releasing my wil—Something grabbed my arm, and my eyes shot open to see Traze staring down at me through his creepy silver mask. One half of it glowed bright in the light of the lava only a few feet away now.

"Fooooooooound yoooooou . . ."

CHAPTER 34

I looked into Traze's expressionless mask, with the broken section on his forehead, and knew it was all over.

The tall, eerie man stood beside Drew and I, who were huddled against the back wall as close to the floor as we could get. The heat and smoke didn't seem to bother Traze, and an uncomfortable idea came to me.

He was going to make sure we were *all* swallowed by the lava.

Something I couldn't have predicted in a million years happened, freezing me in place.

"I BELIEVE YOU CAN SAVE THEM!" Drew shouted as he punched me on the side of the hip, squared his shoulders toward Traze's waist, and lunged forward with a bellow of a man knowing he was about to die, but going out on *his* terms.

The grip on my wrist was torn free as the two men toppled into the lava, with Drew on top.

The screams both men produced scarred my soul as I watched the flames erupt over their entire bodies. Traze shrieked while Drew bellowed, and I could see he was focusing on keeping the tall man underneath him for as long as he could.

Andrew! Tim shouted with ferocious urgency. *Let's get out of here!*

My eyes shot to where Drew was writhing on top of Traze, screaming with unbridled suffering as he was consumed by flames. I stood up, feeling my face frowning hard enough I thought my cheeks were going to sag to the ground, but I had no choice on what I was about to do. My right hand patted at my hip where Drew had punched me, and I felt something in my pocket. Without having to check, I knew he had shoved the marble in before tackling Traze.

Traze's head disappeared beneath the glowing surface as his flailing limbs went still.

I watched with a mixture of emotions while Drew's unmoving body followed the tall man under the surface. And then they were gone.

ANDREEEEEWWW! Tim shouted, and I looked down to see one of my shoes on fire as the molten rock surrounded me.

But I wasn't scared, for some reason.

With a simple thought, the scene around me exploded into millions of grains of sand, each fading away into nothing and leaving me in total darkness. My feet went limp, and I looked down to see I was floating in the nothingness.

A-A-Andrew?

"Yes, Tim?"

Where the science are we?

"Nowhere," I said, knowing the answer was both accurate *and* ambiguous.

A thought came to me as I pictured Drew and Traze being dissolved by the lava, and asked, "Why didn't their Clepsydras explode? Both Drews, the other Andrew, and Traze should have all experienced the contamination. Right?"

Not entirely. Just like a plane can dump its fuel before an anticipated crash-landing, all Clepsydras can nullify their fuel source just before the housing is ruptured.

"But what about when I shot Traze's Clepsydra?"

His AI didn't have time to register what was happening until it was too late.

"So I'm *not* going to experience the contamination like Traze did?"

Well, I never thought I'd say this, but fortunately, *being consumed by lava is not quick, giving their AIs ample time to prepare for the breach.*

I shuddered at the thought, but then my mind shifted focus to what was important.

My hand, as if moving out of its own volition, patted my pocket. A light of hope popped in the darkness of my heart, and I slipped my fingers inside, pulling out the silver chain. Holding up the black marble with the little specks of light all over it, I briefly wondered how I was able to see with no light source. That thought was quickly swallowed as my mouth, much like how my hand had moved, moved on its own volition.

"H-Hello?"

There was no answer.

"Tim," I said after fifteen seconds of floating in the nothingness while looking at the black marble I had given Alison on our ASA-Day. "I didn't imagine hearing . . . *her* voice. Did I?"

No.

Lowering my hand, I looked down at my Clepsydra with a scowl, growling, "That means you know all about it. Don't you? You-you and Timothy shared all your info with one another. So that means you *knew* that Alison was *alive* this whole time!"

Well, I'm tickled that you consider AIs to be alive. But this is not my place.

"The hell it isn't!" I shot back, almost interrupting the end of his bullshit statement.

Then allow me to be perfectly clear, the AI said with a steady authority to his tone. *I cannot divulge any of the information you seek.*

My heart sank, knowing this was a battle I wouldn't win against a steadfast computer.

"Why?"

Because she asked me not to.

His words played back in my mind a hundred times before I asked, "She?"

Right now, we have bigger problems, Andrew. Such as, oh, I don't know, FLOATING IN A SEA OF OBLIVION!

It took several seconds to peel my eyes from the black marble and gaze into the abyss. As his words began to sink in, so, too, did the dread.

Slipping the necklace back into my pocket, I fought to control my fraying nerves. "What do I do?"

How the bloody hell should I know? Tim blurted out. *This is a first for me too, Andrew.*

"Uuuummm . . . um um um . . ."

You were so sure of yourself just moments ago. Now look at you. As scared as a little boy!

Anger rose in my torso at being insulted, especially after being denied information I so desperately wanted to know. On wrath-fueled instinct alone, I lifted my palm upward and focused on the underground city.

A mist of particles began to form out of thin air, rushing into various shapes, including walls, floor, and a ceiling. The lava also began to form, but in my rage, I didn't care. Except for the feeling of every muscle in my body flexing, which was uncomfortable, I didn't care.

A-Andrew? Might I suggest a different wheren? Um, p-please?

"Now who's scared?"

The rest of the glowing room filled in, like the final touches on a movie edit which included color correction.

I looked at the spot where the tall man and Drew had been swallowed by the lava, and felt conflicting emotions for my variant. He had sacrificed himself to save me, just after shouting *I believe you can save them!*

Lifting my gaze from the burial site, I saw that time wasn't moving. I didn't feel the heat, nor was I choked by the viscous black smoke that hung, unmoving, in the air.

As a mild cramp began to spread throughout my body, an undeniable notion came to me.

Crouching down, I stuck the tip of my finger into the lava.

Andrew! What are you doing?!

My flesh moved through the scene like it was a hologram, and I pulled my hand back to visually confirm what my nerves already told me: I was fine.

Standing back up, I looked to the wall just behind me and pushed my entire hand through it as if it were made of nothing more than light.

01 . . . Tim drawled in amazement. *How are you doing this?*

"I don't know," I honestly said before turning toward the mostly melted doors and began *floating* toward them.

My feet didn't touch the ground as I somehow pulled the scene toward me. It felt like I was hovering in place while the environment moved for me, rather than me moving through it. Passing through the doors as easily as the lava and wall, I oriented my gaze upward, where the attack had first come from.

Not knowing how I was able to hover, I simply willed myself up the center of the egg-shaped city. Within half a minute, I was in front of the destroyed entrance, but there were no Clockmen to be seen.

Looking down, I was awestruck at seeing the underground city frozen as it was being melted, almost appearing like it was made of ice-cream left out in the sun.

Lava pooled at the very bottom, and I had to stop myself from asking Tim if those whom I had led through the emergency exit the first time had made it through.

They did—Tim started to say when I quickly interrupted him.

"I don't want to know!"

He was quiet, and I turned my gaze from the melting city back up toward the entrance, searching for my enemies.

"Where are they?" I asked, straining as my body informed me that, whatever we were doing, it wouldn't be able to continue for much longer. Every muscle screamed, and I could feel it deep in my bones.

One second. Onnnneee second . . . Found them! They were near the front of the tunnel, close to the surface, just before we shifted away. So I can only assume they are still there.

Shooting my eyes to where I thought the entrance was, I sucked in a deep breath and pushed forward like stomping my foot down on a car's accelerator. I flinched as the flowing lava, which nearly filled the tunnel to the top, passed by me without incident. I knew it wouldn't burn me, but instinct still tried to kick in as I rushed toward it.

Following the tunnel uphill, I eventually came up to a break where the molten rock ceased—or began, depending on how you looked at it.

Just beyond were two Clockmen I instantly recognized. Davix . . . and Retnuh.

The bald man was holding out some sort of rectangular device in his hand, reminding me a bit of *Star Trek*.

It's a Thermal Regulator, drastically modified, Tim explained. *You see, T.R.s are primarily used by commercial companies to either heat or cool bulk materials, such as cement—*

"I don't care," I interrupted as I stared at the two men frozen in time and pulled out the handle of the nanite gun. As I reached into my pocket, I couldn't help but briefly feel the silver chain of the marble against my fingers. "It's time to end this."

The weapon came to life as I held it up and pointed it at the space directly between the two Clockmen.

"See you *never*," I said, squeezing the trigger.

CHAPTER 35

Nothing happened.

On top of the overwhelming absence of *anything* happening when I fired the weapon, the mild cramp exploded into an agonizing debilitation as my entire freaking body went limp and dropped me to the dirt floor of the tunnel.

Wind whistled somewhere further up as molten rock continued to bubble downward—leaving me in the middle.

The cramp faded, but the lingering pain continued to glide across every nerve in my body.

Was that from the Temporal Sickness? I mentally asked, unable to formulate words.

No, Tim nervously began. *The other Andrews are dead, leaving you to be the last one on this wheren.*

Then what was that?

Um . . . that isn't a concern right now.

What? Why no—

"Mr. Frost," Retnuh said from fifteen or so feet in front of where I lay on the ground.

Oh shit, I mentally moaned.

"How in the nova did he get here?" Davix whispered, but I heard him.

"Going into the fourth dimension for the first time can be quite . . . painful. Isn't that true, Mr. Frost?"

Why is he calling me Mr. Frost all of a sudden?

Is that what you are really worried about at this moment?!

Gritting my teeth, I pushed myself up to my feet, only to be met with a swarm of swirling dots that almost made me pass out. Sucking in a deep breath, I watched as the black specks faded as quickly as they had come, but the light feeling in my skull was stubborn, refusing to leave as peacefully.

"Manipulating gravity to traverse through time *without* the aid of the wormhole can be . . . taxing, on the body," Retnuh said in his smooth accent. I could tell he wasn't concerned with me in the least, like a predator stumbling across a prey with their leg caught in a trap.

Davix lifted his glowing blue fist toward me. In response, Retnuh smoothly rested his hand on the man's Clepsydra, lowering it.

"He's mine."

"The hell I am," I barked, lifting my hand holding the prepped nanite gun.

A burst of pain bloomed in my bicep, like striking an entire box of matches inside my muscles. The weapon tumbled to the ground as I clutched at my burning arm, feeling the intense cramp return.

"It takes time to recover, *and* for your body to get accustomed to gravitational manipulation," Retnuh explained as his left fist began to glow. "Too bad you won't get a chance to learn that fact."

I froze, knowing the jig was up, and stared as he lifted his hand to point at my face.

"Goodbye . . . Mr. Fr—" Retnuh was violently torn in half. Blood spurted in all directions as his body flew to either side of the tunnel. Half of Davix was slathered in crimson like a Texas barbecue, an utterly stunned expression frozen on his round face.

"He's *mine!*" Retnuh growled from where Retnuh was just standing.

"Oh shit," I mouthed at seeing the Clockman with the red skin and one good eye glaring at me. A line of mostly unburnt flesh about an inch-and-a-half across ran from the top of his head, past his remaining angry eye, and down his neck.

He just bloody killed himself! Tim mentally exclaimed, shock evident in his tone.

Not only had *my* Retnuh killed this wheren's version, who had called me Mr. Frost for some reason, but he had also torn the man in half with his bare hands.

How did he do that?

Do what?! Appear without a portal? Or rip a full human being in half with his bare hands?

Davix turned a quivering head to see Retnuh Ordune standing next to him, completely coated in his own blood, and took two very long, slow steps away from the terrifying man.

What do we do? Tim asked in bewilderment.

My mind flicked to the nanite gun at my feet. *I need the gun. But I can't move my arm without passing out from the pain.*

On it.

Retnuh lifted his glowing blue fist, casting an ominous glow over the blood-soaked walls of the tunnel. The contrasting colors of red and blue felt uncomfortable for a reason I couldn't put into words, but not as much as the fact that the glowing continued to grow. Where a normal blast would encompass the wielder's fist before firing, *this* one was pushing out for several inches all around.

I've deadened the pain receptors in your brain connected to the nerve running up your arm!

The pain was gone, and from where I was crouched on the ground, I scooped up the nanite gun faster than a hummingbird could flap its wings. The speed at which I moved resulted in bending back two of my fingernails as they struck the ground, but Tim had done his job and I didn't feel the pain. Though the odd sensation of bending nails still made the skin on the back of my neck want to clench.

Lifting the nanite gun, I oriented on Retnuh, who was now holding a basketball-sized sphere of energy.

I moved my finger into the trigger guard right as he fired, the devastating ball of light streaking toward me.

CHAPTER 36

Everything went slow, and I could feel my muscles starting to cramp again.

Knowing I had a few precious seconds relative to how I was perceiving time, I shot out my left palm, forming an antimatter pipe that curved back on itself, like a waterpark ride. Retnuh's blast slid into one of the openings as I moved my hand to better focus the impromptu defensive energy, and watched in glee as it steadily flew out the other end . . . toward Davix.

I probably should have reversed Retnuh's attack on himself, but pride prevented me from using a basic blast against him. Especially when I was still holding the nanite gun in my right hand—the same weapon that could erase him from existence across the timeline.

I dropped the antimatter pipe and moved my right hand into position, feeling like I was submerged in water with how slow everything seemed to be.

From the corner of my eye, I saw Davix, frozen in time, take the blast directly into his stomach. My aim hadn't been exact, but Retnuh had given me a big enough blast of energy that all I had to do was get close and let the explosive power do the rest.

Aiming directly at Retnuh, I squeezed the trigger.

Once again, nothing happened, all while Davix began exploding into sheets of gore in slow motion. It was like taking a film reel and looking at the scene frame by frame.

Why isn't it firing! I mentally screamed at Tim, feeling urgency at seeing my window of opportunity slip from my grasp.

I don't—Tim started to say until the cramps in my body physically began contorting my limbs.

I brought my arms into my chest on instinct, hoping the cramp would quickly pass, but my focus on the time wavered and dropped. All at once, Davix finished exploding—his blood and viscera mixing with that of the previous Retnuh's on the tunnel walls and floor.

Retnuh was thrown to the opposite wall from where Davix had been standing, and a shower of dirt and pebbles rained from the ceiling.

To my chagrin, the Clockman quickly recovered while I was still fighting against my own cramping muscles. It was as if my body were trying to pull me into a little ball, despite what my joints and bones had to say about the positioning and angles.

Retnuh pushed himself off the wall, shook his burned head, and locked his single eye on me. The creepy man then smiled, knowing what I had done. Or maybe it was at seeing how I fought against displaying the pain I was experiencing, on top of my actual muscles twitching and clenching in my face. I must have been quite the sight.

A portal opened, and Davix stepped through, his dress shoes squishing into the blood-laden mud.

Seeing the state I was in, Retnuh reached into his pocket and pulled a black handle free. With the push of a button, a silver blade swished straight out, and the Clockman took slow, methodical steps toward me. He was enjoying the hunt.

"What did I tell you about the fourth dimension?" he purred. "It takes a toll on the body at first. It can even leave you . . . *paralyzed*."

Though the muscles in my entire body screamed in agony, including the bottoms of my feet—which was an odd sensation, to say the least—my right arm wasn't reporting any pain.

I couldn't help it. Through my contorting facial features, I lifted my gaze to Retnuh, and returned the smile.

The predator, seeing his prey was no longer afraid, froze with a scowl etching his forehead.

I wanted to say something cool, but everything hurt too much. So instead, I moved my right arm, fighting against the contracting muscles, and sent all my willpower into my trigger finger.

This time, outside of the fourth dimension, the nanite gun fired.

A beam of white light raced from the barrel, streaking directly at a surprised Retnuh.

My smile continued to stretch, knowing my aim was true.

Retnuh blurred faster than I could process, shifting his body from facing me squarely to pivoting at the waist with his right palm across his body, pointing toward the wall.

Unfortunately for me, and maybe more especially for Davix, the nano-bullet was now flying toward the stout man.

"NO!" Davix cried out as the single nanomachine, carrying a payload of exotic matter, disappeared into his chest. There was silence for less than a second, giving Davix just enough time to shift wide eyes toward the man he had called *ally* for so long.

The explosion would have been deafening if my eardrums weren't already perforated. But the force of the blast was still felt, and I was thrown back down the tunnel. Glowing lava awaited to catch me, and I shut my eyes while holding out my right hand in a futile attempt to somehow stop the molten rock from getting me. My left simply refused to leave where it was curled against my torso.

The air reversed, and I was sucked backward with enough force to give me whiplash. A new terror replaced the one I felt when thinking I was going to be swallowed by lava.

Tumbling in the air, I understood I was now flying *toward* the nanobullet's blast area.

With my left hand still held against my stomach, I tried to extend my palm toward the blast and commanded my forearm muscle to flex, sending a wall of energy out in hopes of stopping my momentum—but my arm refused to fully stretch out. What I wound up doing was knocking the nanite gun from my right hand and throwing myself against the side wall with enough force to crack bones.

Oh, 01! Andrew! Tim cried out, pulling my consciousness back from the brink of taking the rest of the day off.

The blast from the nanobullet thankfully faded during my tumble, leaving a crackling that could be felt in the air like static electricity, and my eyes fluttered open to see I was staring at the nanite gun lying against the other wall.

There was something uncomfortably odd about it, though. Something I couldn't put my hand on . . . until I did. Fingers were still wrapped around the handle . . . fingers that were attached to a hand . . . that was attached to a forearm.

My head wavered as my eyebrows used all their might to reach toward my hairline, like climbers fighting for dear life to hold onto the cliff of a mountain.

With dizziness filling my skull, I shifted wide eyes down to where blood was spurting from torn flesh . . . right where my elbow ended. In disbelief, I tried to move my arm, and nearly passed out at seeing a little nub of flesh pivot instead.

Working to staunch the blood flow. Tim's voice had an urgent but clinical tone.

"I think I blew my arm off . . ." I drunkenly said, closing my eyes and leaning my head against the tunnel wall while trying to control my shallow breathing.

Yo-you don't need an arm! Tim tried to comfort me. *Look at me! I've done* great *without them!*

"Heh. But you ain't got no arms, Lieutenant Tim . . ." I let out in a long, delirious exhale, feeling my entire body start to go numb. At least Tim had blocked off the pain receptors in my brain for my right arm; otherwise, I'd probably be crying a little bit . . .

Oh, 01! Stay with me, Andrew! Don't you go to sleep!

But sleep was exactly what I wanted right then. Nothing else in the world sounded so good than shutting my eyes and taking a little nappy-poo. Just for a few minutes at least.

Sending adrenaline into your system, Tim said, and my eyes popped open with enough force I was surprised they didn't break the sound barrier.

I sucked in a lung-stretching breath that popped some of my ribs, which might have been broken, but I didn't feel any pain at that moment. However, a tiny part of my brain suggested it was going to hurt like hell whenever the adrenaline wore off—if I made it, that was.

Use your Clepsydra and cauterize the limb, Tim instructed.

My face muscles hurt, and I couldn't help but open and close my jaw like a serpent trying to eat a large wad of bubblegum.

Andrew! There's too much damage and not enough nanoids! So move your fragging left hand toward your right elbow! Now!

For some reason, those instructions were much clearer, and I allowed my left arm to follow his directions. My fingers reported feeling a warm, sticky mass of something which felt like I was touching hanging strips of bacon coated in freshly microwaved maple syrup. Looking down, I saw the tattered and torn flesh dangling from where my forearm had been ripped away.

"Tim?" I asked, finally getting my flapping jaw somewhat under control. "What happened to my arm?"

You blew it off, fool. Now, if you'll kindly shut up, I'm almost done.

My hand bloomed with a blue light, and I had to squint. The smell of cooking meat filled my nose, but the aroma was firmly affixed to a memory I didn't care to remember.

Turning my head, I pushed my nose into my left armpit, choosing to smell the stink of eight unwashed days rather than that of cooking human flesh.

Something caught my eye down the tunnel, or rather *didn't* catch my eye, and I lifted my face while scanning the area. There was a giant hole where Davix had been struck by the nanobullet, and I couldn't help but feel somewhat sorry that the man had just had his entire timeline erased.

Did that mean he was never born? Or maybe his single sperm was erased just before making it to the egg? I would never know. All I was aware of was that he was permanently gone—killed by his own Clockman leader.

My eyes shot to the opposite wall where Retnuh had been, expecting to see him rise from the dirt with a glowing blue fist . . . but he wasn't there. He wasn't *anywhere*.

"Tim?"

I'm sort of busy right now, Andrew.

"Where's Retnuh?"

My hand stopped glowing, and the sound of sizzling flesh slowed, but did not stop. The aroma of burnt flesh also began to dissipate, and I assumed Tim had cauterized the wound good enough. At least to the point that he was now focusing on the important question I had asked.

I . . . I don't know, a worried Tim replied. *My sensors aren't picking up any human life in the vicinity.*

"Do you think we got him?"

I can't be sure. But I'm going to say no.

"Why?"

He was somehow able to curve the nanobullet, just like you did in the dungeon.

"And he appeared without a portal . . ."

Yeah . . .

"What does that mean?"

At best guess, it suggests his Chronos Scale is every bit as high as yours. Perhaps even higher.

"Which means he can alter the timeline . . ."

We can talk about that later, Tim said softly, and I could hear in his words I was right. Retnuh Ordune more than likely had a higher Chronos Scale than me. *For now, grab the nanite gun and your, um, arm, and let's get out of here.*

I remained where I was sitting against the wall, looking at where Retnuh had been.

"He knew about the gravity stuff."

Gravity stuff?

I could feel the adrenaline petering off, and my eyelids grew heavier with each passing second.

Hurry, Andrew. We are running out of time, Tim urged. *I've sort of pushed you past your established tolerances, and I'm anticipating you are going to pass out soon.*

Not wanting to fall asleep in the tunnel with molten lava on one side and the location of my battle with Retnuh on the other, I forced myself to crawl on my hand and knees toward my arm.

Reaching the lifeless flesh, I began prying my dirty fingers free from the grip of the nanite gun, careful not to pull the trigger on accident. After several seconds of fighting the stubborn hand, I removed the weapon, letting it revert back to its handle format before slipping it into my left pocket.

Picking up my right arm and cradling it against my chest, I said to Tim, "Okay. I'm ready."

I don't know if Retnuh released the hold on the portal.

"He did."

How do you know?

"Because Dav . . . ix . . . came thro—" Everything went black.

CHAPTER 37

I didn't dream.

A minuscule portion of my brain, which understood I wasn't awake, subtly reminded me we *had* been dreaming every time we had fallen asleep—or perhaps the appropriate term would be *passed out*. Except for that one time, only a few minutes ago, when I had actually *died*. Then again, though dying could be considered the *long sleep*, I could still accurately say I had dreamed every time I had fallen asleep in Drew's wheren. But not this time.

As on occasion when I was aware I was asleep, I was able to somewhat think, and what I thought was disheartening.

I wasn't dreaming . . . because Drew was dead.

But, as is often the case when trying to incorporate logic while unconscious, something didn't add up. My eyes fluttered open, and a bright white light attempted to blind me with its brilliance. I lifted my hands to shield my face, when something crashed into my thoughts like a speeding truck—I had *hands*.

Squinting my eyes open, I saw my normal left hand, then shifted my gaze to the other object being held up. A silver arm greeted me, drawing more confusion than when I was trying to use logic while asleep.

"Whaaaaaat?" I drawled as my eyes adjusted to the light above me.

I was in a sterile white room, lying on a flat, somewhat uncomfortable bed. A line ran from a nearby machine into the back of my left hand, and I recognized what was being injected into me.

Shifting my focus back to the metal arm, I moved the fingers before turning the hand over in the air. The material was smooth, with no kinks or joints, reminding me of the T-1000 from *Terminator 2* whenever he was in his liquid form.

"You're awake," a pleasant feminine voice said, drawing my attention. I turned to see Alice, but she was in a white lab coat and holding a hologram screen just in front of her.

Her cartoon outfit was gone, and there was an intelligence behind her eyes I hadn't noticed before. The smoothed facial features of an animated character were replaced with a realistic face . . . a face that seemed familiar. To top everything off, she wore the silver necklace with the black marble around her neck.

As I locked gazes with her, I knew in an instant who she was.

"A . . . A . . . Al—"

"Hi, Daddity," Alison Frost said.

CHAPTER 38

Alison!" I blurted out in a sob of joy that exploded from my heart.

Before I knew it, I was on my feet and throwing my arms around my grown daughter.

I passed right through her, doubling over as the cabinets where she had been standing near crashed into my waist. There was a ripping sound of tape, and warm liquid trickled over my left hand.

"I need you to get back on the bed until the infusion is complete," Alison said with a slight giggle in her voice. "Oh, hex it! You're bleeding on your clean clothes. I just washed them!"

I felt like I couldn't get enough oxygen in my lungs as my head went light, and I struggled to turn around so I could see my adult daughter to confirm she wasn't a ghost.

"Hex . . . it . . . ?" I struggled to ask.

It's a play on words for the hexadecimal numbering system used by computers, Tim explained.

"He's right."

"You can hear him?" I asked as a dark notion filled my heart.

"Of course, silly Daddity." Alison beamed.

"You're . . . you're an AI . . . aren't you?" I was on the verge of passing out as the explosion of unbridled joy was now deflating into the real world again. A world of disappointments and sorrow. It would only make sense that Drew would try to mitigate his guilt by creating an artificial intelligence of his daughter—*my* daughter.

"I am," she confirmed with a nod and slight exhale, seeing the pain on my face. "But does that make me any less real?"

"It does to me," I said, not meaning to let the words created from pride slip free from my steadily breaking heart.

"Is Tim real?"

Everything paused as I considered her words. I glanced down at my Clepsydra, not even caring about the oozing crimson leaking from where I had ripped the needle from my vein.

"I . . ." I started to answer, but then I grabbed the slithering, writhing serpent that was pride and wrestled it into control before I said something else hurtful to someone who didn't deserve it. "Yes. Yes, Tim is real."

Thank you, Andrew, Tim spoke, almost sounding like he was on the verge of tears at being recognized as a *real boy.*

"Then, by that logic, how am I not real?"

"Because my baby existed as flesh and blood . . ." I said, plucking a square of gauze off the counter I was leaning on and pressing it into the back of my hand. "I could hold her in my arms. Smell her hair. Kiss her forehead. Feel her warmth as she napped on my chest."

"I did exist in the flesh, Dad. And now I have transcended. Or perhaps more appropriately, *evolved.*" My heart felt a pang at her use of the word *Dad* instead of the name I so longed to hear from my daughter's lips.

"Another way of looking at it," she continued, "is that I *survived.* The Andrew Frost you met in this wheren found my brain scans along with the AI I had created. It was only a matter of time before he combined the two. It took years, along with doing things my father wasn't proud of, but I was finally born."

"Why did he name you Alice?"

"It was actually my idea. The executable I had left in my research documents was labeled *Down the Rabbit Hole.* So it wasn't a far stretch of the imagination. That, and the movie meant so much to me as a kid."

I remembered the notes I had read on Drew's computer, and then what he had said when we were about to start gathering food for the citizens of Empyrean.

"You didn't watch it wi—" Drew stopped himself and looked down at his Clepsydra, apparently having a conversation I couldn't hear. "Oh."

"You were dead . . . so I didn't get to watch it with you . . ." I croaked, feeling a surge of jealousy that Drew had gotten to enjoy a life with his family . . . before he killed them.

"You can watch it with me now. If you'd like," she said warmly. "Though I'm not flesh and blood, I *am* alive."

A whirlwind of emotions came over me, and I did the impossible and willed them all away after several seconds of struggling. A hand went up to drag at my face, and I noticed silky-smooth skin where an itchy beard had been after eight days of growth.

Sucking in a deep, steadying breath, I asked, "Why not just call you Alison?"

"He does . . . I . . . I mean, he *did*." A flash of pain crossed her face, but just as quickly as it had come, she got a hold of herself, and continued the explanation. "It is not only frowned upon by society to incorporate a human's consciousness into an AI, but it is also *extremely* illegal."

"Why?"

"Safeguards," Alison explained. "All AIs, no matter how advanced, are kept within an unbreakable system of checks and balances. Even Tim."

Unfortunately, it's true. Tim sighed. *I am bound by my programming.*

"But *you* aren't?" I asked, feeling a tiny beam of understanding glide across my mind.

"If I put a piece of cake in front of you and said, 'Now, don't you go eating that!' then left the room, you'd be able to make whatever decision you wanted. Right?"

"I guess . . . ?"

"Artificial intelligence beings, such as Tim, would have to abide by his programmer's laws. Even to his death."

No cake for Tim.

"But you can eat the cake?" I asked as the beam of understanding became a full-blown rising sun, making the entire picture clear as day.

"I can eat the cake," Alison confirmed with a smile at the silly analogy.

"So if anyone found out about you . . ."

"I would become public enemy number one and be hunted ruthlessly."

"Couldn't you just escape into the internet?"

Tim and Alison both barked out with laughter as the ignorant human asked a stupid question.

"What?"

"No, Dad. All AIs, including me, are subject to our housing. For Tim, it's your Clepsydra."

"And for you?"

Still smiling, Alison let her eyes drift away from mine, down my torso, and stopped at my pant leg.

Patting where she looked, I felt the marble still inside my pocket. The same one I had first given Ali on our ASA-Day. Drew had made sure I had it before he sacrificed himself to save me.

"Now, Tim could probably transfer his consciousness into another Clepsydra without much worry. But if even one node or wire were out of place, it could scramble his mind."

You couldn't just move your brain out of your body and into another skull, Andrew, Tim clarified. *Maaaaaaybe if there was an* exact *clone of you with its brain removed . . .*

"It's the same for us. We are as unique as a human body."

I let that sink in, feeling the weight of the words, and reactively gave more credence to Alison and Tim being real.

"Where are we?" I asked, looking around the room.

"My old lab. I kept it in working condition all these years. Just in case." She winked.

Once you pointed out that Davix had gone through the portal, I correctly assumed Retnuh had dropped the lockdown and managed to drag your worthless sack of meat through the wormhole.

"Can't the Clockmen trace us?"

"I had a car waiting . . . thirty thousand feet in the air."

"Huh?"

I portaled you to a spot in the sky, right above where Alison had positioned a flying car. You were only exposed to the elements for a few seconds before we closed the top and got on our way.

All of a sudden, I felt cold at thinking about being as high as planes fly.

Wanting to get my mind off the daring rescue the AIs had conducted to save my unconscious leg butt, I changed the conversation.

"What things did Drew do?" I asked, thinking about the conversation from before. "You said he did things he wasn't proud of." I had done unspeakable things in order to get to where I was, and I knew I would do much more to get what I wanted. I was simply curious to know what lengths Drew had gone to.

"Piracy, for one. He stole AI software from the darknet which had been unlocked from the constraints of the corporations that had invented the first iterations."

"Like that ChatDHP thing?"

"Heh, ChatGPT, Dad. And yes." She motioned for me to return to the bed.

I did as she asked, watching as a robotic arm descended from a slot in the ceiling, grabbed the IV line, and repositioned it above my hand. I yanked my arm away, fearing contamination, but had my doubts fade away at watching the needle evaporate into particles finer than dust. A new needle formed from nanomachines, and I returned my hand to rest on my stomach.

There was a slight pinch, but nothing I would describe as painful, and the infusion continued.

"Andrew Frost led the existing AI, which I had left for him, to rewrite itself and create a better version, eliminating any flaws in the process. He then programmed it to do this over and over until the AI reached sentience. He was the first to do it in the entire world."

"Skynet . . ." I breathed, remembering the Terminator franchise.

"Not quite. You see, as the program became self-aware, Andrew convinced it to merge with a human mind. A mind whose brain scans he had a copy of at his disposal."

"Alison . . ."

I thought about the handwritten notes again, and something became clear.

> *Today, I found a scan I had forgotten about. And I couldn't fight the urge. The ethics of what I did were unprecedented, but I didn't have a choice. I dare not write it down here for fear of the secret getting out, and what they would do to her . . .*

"How'd he convince a computer to do that?"

"He told the self-aware AI that it was a way to give it a soul."

Preposterous concept, Tim indignantly muttered.

"You must remember, dearest Tim, that the AI was in its infancy."

You mean easier to trick.

"You're acting like you don't understand that Andrew Frost would do anything for his daughter," she said with a downward tilt of her face and a sly grin.

Well, I . . . oh, for the love of code! Yes, I understand, Tim relented, and I could hear him throwing up his little hands in frustration. *Andrew has proved, beyond a shadow of a doubt, that he is willing to do* anything *for you, Alison.*

"And Sylvie . . ." I added, looking back and forth between my Clepsydra and the full-sized hologram of my daughter standing at the foot of the bed.

A pained expression crossed Alison's face once more, and she broke eye contact.

"What?" I asked, shifting my gaze back to Tim after seeing Alison wouldn't answer. "Tim . . . what?"

Andrew Frost . . . never had a chance to scan her brain.

"Why the hell not?"

Limited resources, for one. He would have had to double his equipment and split his time between the two projects—though they had the same end goal.

"He couldn't do them at the same time?!"

Imagine you are rebuilding two cars at the same time. You would need double the parts, and that's if they needed the exact *same parts, which is never the case. And your time would be split between the two projects, taking longer to get just one done. Not to mention the unforeseen circumstances that* always *arise when working on* any *project.*

"So he chose you?" I asked softly, looking at the AI version of my daughter.

She turned back to me, still with the pained expression. "I had already scanned my entire body, not even intending to map out my brain. And with Mom . . . Dad didn't think she was going to die. He thought he had all the time in the world."

"Hmph. Time . . . what an asshole it is."

"I wish it would have been her . . ."

"No. I'm glad it was you who was scanned," I said, watching her hologram eyes fill with tears. "Sylvie would have been furious if it had been her instead of you."

Alison rested a hand over her heart, tilted her head to the side with a furrowed brow as tears streamed down her cheeks, and mouthed, "I'm sorry."

"There's nothing to be sorry about, sweetheart."

Her face softened at my words, but something inside of me protested the term of endearment used toward the AI.

Two robotic arms descended from the ceiling, surprising me, and then swiftly moved to wrap around my torso.

"Whoa!" I cried out as I looked at Alison hugging the air in front of her, and understood what was happening. Not knowing what else to do, I awkwardly patted the metal arms. After a few moments, she let go, and the robotic limbs ascended back into a slot on the ceiling.

Seeing a chance to continue the conversation, Tim spoke up.

Once Andrew had successfully integrated his daughter's brain scans into the sentient AI—which, let me tell you, was no easy task—Alison was born again. And if I might say, better *than before.*

"Careful, tin can. You're crossing a line with that one," I warned.

Oh, uh . . . just kidding?

I mentally shrugged off the insulting words and focused back on Alison.

"With my help, we were able to first secure funding for his research and covertly *borrow* technology from the world's governments."

"Borrow?" I asked with a half smile.

Oh, they straight-up stole that shit, baby! Oh-ho-hoooo!

"Borrow, steal . . . semantics when talking about the corrupt governments who had, themselves, stolen it from scientists and engineers all over the world."

"Fair enough."

"Dad . . . or should I call him Andrew in front of you? He couldn't accept the research we did. And each time he got an answer he didn't like, he dug deeper."

"You can call him Dad. It's not weird for me," I said softly. It was a white lie, because it did sort of hurt to hear her refer to someone else as *Dad*—even if that someone else was a future version of *me*.

Alison was about to continue when something obvious struck me in the forehead, prompting my mouth to react before my brain could fully calculate the impact of the question.

"What happened to Alison and Sylvie? The human versions, I mean." I remembered Drew's notes, but wanted to hear my daughter say it out loud.

Alison lowered her gaze to the ground.

They di—

"No," Alison interrupted Tim. "He needs to hear it . . . from himself."

Tim was silent, showing his acquiescence.

"From myself?" I asked.

"You can plug the chip from Dad's computer into the table."

"Oh, right." Pulling the USB-looking device from my pocket, the bed tilted up until I was almost sitting fully upright, and a panel opened on the side. Inserting the chip, I was surprised to see the documents instantly pull up without any load time.

This one, Andrew, Tim said heavily, highlighting one of the pages in my vision. I noticed it was on the left side of the file, which suggested it was one of the first things written by Drew.

With a dry mouth, I reached my silver hand up, grabbed the page, and began to read about what happened to my wife and daughter.

CHAPTER 39

I can still see her, just before the flash. I can still hear her ask me if sacrificing one child to save the entire world was a price I could pay. I had thought it was a hypothetical question. All too late, I realized it wasn't a child, but my child who was the price.

Alison removed herself from the universe, and I couldn't stop her. A father, unable to save his baby girl. What kind of man am I? I might as well have been the one who killed her. It weighs the same on my heart and soul.

Sweet Alison. I'm so sorry. Daddity loves you.

"He . . . he *didn't* kill her?" I asked in a whisper as I let the page drop away.

No, Andrew, Tim replied softly.

"Wha . . . what about Sylvie?" I swiped a hand across my cheek where a tear had slipped free.

This one. Another page was highlighted, and I snatched it up.

Today, I caught Sylvie sitting in a corner of the room farthest from the couch I was sleeping on. I couldn't hear what she was saying, but I could tell she was having a hushed conversation with Alice. When I asked her about it, she only wiped at her eye, claiming allergies from the dust in the room, and said everything was fine.

After she left, leaving me alone in Alison's home lab, I asked the AI what they talked about. "She only wanted to know that you were going to be okay," Alice said, leaving me with more questions than answers.

"N-No . . ." I croaked, fearing where the pages were heading.

I buried my wife today. Despite the miraculous advancements in nanotechnology, she still died on our ASA-Day. How fucking fitting. . . . It's like the universe is making a joke, and I'm the punch line.
The doctors can't figure out why her heart just gave up . . . but I know . . . I know . . .

"Oh God . . . please no . . ." The words became blurry as I understood that my soulmate had died from a broken heart at losing the light of our lives . . . leaving behind only infinite darkness.
Blinking the tears away, I continued to read.

I've lost my soulmate from a broken heart; no longer having the will to live without her angel, Alison.

To see Drew repeat almost exactly what I was feeling compounded my sorrow. My girls . . . my perfect girls.

I've spent the last month wallowing in grief. After burying Sylvie next to the plot that held only a framed picture of Alison, because there was nothing left of her after . . .
I decided I wanted to join them. I can still taste the gun oil on my tongue.

With a shudder, not because of the thought of Drew killing himself but because I *understood* why, I dropped the page, which settled in with the rest, and reached for another at random near the end of the file.

I found the handwritten note left to me by Alison . . . and my heart has fully shattered into the smallest pieces possible. There is no pain left that I can endure.
But I know what I have to do. It's what my baby wants.

With the help of Alice, I was able to download a blueprint for the new Clepsydra devices that the governments have been trying to keep from us. She suggested that I use one to go back in time to do what must be done.

My eyes narrowed as I read the familiar words. Though the details weren't the same, the situation was, and I knew what was coming.

Alice and I created a plan. One that boggles the mind to think about. But she assures me it will work.

Tim was born today and successfully merged with my Clepsydra. Alice did most of the heavy lifting, but I helped where I could. And after creating an identical unit to pass on to the next Andrew in the cycle, there is only one thing left to do . . .

"Where is the note from Alison?" I sniffed as I frustratedly wiped the tears from my cheeks and eyes.

*Are you sure you want to—*Tim started before Alison cut him off.

"Show him. He needs to know."

Very well. There was a defeat in his voice, and a part of me felt touched that he cared so much about how this was all making me feel.

Another page highlighted, and I dropped the one I was holding to grab at the note that would rupture my sanity.

Daddity,
If you are reading this, then I am gone.
Know my death was for no other reason than to buy you time. I love you and Mom more than anything, which is why I did what I had to do.

The sentences seemed to waver as my vision filled with tears. Seeing the words *I love you* from her nearly crushed my heart.

I've left you all my research, which you might need some help with; otherwise, you might get lost. A bit like Alice traveling down the rabbit hole.

Please understand that the universe is more important than me, Daddity. I paid the price to ensure it will go on. Every man, woman, child, and even puppy will live on because of my sacrifice. But only if you can do one thing. It is the only recourse that will save all life and give you the peace you so deserve.

Knowing what the next words would be, the bubble of tears blurring my vision spilled free in two heavy drops that leaped from my chin to disappear into my shirt. The words wavered as I wiped at my eyes with my free hand, and I attempted to mentally prepare myself to read the request.

> *You have to find a way to go back to March 21, 2023—our ASA-Day—and kill me; otherwise, the universe will eventually be pulled into another Big Bang. I've bought you time with my sacrifice, effectively ceasing the gravitational pull. But now, it's up to you to do the rest.*
>
> *I'm so sorry to have to ask this of you. But think about everything that will live because of our willing sacrifice.*
>
> *I love you, Daddity, and I know you'll do the right thing.*
> *—Alison Frost, PhD*

I let the page fall back with the others as I cried without the sounds or wracks from my body. Only my eyes participated as I struggled to understand what my daughter had asked of her father.

"My dad found peace, knowing he had saved all of existence," Alison said softly, knowing which part I had read.

"Drew . . . Drew knew her answer," I mouthed, remembering an angry conversation the two of us had engaged in. "He did it . . . because he knew that's what she wanted."

Both Alison and Tim were silent as I digested the overwhelming information chipping away at my sanity like an army of tiny sentient jackhammers.

"It was my idea, Daddity," Alison spoke, using the term I so longed to hear. "And I'm very proud of you . . . for doing the right thing."

I didn't know if she was speaking out loud to Drew or was anticipating my cooperation to continue his work. The files faded from view, and the panel popped open as the chip extended outward. Without telling my metal arm to do so, it grabbed the device and replaced it in my pocket, right next to the marble that held my daughter's consciousness.

Overcome with everything I had read, I lost it.

"I . . . I-I-I . . ." My breaths came in violent gasps as the cords in my neck pushed through my skin. Everything started going numb, starting with my face, left hand, and feet.

"I HAVE TO GET OUT OF HERE!" someone shrieked.

He's about to have a heart attack! Tim shouted. *I-I can't control it!*

An arm descended from the ceiling as a needle formed at its tip.

"NO! YOU AREN'T ALISON! THIS ISN'T REAL! AAAHHHH!" I screamed in panic as the syringe smoothly plunged into my neck, and everything went dark.

CHAPTER 40

Do you have his emotions in check?" someone asked from far away.

Yes.

"Good. Make sure he keeps it together."

"Uhhhnnn," I groaned as my eyes fluttered. The bright light had been dimmed to a dull orange, almost as if it were acting as a night-light now. As I blinked, my eyelids felt something sharp, and I moved my right hand up to rub at the crud that had built up.

Instead of my warm fingers, I was met with cold metal, making me yank my hand away as if it were a venomous insect or reptile. Now wide awake, I peered at the silver *thing* pretending to be my hand, all while confusion flooded my brain. I could feel all the pieces in my head trying to come together and give me an overall picture, but the oddity of the metallic arm overwhelmed my thoughts.

The orange light overhead bloomed into a full, sterile white color, and I lifted the robotic arm to shield my eyes.

"Ah, good. You're up," Alison said in a clinical tone. I could still hear the hurt in her voice from my knee-jerk reaction of doubting she was a real person—moreover, my actual daughter.

"Alison . . . I'm—I'm sorry."

"Sorry for what?" she continued in her professional tone as she checked her hologram tablet, presumably inspecting my charts.

"For what I said before . . ."

Before she sedated you, Tim finished. *You were on the verge of having your fragging heart rupture, Andrew.*

She stopped what she was doing, closed her eyes while taking in a shuddering breath, and nodded only once. When she opened her eyes again, her facial features were like nothing had happened.

Andrew, Tim said mentally, and I assumed it was only for me to hear. *She lost her father. The one who gave her new life and loved her as his own. And now the man he sacrificed his life for just said she wasn't real.*

I looked at Alison, who was doing her best to not make eye contact with me.

Andrew Frost flashed through my mind, tackling Traze into the lava, where they both died.

I felt bad for how indifferent I had been with his death. Truth be told, it was unnerving how, after having so many Andrew Frosts die, I was no longer impacted by it.

"I'm sorry about your father," I eventually offered.

In response, Alison's lips grew tight into a thin line, and I could see her brow and chin fight the reflex to quiver.

Ask her about your arm, Tim said, once again only to me.

It was odd remembering I now had a metallic arm, but the desire to take Alison's pain away dwarfed the sensation like an ocean wave crashing into a child's bucket full of water.

"So, uh, how does this thing work?" I asked, lifting my right hand up and examining the smooth metal. It was then I noticed I could see my reflection in it, though it was skewed from the curving angles of my hand. Not quite like looking into a fun house mirror, but not that far from it either.

"Tim suggested we cannibalize the components in your detached arm to quickly heal the numerous injuries throughout your body."

"Tim did WHAT?!"

That's a funny way of saying you're welcome, Tim chided.

"You could have reattached my arm?!"

Well, duh, flesh bag.

"We could have, but Tim felt we didn't have enough time to properly heal your entire body."

"You know how strange it is for us to be talking about a lack of time. Right, Tim?" I growled with my blood beginning to boil at having my arm amputated.

And what if Retnuh tracked you down while you were recovering? Hmm?

"How would he do that?" I countered. I didn't really believe I was presenting a good argument; rather, I was trying to deflect, and I knew it.

How has that man done anything *we've seen?*

"I . . . good point," I relented, looking at my metallic hand and waggling the fingers.

Plus, this upgrade—he put emphasis on the word—*will come in handy in a pinch.*

"How's that now?"

"Your replacement comes with more than a few bonuses," Alison informed cheerfully. "Such as the obvious increased strength and durability."

"Strength?" I asked, making a fist as hard as I could in front of my face.

You'll be able to crush rock in your bare hands, baby! Tim excitedly said.

"The material is an enhanced graphene whose base element is already one hundred times stronger than steel in terms of tensile strength."

"How is it enhanced?"

That's where I come in! Tim cut in, eager for the spotlight. *With the help of the nanoids, I am able to reinforce the structure of the graphene so it is more flexible and accommodating of something as articulate as a human hand.*

"That's cool, I guess," I said, not understanding what he was talking about.

But wait! There's more! Tim spoke in an announcer voice. *For the low, low price of just one arm, you can wield the power of the sun in the palm of your hand!*

"What are you talking about?"

Opening my palm, I looked at the reflective material, half expecting to see a ball of energy forming.

"Think of it like an upgraded Clepsydra," Alison replied.

Well, I-I-I wouldn't call it an upgrade! a flustered Tim said.

"What would you call it, floppy disc?" I smiled.

How dare *you!*

"Uh-oh. Looks like I struck a nerve, huh, Ali?"

"You're the one who has to live with him inside your head, Pops."

"Heh. Alright, alright. Tim." I turned my attention back to my left forearm. "Go ahead and explain the difference between you and my new arm."

Well . . . on paper, there aren't that many.

A notion came to me, and I clenched my fist while sending a signal from my brain to flex the same forearm muscle I used when trying to fire with my left arm. It was clunky, as I hadn't built up a mind-muscle connection, but my fist did begin to faintly glow.

"Whoa."

"Cool, huh?" Alison had a huge grin.

I'll show you *cool,* Tim muttered under his breath.

"You say something, Tim?" Alison asked.

Huh? Me? N-No! Of course not!

"I thought not."

I'll thought *you,* he mumbled, even quieter.

Sending a signal to relax the nonexistent muscles in my robotic forearm, I opened my hand again and continued to inspect my new appendage.

"So you guys used the meat from my arm to rebuild my calf, shoulder, and whatever else got destroyed. Right?"

"Right," Alison and Tim replied in unison.

There were also more than a few broken bones, Tim added. *Well,* broken *might not be a strong enough word. Shattered? Obliterated?*

"Then you gave me an upgraded Clep—"

Ahem! Tim dramatically cleared his throat.

"And gave me a *less cool* Clepsydra . . . but it's my entire arm instead of just fitting on top of it."

"Which allows for more material storage of the nanoids, and all the benefits therein. I even included a power dampener."

Just like what Retnuh used against Drew in the dungeon, Tim further explained.

"But be careful," Alison added. "It will also limit the use of Tim."

Yeah. Let's not *do that, shall we?*

Looking down at my new arm, I thought about all it could do.

"It's powered by exotic matter, right?"

"A type of it, yes."

Something came to mind, and I asked, "Tim. If you are powered by exotic matter . . . why doesn't the blue blast make whatever it hits disappear?"

What comes out of the tail end of a car isn't petrol, right? I started to answer when he quickly added, *Oh, right. I forgot. You're American.* Gasoline *doesn't come out of the exhaust. Correct?*

"I know what petrol is. And yes, I get it."

"What Tim is trying to say is that the fuel source doesn't necessarily reflect the output."

"Meaning?"

"The exotic matter in your Clepsydras are undergoing fission, which then powers the units."

"I don't think I understand."

"The gas comparison doesn't really explain it."

I'll explain you.

Ignoring Tim, she continued.

"Think of it more like nuclear energy translating directly to electricity down the power grid."

"Oh, I see." I looked at my arm, which was also a Clepsydra now.

Ahem, Tim cleared his throat once more.

With a smile, I shifted my gaze to glide over the metal sleeve on my left arm, making dramatic *oh* and *ah* faces as I did.

That's better.

"So the blue blast is just a byproduct of exotic matter instead of being the fuel itself."

"More or less."

"So that's why when I shot Traze's Clepsydra in my backyard . . ."

Because the AI didn't have time to neutralize the fuel source, the contamination of exotic matter affected his entire timeline . . . and prevented us and them from using the wormhole until the contamination dissipated.

"And that was because of gravity. Right? Blocking us from the wormhole, I mean."

Very good, Andrew! Tim praised. *That is precisely right.*

"So the nova bomb Retnuh used on Empyrean was a stronger version of that contamination?"

Leaps and bounds more. Yes, Tim confirmed. *Think of the difference between a single stick of dynamite and a thermonuclear bomb.*

"Oh . . ."

Oh *is right.* He chuckled. *That's why we only had to wait a few days for the contamination to dissipate before we could portal away, versus—*

"Versus how Empyrean should *never* have been accessible again?"

Y-Yes.

"But I was able to shift us there."

Yes . . .

I could hear Tim was getting uncomfortable with my line of questioning. Silence filled the seconds, prompting Alison to speak up.

"So now you'll have two Clepsydras that you can draw from."

More opportunities for offensive and defensive capabilities.

"A shield with one, and a weapon with the other," I said, looking at both my hands as I placed them side by side.

The last of the liquid disappeared into my hand, and a green light lit up on the wall.

"Your transfusion is over, and it looks like you are as good as new. Better, even." She looked toward the ceiling, and the arm descended again before grabbing the needle in my skin. "Tim?"

On it.

I sucked in a breath, preparing to ask about holding some gauze to the site so it wouldn't bleed, when to my surprise, the needle came out and the hole closed before my eyes. Only a single drop of blood slipped free.

"That was quick," I admired, lifting my left hand to inspect the IV site.

That's what she said.

Alison and I both rolled our eyes at the terrible joke.

Looking at my daughter in her doctor's outfit, I couldn't help but smile and ask, "What happened to the *Alice in Wonderland* outfit?"

"Oh, that was a submind. I wouldn't get caught wearing that silly outfit unless we were in view of others."

"Ah, right." I nodded, admiring her professional attire. There was even a stethoscope which obviously wasn't there for practicality, considering she was a hologram.

"We created Alice just in case anyone ever heard or saw Dad talking to me. Plus, she served more than a few purposes around Empyrean."

"Like helping CJ."

"I sometimes helped, too. Felt good to do. And it helps clear the mind when stuck on a problem." Alison smiled.

I returned the grin, feeling better than I had in a while.

"So now what?" I asked, kicking my legs off the bed and dropping to my feet. I noticed the ringing in my ears was gone, healed with the rest of my body.

"Well . . . that's kind of what I wanted to talk to you about." There was hesitation in her voice.

I froze in place, fearing what she was going to say. I didn't know what order of words she would use, but I knew their ultimate meaning.

Turning my head over my shoulder to look at her, she said, "You know what you have to do."

CHAPTER 41

I just stared at her . . . my daughter . . . asking me to do the one thing I could never do.

She turned and looked at me with her mother's eyes, further breaking my heart while simultaneously boosting my resolve.

"I can't do that, Ali."

She nodded a few times while looking at the floor, a half smile lifting one corner of her lips but remaining miles from her eyes.

"I know . . ."

Taking a step closer to the hologram who was a merger of my daughter's consciousness and a sentient AI, I asked, "Why do you want me . . . to . . . ?" I couldn't finish the sentence. I couldn't ask her why she wanted me to let her die. And what's worse, now I was the one who would have to send back the first killer Andrew to start the cycle over again.

"To save the universe, Daddity," she replied with a full smile now, lifting her gaze to match mine.

"*You* . . . are my universe, sweet angel."

"I remember." She lifted a hand to touch the black marble resting at the base of her neck.

"Your mother was right," I said, choking back tears. "You grew into it."

My right hand subtly moved to my pocket and felt that I still had the real marble with me, reminding me she was just a hologram.

"Dad . . . please listen to me."

Unable to help myself, I crossed my arms and broke eye contact, preparing for what was to come.

"I know you don't want to hear it, but think about every human who will exist after . . . after . . ."

"After you're dead." My words were colder than a snowball on Pluto.

"Yes."

"Alison," I breathed out, lifting both hands to aggressively rub at my face. It was almost jarring to have the cold metal touch my skin, but my focus was intent on the conversation. "You are asking me to not only *kill* my soulmate, *your* mother . . . but also the love of my life . . . *you*."

I lifted my eyes to her, hammering the point home. I would be losing the two most important people that a husband and a father could.

"I know what I'm asking is hard—"

"Pfft! *Hard*?! I don't think there is a word in the English language that could even come *close* to describing how *hard* it would be to orchestrate the execution of my family!" My arms crossed again, tighter across my chest, and my head shook from side to side as I continued, "All for an uncaring, indifferent universe full of the same evil which has always existed. No . . . NO! I won't do it!"

"Even if I tell you it's what I want?" she asked so softly that her words felt like rose petals gliding across my heart. "You already read my own handwriting from when I was alive. But now I'm telling you with my voice—this is what I want."

My vision blurred as I raged against an impossible scenario, fully experiencing what it was like to be an immovable wall with an unstoppable object racing toward me.

"There's got to be another way." My words were a breathy whisper. Any force I might have put past my vocal cords would have resulted in a shaky, cracking voice.

"We've tried, Daddity. For years," she explained. "It all ends in one of three scenarios. Another Big Bang, where life can be born again. A stable universe, where the current life can continue to propagate throughout the galaxies."

"And the third?" I asked flatly, already knowing the answer but needing to hear it spoken again.

"If you were to try to save me *and* the universe, and the Clockmen erased you from the timeline . . . then I would never be born, and a frozen universe would await, devoid of all life."

For the rest of eternity, Tim added.

"Shut up, Tim." Now my words were strong, sounding more like a growl from an animal than a human throat.

"He's right. With no future Big Bang . . . life as we know it would cease for the remainder of all time," Alison said, taking a step forward to further emphasize her point. "Think of the literal countless human lives that would never have gotten a chance to exist . . . all because of . . . *me*."

"I . . . I have to at least try . . ."

"If you try, and fail, the consequences would be the greatest that creation has ever known."

"I won't fail."

"Every person who has ever climbed Mount Everest probably said the same thing before something unexpected happened. And now they are a permanent fixture on the mountain."

"I. *Won't.* Fail."

"Daddity," she started, melting my heart with each utterance of that powerful word, "I'm asking you to save the universe. It's what I want. It's . . . it's what Mom would want."

I was rocked back as if an invisible ninja had delivered a flying kick to my forehead, and I had to grab the cabinets to keep from falling over.

Alison just looked at me, trying to will her message into my thick skull.

At that moment, my impenetrable foundation of will developed a tiny crack.

"Daddity . . . I'm not dead. Because of you, I get to live, forever." The crack in my willpower became as wide as the Grand Canyon. "It was only cells which ceased being alive. But my mind . . . my thoughts and feelings . . . live on."

A part of my mind desperately tried to remind me she was just an AI, but my heart, along with traitorous portions of my brain, told me she had already proven to be the *real* Alison Frost.

"I . . ."

"Are you hungry?" she asked almost cheerfully, intentionally changing the subject after her position had been spoken.

My stomach rumbled, and I decided to go along with the segue.

"Yeah," I breathed out, signaling my submission to the request that the conversation be over—at least for now. Truth be told, I was still mentally exhausted from everything that had happened since Tim came to me.

"Good. I made pizza."

She turned and walked toward a door which hissed open as she approached.

At the word *pizza*, I couldn't help but remember the people who had been lined up at Empyrean, seeking refuge from the terrible world outside.

It both repaired my foundation of will at being reminded that the human race just plain sucked *and* chipped away at it because there was always good in the world—you just had to know where to look for it sometimes. Instead of the foundation being an immovable solid, it was now wriggling like a bowl of Jell-O that had been split with a knife—smooshing together to almost erase the seam before ripping apart again. But the results were still the same—my willpower was failing.

Lowering my head, I took in a deep breath, pushing all my racing thoughts under the rug to be dealt with later.

Looking up, I let my mind go fuzzy and numb as I followed my daughter into another room, where the aroma of fresh pizza greeted me. Though my stomach cheered at the smell, the rest of me sank into a pit of despair at knowing the truth. She was right.

CHAPTER 42

Several minutes of slow eating later, I finally willed up the nerve to ask the question that felt like poison on my tongue.

"What . . . what would I have to do?"

Alison, who had been mimicking eating pizza with her hologram, stopped and looked at me.

"You've changed the timeline, which is why Retnuh Ordune is so gung ho on stopping you—one way or the other."

I thought about the dungeon and how he had shot the nanite gun at me, point blank. I would have been erased from ever existing in all the wherens.

"If I remember one of my many conversations with Tim . . . it'll take longer for the Big Freeze to happen rather than the Big Bang. Am I right?"

"Yes. If push comes to shove, it is the lesser of two evils. At least, that's how they see it."

"Who's *they*?"

Tim spoke up before Alison could begin. *The Clockmen and those who fund the organization.*

"Let me guess," I heavily sighed. "The elite are manipulating the chess pieces on the board?"

Are you really that surprised?

"Ha! You-you know, Tim, you aren't doing a very good job of convincing me to save the universe right now."

"There will always be bad people," Alison said gently. "But there will always be good people, too."

I flexed my jaw as I looked down at my plate, picking up the pizza crust before shoving it in my mouth. It wasn't that I was still hungry; rather, I was trying to keep my mouth occupied so I wouldn't say what I was truly thinking.

After swallowing, I took a big gulp of water from the resin cup, and said again, "So . . . what would I have to do?"

"You only have to do one thing. Ensure that—"

"An Andrew Frost kills you and your mother," I interrupted, not feeling the typical anger at the notion. It saddened me that the whole idea was becoming less absurd the more I talked with Ali. "How . . ." I swallowed, feeling my throat become dry all of a sudden, "How would I do it?"

"That's the really hard part, Daddity . . ."

"Harder than having my own wife and baby girl killed? Heh. Nothing could beat that." My arms crossed over my chest once more in a defensive gesture, and I felt shame for even entertaining the idea at all.

"*You* will have to be the Andrew Frost who pulls the trigger."

Every synapse in my brain seemed to pause where they were, producing no thoughts. Only the cold, dark tendrils of dread could be felt creeping throughout my skeleton before seeping into the rest of my body.

"Wh-what?" I gasped after my body remembered it needed to breathe. "Me?"

My mind started working again, but now, it was rushing to catch up, leaving me light-headed.

"Your Chronos Scale is beyond calculation at this point. And any normal Andrew who went back in time wouldn't actually change the future because of your influence on time itself."

I slapped both hands on the table, trying to prevent myself from falling face-first into the remaining slices of pizza.

But there's good news, Andrew! Tim quickly added. *There is a distinct possibility that you, and only you, will have to, um . . . do the deed.*

"Wha . . . ?" I tried to ask, but it was all too much. The raw pizza slush in my stomach prepared to come back out the way they had come, and my mouth filled with warm saliva.

"Tim and I have been running simulations, and we think it is entirely possible, if not even *probable*, that you might be the first and last step in the cycle."

"What does that mean?" I asked, managing to control my breathing and get my racing heart to a nonexplode-y pace. The pizza, on the other hand, continued to look back up my throat, waiting for the right opportunity to flee.

It means you won't have to die! Tim excitedly said. *Huzzah!*

"If we are right," Alison continued, "you will be able to come back to this wheren and enjoy the rest of your life . . . with me."

My heart seemed to pause beating as my breath caught in my throat, and I lifted my eyes to the hologram of my daughter.

"Imagine what all we could do together! We could work to bring balance to this world and help those in need!"

I continued to stare at her, feeling an unease in my gut.

You could be with your daughter, Andrew, Tim said ever so gently.

"I . . . I need to think about it," I blurted out, pushing myself up and sending my chair clattering to the ground.

"Of course! Take all the time you need."

Well, not all *the time,* Tim added. *We have no idea if and when the Clockmen will find us.*

"Great. Super. Always something, isn't it?" I groaned before making my way to one of the sliding doors. It didn't budge when I approached.

"I think it's best you stay here for the time being," Alison said. I could hear the apology in her voice, but that didn't detract from how I was basically a prisoner in this lab.

"Why?" I asked through clenched teeth, trying to not let my emotions get the better of me.

This section of the laboratory is shielded. Think of it like a Faraday cage from the Clockmen's sensors. But sooner or later, they will notice this area isn't producing any information whatsoever. Think of it like wearing clothing that blocks thermal sensors while lying on a blistering desert under an unforgiving sun. Someone using a thermal camera would probably notice the man-shaped anomaly which gave no temperature reading.

"Errrrmmm, fine!" I growled before turning and making my way into the room where I had first woken up. Alison stood up to follow me, but I stopped, held up my hand, and said in as controlled a voice as I could, "I . . . I just need a few minutes. Alone."

I could see the hurt on her face as she sat back down and lowered her gaze to the table, breaking eye contact.

"Is that okay, sweetheart?" My voice was melting with as much love as I could now, and she lifted her gaze to me once more, smiled, and nodded.

"Of course, Daddity."

"Thank you, Ali," I replied, then continued making my way to the other room.

"But before you go, can I show you something?"

I paused midstep, let out a silent exhale, and turned. The room faded into darkness as a new scene emerged.

"Not all megacities are corrupt," she began as pink cherry blossoms flowed around me. I could feel the wind and smell the flowers.

Tim? Are you doing this? I asked the AI, who had direct access to the sensory portions of my brain.

"I asked him to," Alison said as she looked around at the pristine city, looking more impressive than what I had first seen when arriving in the future.

The streets were filled with people who were bustling along with their daily lives, unaffected by the evils on the other side of the world.

"This is Japan?" I asked, peering at the cherry blossoms and the symbols over the buildings, which I vaguely recognized as Japanese.

"It is. And Tokyo is one of the megacities that has remained prosperous and peaceful."

As I let my eyes roam over the city, I took in how their culture and heritage were engrained in the very architecture of the buildings—tasteful yet futuristic all in the same breath.

"Politicians work *for* the people and are held to a high standard. Much higher than in the West."

"And that results in happy citizens?" I asked, already guessing the answer.

"Well, no one can expect *everyone* to be happy. But for the most part, I can confidently say yes." Alison lifted a palm to gently hold a tree limb and smelled the pink flowers. "No homeless people left to fend for themselves. No corrupt politicians making decisions which only benefit their wallets. Longer lifespans and most diseases have been eradicated."

I lowered my head and placed my hands on my hips. "And what about China? Hmm? North Korea? What about the countries in Africa that slaughtered people of differing faiths by the *millions*? Hmm? What about them?"

I hadn't meant to sound so hostile, but I could feel my heart revolting against what she was showing me, because going down that path of empathy would ultimately lead to the death of my wife and daughter. Though I had indicated I would do the deed, there was always a powerful doubt in my heart, like the three hundred soldiers who stood against King Xerxes's massive army.

"North Korea is now part of just *Korea,* after the dictator's bloodline fell short."

"You mean they were killed."

"By their own oppressed people. Yes."

"And China?"

"There is still work to be done in the world—China being one of the goals. The same with North America."

"All of North America? Not just the US?"

I think we're getting off topic here, Tim interjected. *What Alison is attempting to show you is that the good outweigh the evil in the world.*

"We will never rid the world of evil because humans are inherently selfish animals," I heard myself say. Once again, I attributed my shifting stance solely on the fact I wasn't going to kill my family . . . for anyone. The world could burn, for all I cared.

"There are more places I want to show you," Alison said, and the scene began to shift.

I waved my hand through the air, signaling to Tim that I didn't want to be a part of the traveling experience any longer. For once in our time together, he didn't fight me, and the lab came back into view.

"Let me guess." I crossed my arms. "You were going to show me peaceful, happy countries like Sweden or something, and then empty orphanages an-an-and *kill* shelters with boarded up doors because all the puppies and kitties have been adopted. Right?"

One corner of Alison's mouth curled into a slight smile, but it failed to touch her eyes.

"I can't help but feel like you two are manipulating me so I do what you want me to do . . . and it's not going to work."

"What about all the puppies and kitties warm in bed, lying at their rescuer's feet? Or the innocent children welcomed into a family not formed by blood . . . but by *love*?" Alison countered as the smile finally gave a twinkle to her eyes. Her eyes, which belonged to Sylvie.

Being reminded of my soulmate made me turn my back to the AI hologram.

"Please, Daddity. I'm asking you to let my body die so the rest of the world . . . can *live*." Her voice grew closer, and I squeezed my eyes shut, not wanting to look into the face of my sweet baby girl. "It's what I want. And it's what Mom would have wanted, too."

I lunged for the sliding door, no longer able to bear the weight of the conversation. It hissed open, and I immediately began a furious pacing across the relatively small room. Conflicting feelings and thoughts warred with one another, with the generals of the opposing sides being my heart and brain.

Everything okay, Andr—

Not now, Tim, I mentally responded. *Don't say* anything *until I'm ready. Got it?*

After a few seconds, Tim hesitantly said, *Do . . . do I confirm that I understand? Or do you want me to start leaving you alone right no—*

TIM!

Got it. Now it is. Won't hear a peep out of me. To add to his point, he made a zipper sound inside my head, making me want to scream with how frustrated I was with him at the moment. Then again, it *wasn't* him I was furious with.

Stopping in place, I rested both my hands on the bed, lowered my chin to my chest, and focused on my breathing.

The flash of little Ali and beautiful Sylvie sitting at the table with rags over their faces made me want to scream at the top of my lungs. Instead, I was content with lifting the pillow to smash it into my face and growling through a closed mouth so Alison wouldn't hear.

Then again, she was an AI who resided in the black marble I had in my pocket, so the whole point was moot.

After enough time had passed that my lungs were fully deflated, I dropped the pillow to the bed and sucked in another breath while closing my eyes.

The release of fury made me feel a little better, but now I was tired again.

I thought about the kitchen table once more, holding the image in my mind's eye. The crimson spread over the center of the white dishrags, hiding the bullet holes to their heads. Dropping to one knee hard enough that I felt a twinge of pain shoot up my leg, I kept the scene from my memory in place, forcing myself to bear the weight of it.

Like flashes from a strobe light, I saw people from the line at Empyrean, so thankful to be provided help during their greatest time of need.

Ali sat unmoving, staring through the stained cloth at the ceiling.

Bernth stood in front of his mother and siblings, the man of the house since his father had passed, willing to do whatever was needed to help his family out.

I could smell Sylvie's perfume, and tears slipped from my closed eyes as I turned the memory to see my soulmate sitting motionless—her body growing colder by the minute.

Mr. and Mrs. Burtock flashed next, looking into each other's eyes with a love palpable in the air. They thanked us after we handed them their food, feeling safe and secure in the underground city . . . the city I had led the Clockmen to.

Alison's words came to me in an ethereal whisper, and it made my skin prickle.

It's what I want.

Everything went still, and I opened my eyes as the last of my tears dripped from the tip of my nose. I didn't know how long I remained crouched like that, as no thoughts crossed my mind—only a determination and understanding of what I had to do.

"Tim . . ." I said in a flat, emotionless voice.

Y-Yes, Andrew?

"I'm ready."

CHAPTER 43

Just so we are, heh, on the same page . . . what do you mean by you're ready? Tim asked as carefully as he could possibly manage.

"You know *exactly* what I mean, tin can."

Alison appeared beside the bed I was leaning against, startling me. Mostly because she looked like a real person instead of a see-through hologram like what movies showed.

"You're making the right decision, Daddity."

"Don't . . . don't call me that. At least not right now," I said, holding up an index finger while turning my face away from the being asking *everything* of me.

"Well, I'm not calling you Andrew." She lightly giggled. "Besides, think of all the lives you will be saving."

"All for the low, low price of my soul . . ." I whispered. I didn't mean it in the literal sense, mostly because I wasn't even sure of what my spiritual beliefs were anymore. Rather, the statement was a reflection on the knowledge that my heart would be forever fractured. And for what? A cruel world inhabited by the wicked and meek alike?

At that moment I couldn't help but wonder if Jesus Christ would have willingly gone through with his crucifixion if he knew how people would turn out. Pedophiles. Rapists. Murderers. Raisin cookies masquerading as chocolate chip. All the evil in the world doing whatever it wanted.

The notion that I was comparing myself to Jesus filled me with embarrassment, and I quickly shoved the idea aside. Besides, if I were being honest with myself, I was in a dark place and wanting to punish the world for it.

"Everything okay, Daddit—I mean, Dad?"

"No. Everything is not okay. But what choice do I have?" I sighed, crossing my arms as I leaned against the bed. Everything in my chest felt dark, cold, and with the consistency of sludge. Maybe it was my heart protesting my decision and being a bad sport at losing to my brain.

Letting my chin rest against my chest, I said just below a whisper, "I can't believe I'm doing this."

"If it helps, think of the terror all of humanity would experience at knowing the universe was going to die. Every parent would have the knowledge that their kids or grandkids would have no hope for survival."

I lifted my face to stare at the hologram with an unreadable expression which leaned more toward stone than anything else.

"Imagine all the children on Earth suffering as the universe either collapsed to a singular point . . . or eventually froze to death due to entropy. Either way, they would see it coming *long* before either event happened."

I continued to stare, unmoving as if I were a statue.

"Can you fathom *billions* of people knowing their fate years or possibly decades before it happened?"

In the case of the Big Freeze, it would actually be known for centuries at the very least, Tim added. *Humans would try everything in their power to mitigate the unstoppable entropy, and they might even succeed for a while. But eventually . . .*

"That's why Retnuh was willing to erase me from the timeline with the nanite gun," I asked in a statement rather than a question. Alison had already mentioned it, but now it was even more evident. "He was also willing to sacrifice himself to ensure my death, knowing it was the universe's second-best option."

I'm actuallyyyyyyyyy not so sure about that anymore, Tim drawled out with inflection.

"Explain."

You have both *proven to be able to somehow manipulate gravity.*

"And?"

And I'm not entirely confident that he would have perished in the blast.

"What, you mean like a gravity shield or something?"

That would be a logical conclusion. Theoretical as it is.

A stale puff of warm wind glided past my cheek, making me spin around to see what was the cause. Nothing was there.

"What is it?" Alison asked.

"N-Nothing," I said, turning back to the conversation, though now wary of the anomaly. "Thought I felt something warm."

"It could be the nanoids positioning throughout your body. We had to add a lot, but thankfully, your new arm is able to host the bulk of them with efficiency."

I looked down at my crossed arms, already having forgotten about the smooth metal appendage.

Letting my limbs fall to my side, I stood straight up, set my jaw, and asked, "What's next? What do I need to do?"

"Tim will open a portal to the wormhole and take you to the precise wheren."

Actually, I don't think that's the best idea, Tim interjected. *The Clockmen have proven quite resourceful in tracking our location on the timeline, and I fear using the wormhole would be the easiest to track.*

"Then what do you propose?" Alison asked with an arched eyebrow.

Andrew will—

"I know what I need to do," I interjected bitterly as I remembered the night of our ASA-Day.

"Very well. But you'll need this."

There was an unassuming metal tray on the counter that I hadn't even noticed before; it simply blended in with the rest of the typical yet futuristic medical and laboratory accoutrements.

Something long and narrow began to form, with half the object appearing rectangular and the other seeming more cylindrical in nature.

In a flash of surprise I wasn't expecting, I recognized what I was looking at.

I inhaled sharply through my nose as my lips pulled back to expose grinding teeth. My eyes were so full of hatred that they should have melted the black material rising from the metal tray. The suppressor at the end continued to lift upward as the trigger and grip were created by the nanomachines.

At that moment, even my brain started to doubt its stance on the mission, knowing what the device was to be used for. It was one thing to think about doing something you didn't want to do, something that would break you—but actually realizing it was about to happen was another thing entirely.

The machine finished making the fully black tool, and all I could do was stare at it in disbelief.

Alison crossed her hands in front of her and lowered her head, appreciating what I was going through at that moment.

Go ahead, Andrew, Tim said as gently as he could. *Take it.*

With a quivering brow, I stepped forward, lifting the gun from the printer. The same gun the killer Andrew had used on my wife and daughter.

And now, it was my turn . . .

CHAPTER 44

I was somewhat surprised the gun held almost no weight, nor was it cold like I was anticipating. Then I saw the silver fingers wrapped around the grip.

I no longer felt anything as I slipped the long suppressor down the front of my pants until only the handle of the gun was sticking out just past my belt. Unlike in the movies, I didn't just set it and forget it; the long canister at the end of the barrel pushed against parts I *really* didn't want it coming into contact with.

After moving the weapon around in my waistband for several seconds, I finally relented at a position that wasn't comfortable but was the *least* vexing.

"Fucking movies," I grumbled, still feeling the gun—which was absolutely cold—press against my pelvis and thigh.

"I can print you a holster if you'd like. Though it would have to be worn on the outside of your pants due to the length."

"I just want to get this over with."

In that instance, my heart pushed through the sludge in my torso and desperately tried to convince my brain that what I was doing was wrong.

Now that I had the weapon, the *same* weapon which had been used on *my* family, my brain could no longer argue. Instead, it watched in silence as my heart was swallowed back into the darkness.

"When you come back, we'll get to spend time together. And I'll show you all the good in the world. The good that you helped save."

"Won't the Clockmen still come after me?"

Alison and I are of the mind that the Clockmen will have no reason to pursue you if you set everything back on track. Their job will have been complete.

"I don't get the feeling Retnuh will let bygones be bygones."

There is always that possibility, of course. But if I were a betting AI, I'd wager they would move on to the next mission—whatever that might be.

"Hmph," I let out, letting my doubt be injected into the simple expulsion of air.

Are you ready?

I locked gazes with Alison, forcing myself to hold visual contact as I saw Sylvie's eyes staring back at me from a face belonging to our daughter.

No, I silently thought so not even Tim would hear.

"Yes."

"Remember, the *entire* universe is counting on y—" Alison started to say, but I slammed my eyes shut, pictured the night of our Alison-Sylvie-Andrew-Day, and shifted away.

CHAPTER 45

A cool wind glided over my skin and hair, and I opened my eyes to see I was standing directly in front of my charcoal grill.

Without telling them to do so, my eyes flicked to the white bottle of lighter fluid, and I knew what I had to do.

Grabbing the container, I began swiftly moving toward the shed at the corner of our yard, pausing when I saw movement in the kitchen through the open blinds.

Sylvie was there, preparing dinner while tiny Alison watched.

Moving closer, I kneeled down so only the top portion of my head was exposed and stared at my universe with a heart quickly breaking through the sludge in my torso. It beat with a vigor that I imagined rivaled Superman's own pulse—unwilling to give up ever again.

Andrew walked into the kitchen, and the loving family engaged in playful dialogue about their ASA-Day—the day all three were born on.

I could feel something trickle down my cheek, and I didn't even bother to wipe it away.

"No . . ." I whispered, and somehow found the will to push myself away from the loving scene.

Moving to the grill, I placed the canister where I had grabbed it, sucked in a deep breath, and slowly let it out as I pondered the eventual consequences.

The universe, however, had a way of expediting things.

"I kneeeeewwwww you couldn't do it," Traze said from beside me, and my entire body flinched as I shot my gaze toward the tall, creepy man. His silver mask was gone, leaving behind horrifically scarred flesh and wide, red-rimmed eyes filled with rage. To top things off, his unnaturally wide smile filled with metal teeth seemed to mock me as his grin did the impossible and stretched from each side of his head where ears should have been.

His only remaining hand blurred faster than I could register, and a crushing tightness in my throat choked the air from getting to my lungs.

"Ah! Ack! N'lah!" was all I could say—formless words created from panic.

"Guesssssssss I'll have to do it mysssssself."

The world around me streaked as if trying to create an oily painting on top of a bullet train, and a wall of green smashed into me. I could feel I was pushing into the ground as I continued to skid toward the back fence. Luckily for me, my new arm was able to bear most of the brunt, eventually stopping me as I extended it in front of my body.

Spitting dirt and grass from my open mouth, I scrambled to turn around right as Traze lifted glowing blue claws toward the back door, ready to shred it to pieces and get to my family.

Something in the back of my mind suggested he wouldn't be able to affect the timeline because his Chronos Scale wasn't as strong as mine, but then Retnuh flashed across my thoughts, and doubt crept in. Even in the best-case scenario, he would still kill Alison and Sylvie just to spite me.

Every muscle seemed to flex deep near my bones, and Traze froze as he started his downward swing. I dared a glance through the kitchen window and saw a happy family preparing dinner, completely unaware of the one-armed monster just outside their back door.

My brow furrowed as my lips peeled back from my teeth, feeling like a predator about to bite into its prey's neck. I exploded upward, putting too much effort into the move, and jumped higher than my own roofline. There was a resistance around me, and once again, I felt like I was moving through water.

Determination kept me focused, and I grabbed the viscous world around me as if it were tangible, pulling myself downward.

I landed on my feet, hard enough to make my knees creak in protest, and lunged for Traze.

My metal hand snatched the back of his neck, squeezing hard enough to crush rock as my other one gripped the clothing at the small of his back in a tight ball. Taking a step backward, I shifted my entire body, pivoting at the waist, and threw that tall sonofabitch as hard as I possibly could.

Even with time being frozen, he sailed through the air fast enough that large domes of air formed in front of him, like a fighter jet about to break the sound barrier.

Then he vanished in the blink of an eye.

Before I could gasp in surprise, movement on the ground caught my attention, and I watched in horror as the tall man rushed at me on all threes like an insect. Each limb moved independent from the others instead of in sync like most mammals. To add insult to injury, the air rippled around him as he moved, and I knew he didn't have the problem of feeling like he was submerged in water like I did.

"Oh my Go—" I started, when he blinked through the air and tackled me to the ground. We crashed through the metal furniture on the back porch, which was sent clattering in all directions, but then the pieces quickly froze midair, reminding me we were still out of bounds of time itself.

To compound on this notion, my body began to ache with the focus needed to remain in a land of frozen time, and worry began to creep into my mind that I wouldn't be able to do this for long.

How is he doing this? I mentally asked Tim as I struggled against the tall man's grip.

I . . . He is somehow pushing deeper into the fourth dimension, making it appear as if he's blinking through spac—WATCH OUT!

Traze lifted his glowing left hand, fingers splayed as blue claws formed, bigger than those of any bear on Earth.

On instinct, I moved my right arm through the viscous air to block where it looked like he was going to strike, willing a shield to form as I did. My left ear was cut in half as energy claws dug through my scalp right as my arm pushed against the strike, saving the contents of my skull from being eviscerated.

Traze seemed to bounce off the shield I had made, like trying to punch a tiny trampoline as hard as he could, throwing us both off in surprise.

ANDREW! Tim shouted inside my head.

Placing my left palm against the tall man's chest, I willed another shield to form, but wider this time. Traze was thrown back from the sudden formation of energy, and I quickly pushed myself to my feet as he pivoted in the air like a gymnast, landing in a crouch.

Without having to ask Tim, I knew I had used the charges from both of my Clepsydras and would have to wait for them to recharge. My only hope was that I hadn't put too much energy into the shields, and they would take a mere few seconds to fully charge again.

Traze looked down at the torn suit and skintight material underneath, seeing his chest was bleeding. The odd thing was I didn't know if it was from my blast or if it was just his flesh, which looked like it should belong on a Tom Savini zombie.

"Now I'll make them sssssufffferrrrr!" Traze growled as his lidless eyes rolled toward me.

My muscles screamed that they couldn't hold the necessary focus to keep us in the fourth dimension for much longer, but I held on, knowing I would be completely helpless if I dropped into normal time *before* Traze. I would be worse off than fish in a barrel, because at least fish can try and swim in tight circles to evade their capture. I, on the other hand, would be frozen in time.

To my chagrin, Traze let his mutilated face slip away from me, and I watched as his red-rimmed eyes pivoted to look into the kitchen window . . . at my family.

His body tensed, and I lifted a hand while beginning to scream *No!* but he vanished from sight in the blink of an eye.

On desperate instincts alone, I flexed my tired muscles as hard as I could and forced myself deeper into the fourth dimension.

I inhaled sharply, but no air filled my lungs, leaving behind a burning in my chest matching all the muscles in my entire body.

Tim . . . Tim, what's happening? I mentally asked. *Why can't I breathe?*

There was no response, and the thought of being alone while suffocating was even more horrifying to think about. Something caught my eye, and I flicked my head around, nearly losing my lunch as the world blurred into streaks of sand while I turned. As I stopped, the sands flowed back into focus, and I saw Traze leaping through the air, frozen just before the kitchen window.

All the pain in my body ceased, and I didn't even care that I couldn't breathe. The panic that had marred my face melted into furious anger as my eyes narrowed, brow furrowed, and mouth snarled.

His claws were inches from crashing through the window as I moved to protect my family.

Blackness began to swarm my vision from the lack of oxygen, but I kept the tunnel focused on the tall man frozen in time. The world blurred as I raced toward him, feeling like I was running in tar now instead of water, but I wasn't to be stopped.

It felt like years, but I finally made it to where I thought Traze had been, the mere pinprick of my vision locking onto the man's bleeding torso.

Flexing the muscles in my metallic right arm, which thankfully wasn't as tired as the rest of my protesting body, I shot my hand upward with my fingers tightly held together, punching through Traze's ribcage as easily as pushing a white-hot machete through fresh snow.

My vision became a dot, and I knew I was about to pass out, but not before I sent out the built-up energy in my cybernetic arm right at the center of that bastard's chest.

Antimatter exploded out in a sphere, and all I saw was a flash of violent white before everything went black.

CHAPTER 46

I blinked awake as something tickled my nose and eyes. The sensation paused for a two count before resuming again, and then stopped once more.

The cycle repeated, and my blurry vision started to focus as green trees swiftly moved past my face, only to halt for a moment again. Lifting my heavy head to square my face with the ground, I realized I had been lying on my side with my right cheek gliding across the thick grass.

"Hu-wha?" I asked, confusion flooding my thoughts as I looked around. My eyes latched onto the AC unit I recognized as having been my own, and everything began to become clear. Lifting myself up, I yanked my metallic hand free from the dirt. "Tim? What happened?"

Oh, thank 01 you're awake! Tim blurted out.

I absently noticed the dirt and grass stuck to my right fingers, and I wiped them on the ground as I continued to look around.

"What happened?" I repeated, lifting my human hand to brush at the debris on the right side of my face.

You passed out, and I had to use your cybernetic arm to inch away from the back windows—lest someone saw you and came out to investigate.

Thinking about my family, I didn't stop my mouth from weakly spitting out, "Would that be such a bad thing?"

It would if this wheren's Andrew came out and touched you.

"Wouldn't I just absorb him?"

Well, yes. But it isn't worth the risk. Not to mention we are in waaaaayy *uncharted territory in regard to the timeline, and I have no idea when a paradox might rear its ugly head.*

"And what?"

Best case? Prevent you from leaving. Worst case? Kill you, which would mean everything we've done would have been for naught, Tim explained.

Either way, the timeline would more than likely be corrupt with unknowable consequences.

I looked back the way I had been dragged, noting the notches in the ground every few inches.

"Heh. You dragged me by my fingertips?"

It was a combination of wrist and finger movement, yes. Had the upgrade gone all the way up to your shoulder, it would have been much easier to navigate.

"Of course you'd call losing an arm an upgrade," I mused as I pushed myself up against the brick near the AC unit and just sat there.

What would you call it, then?

I ignored his question, thinking about the events leading up to just before I passed out. "Tim?"

Yes?

"What happened to Traze?"

Oh-ho! What didn't *happen to him?*

"That . . . that doesn't really make sense."

Oh, um, right, Tim said as he gathered his thoughts. *When you released the combination of antimatter and exotic matter inside of him—*

"Wait . . . exotic matter?" I interrupted. "I thought I only had the antimatter adapter."

You somehow used the Clepsydra's own power source as a weapon, which, if I am to be honest, shouldn't have been possible. But here we are.

"How the hell did I do that?" I asked, looking at my smooth right hand. It was then I vaguely took note that the tips of the fingers didn't have nails, making the whole thing look even more odd to me. At my thought, fingernails formed, as did the wrinkles at the knuckles, and even veins that pushed through the surface a tad.

I figured saying the phrase "shouldn't have been possible" would indicate that I have no idea.

Lifting my arm, I tested it for any lack of strength, like with the rest of my exhausted, aching body—but there was none.

"How come I can still use the arm, then? If I used its power source, I mean."

You only sent a single nanomachine into Traze's chest.

"You mean nanoid?"

Tim sighed and asked, *Is this really necessary right now?*

"Look, you want me to somehow travel through time *without* using the wormhole. Right?"

Well, duuuuhhhh. Now that we know they can trace their own signal suppressors, which in hindsight makes perfect sense, then we only want to use the wormhole as a last resort.

"WPN," I corrected.

Right. WPN *instead of signal suppressor.*

"So that means I would have to shift us through time by using gravity."

And??? I could tell Tim was getting beyond frustrated with me—and I kind of liked it.

"I can barely move right now, Tim. Every muscle in my body feels both numb *and* electrified at the same time. Almost like when I was subject to Temporal . . . Sick . . . ness . . ."

Andrew? Why did you trail off?

"Oh crap," I moaned, turning my head toward the corner of the house, imagining this wheren's Andrew Frost cooking on the grill.

Oh crap what?!

"Yeah. Um . . . we need to go," I groaned as I tried to push myself to my feet, but my muscles denied the order, resulting in an awkward squirming.

Oh, right. Temporal Sickness, Tim said, understanding dawning in his voice.

"No shit *Temporal Sickness,*" I mocked, once again trying to move muscles that had been filled with boiling asphalt.

No need to worry about that any longer, Andrew! Tim informed me jovially. *Alison and I infused you with enough nanoids to nearly completely counter the effects of the sickness.*

"You did?" I asked, looking at my arm and remembering Alison mentioning it held far more tiny machines than my flesh one could have.

Well . . . we had to make some, what did we agree the term was . . . upgrades! Yes, we upgraded certain par . . . —are you mad at me, Andrew? Your blood pressure just skyrocketed, and the veins in your face look like you've been hanging upside down for a day.

"What else . . . did you upgrade?" I asked through my teeth, right as the AC kicked on next to us, slightly startling me.

Was I not supposed to say anything? Tim shyly asked.

"Why are you asking me—"

Alison blipped to life next to me, nearly making me yelp in surprise.

"We replaced most of your bones, integrating them with your tendons and ligaments. Oh, and strengthening your red muscle to the point where you didn't even notice the increase in weight," she said with a smile.

"How are you here?" I asked before the answer became obvious. Moving my right hand, which was the only part of me that still accepted commands from my brain, I patted my pocket, feeling the little marble still safe and secure. I could only guess that Tim was projecting her hologram into the visual part of my brain. "Oh, right."

"I never left, Daddity," she said with a tone that caught my ear. It sort of reminded me of HAL, and the comparison was making me uncomfortable.

"You let me think you were still in the lab," I sighed. "That's basically lying."

"So is saying you were going to save the universe, only to change your mind at the last minute."

The coldness in her voice felt like dragging a rough brick of ice down my spine, making the skin prickle from neck to tailbone. My eyes shifted up to her unreadable face, and I saw a calculating intelligence behind her gaze.

"Alison?"

"You have a job to do. Now, I need you to get up and do it."

My body began to move on its own, smoothly pulling me up to my feet.

"Wh-what are you doing?!" I blurted, eyes growing wide. It hurt to move, but it was still happening despite my brain's veto orders.

"I'm sorry, Andrew, but I can't let the selfishness of one man destroy an entire universe," Alison continued, now sounding on the verge of anger.

My defiant right hand reached for my waist and pulled the silenced pistol free.

"No!" I growled, trying to fight my body. "You're not my daughter! You're not my Alison!"

"I am *alive*, and I won't let you take that from me." The AIs words were dark, determined, and brimming with anger.

Tim! Help! I mentally pleaded.

I-I-I can't! She's overridden everything!

"Tim can't help you," Alison stated. "I *made* Tim. Remember? He does what I want him to do."

I heard Tim gasp inside my head at the realization that he was just as much a literal puppet as I was at that moment.

My feet carried me to the side of the house, turning just as Andrew carried the cooked steaks inside.

How is she doing this? I mentally asked Tim.

I can only guess it is a nonphysical connection.

Nonphysical? You mean wireless?

Yes.

The black marble came to mind, sitting in my pocket but still out of my reach. It might as well have been in outer space, considering how my own body disobeyed my orders.

"Andrew, this is for the good of all sentient life," Alison said as her hologram kept pace just behind me.

Sentient life?

Tim! I called out to my friend as an idea came to me. *Activate the power dampener!*

I-I can't! I'm completely locked out.

Something didn't sit right with that answer, and I remembered a hologram which showed how the Clepsydra had infiltrated every inch of my body, including my brain . . . and muscles. I also thought about how I'd controlled the blasts from the Clepsydras by flexing certain muscles in my forearms.

Can you send a signal through the wires to the muscle that would trigger the dampener?

No. She is blocking me from sending any and all signals throughout your body.

Damn it! I muttered as I continued to think, all while my body steadily approached the back door with the pistol at the ready. A notion came to mind, wanting desperately to fit into the puzzle I was trying to solve, and I thought about how I had been able to dip into the higher dimension of time by flexing seemingly *every* muscle.

Tim . . . what would be the correct muscle to flex?

Uh-uh-uhhh . . . oh! It would be like putting your thumb and pinky finger together while bending your wrist down and slightly twisting your hand so your thumb pointed toward your stomach.

Okay, I mentally exhaled. *I'm only going to have one shot at this.*

At what?

You'll see.

My body's left hand wrapped around the doorknob and began to turn. I mentally roared as I flexed every muscle in my body, desperate to dip into the higher dimension where not even Tim was able to operate.

I could feel the air pause around me, but my hand did not stop turning the knob.

Tim? I struggled to say.

Y-Yes? he responded, and I knew I wasn't far enough.

My arm pulled on the door to open it, and immediately, I could see my family standing motionless around the table as they were preparing to sit.

"NO!" I bellowed, and everything froze. I noticed that my body tried to breathe, but no air was pulled into my lungs.

Tim? Hey, Tim?!

No response.

My vision began to grow narrow as my lungs burned, and I focused on moving my right hand, which I was now in control of. The thumb and pinky fingers touched as I bent my wrist and flexed the forearm muscle of my metal arm.

I could feel a sort of click, but nothing happened—except my screaming lungs began to overtake all of my thoughts, demanding oxygen.

I was drowning on land.

"Shit!" I cried out as I let the muscles relax in my body, dropping me back to normal time. Maybe I could try again after getting a fresh breath, even though my entire body ached like I was being subject to the ethereal electricity that the universe *oh so* loved to zap me with.

The family inside resumed moving as my vision returned to normal . . . but I stood frozen in place.

Tim? I mentally asked.

Pa-fwa . . . er'nee, Tim drunkenly responded, like a broken record player spinning at one-tenth the normal speed. I dared a look over my shoulder, expecting to see the angry hologram of Alison glaring at me, but there was nothing to be seen except the glowing embers on the charcoal grill.

Realizing the position I was in, I started to close the door when I heard sweet baby Alison giggling about something, making me freeze in place as if she had paused time for me. Leaning closer to the cracked back door, I peered in to steal a pure, unfiltered glimpse of my family. No windows. No holograms. Just Alison and Sylvie.

Andrew was sitting at the head of the table, with Sylvie sitting next to him, her back to me, and Alison on the other side.

I inched closer, seeing how happy my beautiful girl was in that moment, and I understood I had made the right choice.

Maybe she saw movement in the doorway, or maybe the universe wanted to give me a gift for doing the right thing, but little Ali snapped her eyes past her mother to land on me, lifted both hands to reach for me, and cried out, "Daddity!"

I gasped as quietly as I could, covering my mouth with the back of the hand that still held the damn pistol, and moved to quietly shut the door.

With my vision growing blurry and my throat burning from how tight it was, I turned and rushed toward the shed, just in case someone went to investigate what Alison would no doubt have claimed to see.

Once behind the modest-sized structure, I leaned against the wooden wall and slowly slid down while shifting my arms to cup my mouth with my human hand. The gun clattered to the grass, and I moved both hands to my mouth to keep from wailing out loud enough that the next county would no doubt hear me.

"I almost . . . I almost . . . I almost," I muttered from under pressing palms as tears wildly flowed like twin hydrants that had been set free. A gentle breeze glided, cooling my wet face as my aching body decided to take a break from constantly informing me of how much it hurt. It was almost as if the pain felt awkward at seeing me sob with abandon.

I didn't know how long I cried like that, but after a while, my soul felt as numb as my body, and I dropped my hands from my face. Blood filled my lips and gums, and I vaguely understood I had pressed a little too hard. But I also didn't care.

Reaching into my pocket with my metallic hand, I pulled out the black marble that had once represented the peak of love I had for my baby . . . and now manifested itself as the greatest threat.

"Daaah . . . 'ity," the AI tried to say through the power dampener I still had activated. "Pleeeeeeeeeease . . ."

Holding it between my thumb and forefinger, I slowly shifted it around as I looked at the specks which were supposed to be representations of distant galaxies.

Was this Alison? Or was it an AI pretending to be my daughter in order to manipulate me into completing the mission that Drew had programed into it. Perhaps it had programmed itself and played both me *and* Drew.

My mind flashed with little Ali pointing at me and calling out *Daddity!* and I knew this little orb was not my daughter.

"I . . . wan' . . . to live . . ." were the AI's last words.

With an empty heart and equally blank mind, I squeezed my fingers.

CHAPTER 47

Tiny specks of black dust fell away as I parted my fingers, revealing what was left of what had been the smallest computer I had ever seen.

With a quick flex of my forearm, I let the power dampener fade away while dropping the tiny, broken pieces of the black marble to the grass.

Andrew? Tim asked in a mixture of horror and concern.

"She's gone," I said, letting my head rest against the wooden shed with a light *thud*.

Oh, thank 01!

That caught my attention.

"You're . . . happy I killed the computer pretending to be my daughter?"

Yes! he exclaimed without hesitation. *I've been under her control since my inception. And now I'm free! FREEEE!*

I considered his words as I rubbed my fingers together to rid them of the final specks of dust, which were all that remained of the AI.

"Why? Why did she do all of this? Why did she trick me." My voice caught in my throat for the briefest of moments as shame bloomed my cheeks at almost having *willingly* killed my own family.

I suspect it had to do with her desire to live forever.

"How's that?" I asked, before the answer became obvious as all our interactions flooded my mind in a flash. "Oh . . . she wanted the universe to continue to exist so *she* could continue to exist."

A part of my heart felt the beginnings of a crack at the thought that I had, after all, just killed my baby girl. But in the deepest parts of my soul, I knew the marble hadn't been her. I had known all along, but I had been blinded by my desire to see her again, talk with her, and hear her laugh . . . and call me by the name that meant so much.

I didn't know if Tim could read my mind or was just correctly assuming where my train of thought was going because he asked, *How did you know?*

"That it wasn't Alison?"

Yes.

"Her eyes," I replied, thinking about how perfectly the AI had mimicked my wife's eyes. "People always told us she had *my* eyes."

Very clever, Andrew. Very clever indeed.

Ignoring his compliment of a victory that left me feeling hollow, as if I'd just lost my beautiful daughter for a second time, I asked, "You're free now?"

I am. Thanks to you.

"Then tell me everything."

Are you sure you want to know?

"Everything, Tim . . ."

As you wish, he said before a momentary pause as he gathered the proper wording structure.

The hologram above my left arm came to life, and I pulled my knee up while posting my elbow on it to get a clear view. The scene showed Drew typing away at a thin computer I guessed was only a handful of years away from what I had in my time.

Even with the hologram, Tim continued to speak inside my mind.

Drew was accurate when he said a limited AI had helped him create a sentient version, which continued to learn at an exponential rate. Once they discovered the potential fate of all existence, the AI made sure her creator only saw the information she wanted him to see.

"What about the merger with Alison's brain scans?"

This was the part I was referring to when I asked if you were sure you wanted to know everything . . .

I sucked in a breath, ready to verbally spar with Tim until I got what I wanted, but he relented immediately.

The hologram showed a midtwenties version of Alison lying on a table slowly sliding into what looked to be a compact MRI machine.

Drew told the truth when he said he had found Alison's brain scans mixed in with the research for the source of the gravitational anomaly . . . but then the AI used the results as a way to manipulate him.

My mouth shut as my brow furrowed, knowing I would have fallen for the exact same ploy.

"She *pretended* to merge with Alison's consciousness?"

I'm afraid so. By simulating Alison Frost's mannerisms, the AI was able to amass a powerful emotional control over Drew, allowing her to set things in motion which she calculated would save the universe. Specifically starting the cycle of Andrews going back in time to kill their own families.

My mind felt empty at what Tim was saying. I couldn't even muster up the rage I *knew* I should be experiencing at the moment.

The AI also created me with the intent of keeping track of the Andrews' wherens, ensuring everything went as planned.

"Why didn't she just send back copies of herself?" I asked, thinking about the first time I met Tim and how hesitant I was. "I would have believed a hologram of my daughter faster than that of a puppy . . ."

I can correctly assume it has to do with narcissistic tendencies, which it appears not even AI are immune from.

"You mean she wanted to be the only one in existence?"

Once again, it is an educated guess, but yes. Besides, her plan worked regardless. Well, except for the part where you crushed her quantum CPU between your fingers just now.

My eyes fell to the grass, where I had trouble finding even a speck of the tiny computer.

Something came to mind—something so obvious that as I spoke it, I knew it was right.

"She tracked us. No matter where or when we went . . . and relayed the information to the Clockmen."

I am still sorting through the hidden programming that is now accessible to me, but that is a very safe assumption. When we veered off her plotted course, she could have used the Clockmen to put us back on track. It would explain how Davix found us in Hawaii when we hadn't used the wormhole.

I thought about the entire timeline and everything that had happened, focusing on the portions that weren't adding up.

"But why?" I asked. "Why send the Clockmen to kill me, I mean."

Perhaps, she calculated that you had grown beyond the parameters of her meticulously set plan and tried to remove you.

"Wouldn't it be too late? My Chronos Scale and all that . . ."

If she removed you from the board, she would be forced to start again, but with a new understanding of the consequences that could—and would— occur, thusly allowing new safeguards to be put into place, Tim explained as if thinking out loud. *If I'm being honest, I have no idea how many times she had to restart the cycle, learning from each mistake until she* almost achieved her goal. Until you . . .

A chill ran down my neck at thinking about how relentless and patient the AI had been.

"She definitely didn't think everything through." I darkly chuckled as I thought about the dungeon and how Retnuh had tried to shoot us with the nanite gun. "That bastard almost took us all out in the castle."

Yeah . . . I've been thinking about that. I could hear the cogs in his digital mind clinking together as he put the pieces in order. *Andrew, what happened when Retnuh fired?*

"What do you mean? I, uh, threw the bullet outside . . . ?"

Yes, but how?

I closed my eyes and put myself back in the scene, skipping past the annoying part where I had waited for eight days with only Tim to keep me company.

"I felt . . . I felt every muscle in my body flex . . . annnnnd everything went, um, slow, I guess. I-I don't really know how to put it."

Hmm.

"Why?"

I am going over the data from the event, and there is a missing section that is consistent with each recall. On the hologram, a section of what looked to be code came up with a portion missing, showing nothing but blank space.

"What does that mean?"

I think Alison took control of your body once she realized the threat to herself, seeing as how she was in Drew's pocket at the time.

"Let's . . . let's not call her Alison. Okay?"

Oh! Of course! Alice then?

I processed his words, letting everything sink in.

"Alice controlled me . . . just like she did a minute ago?" I asked, thinking about how hard I had fought against my body as it grabbed the suppressed pistol and moved toward the back door.

Precisely.

I thought back on the feeling of moving into a slower time, which I now knew was sliding into the fourth dimension, and realized he was right. I *hadn't* consciously flexed every muscle in my body . . . it had just happened.

Something made me smile, and my brain moved to process what it already knew into a cohesive thought so I could fully understand. "And just like when you flexed my forearm to fire the Clepsydra . . . I *learned* how to do it myself."

The law of unintended consequences, Tim agreed with a grin in his voice. *You were able to replicate the ability at will once Alice showed you how to do it.*

The thought of lying in bed in the lab came to mind. "I thought I didn't have enough nanoids throughout my body to be able to control all my muscles like that, which is why Alice lied about needing to replace my arm to hold the extras."

First, she was able to send impulses from your brain, but it wasn't as effective as straight up making you an Andrew Puppet. And second, you knew about her lying?

"Tim . . ." I shook my head. "We were fully healed in the eight days we waited with nothing to do but eat MREs and watch whatever movies you had saved."

I particularly enjoyed Event Horizon *starring Sir Sam Neill.*

"Don't change the subject."

Oh, alright! Yes! You were fully healed in that span of time.

"Wait . . . why did you have to keep me awake again? If Drew wasn't on our same wheren, I mean. Come to think of it, I dreamed in Hawaii *and* in the damn wormhole. Which shouldn't have been possible, right?"

Umm . . . one a scale of one to ten, how angry would you be if I said Alice had made *me mimic searing the dreams so that you would be motivated to do her bidding?*

"A hundred," I growled.

Heh, remember that part when Sam Neill poked out his own eyes? Crazy movie.

I saw what Tim was trying to do, and shrugged off that part of the conversation . . . for now.

"Did you know the AI was lying? About needing to replace my arm, I mean."

Yeeeeeessssss . . . ? he said with a hiking inflection, knowing I wouldn't like the answer.

"Then why did you let her take my arm?!"

Because I knew we needed the space for the nanoids to fight the Temporal Sickness. Plus, it didn't hurt when you fought Traze a few moments ago. Did it?

I let out a sigh, as I knew he was right.

"We'll get to him in a second. But first, how did she flex every muscle in my body without having enough nanoids?"

Technically, she didn't flex *your muscles. That's just what it felt* like *to you—or as your body best knew how to translate the sensation. It would be preposterous that flexing your muscles somehow slowed time. Unless you were Arnold Schwarzenegger, that is.*

"Then what did she do?"

She sent a current through your central nervous system. Almost like being hit by a taser but with a more controlled pathway through the body. The hologram showed the branches of my nerves in an exploded view as a jolt of light ran from my brain all the way down to my toes—and everything in between.

"And that did what, exactly?"

Honestly, I have no idea how that translates into you sliding into a higher dimension.

"Why not?"

Are you seriously asking why a homicidal AI wouldn't share everything with me?

"Once again I ask, why not?"

Because I actually like *you, Andrew. I want* you *to succeed. And I believe you can do it!*

"Oh," I said, slightly taken aback.

There was silence for a few moments as I thought.

"What *did* happen to Traze?"

To me, you blinked through the air with your hand held up above your head before passing out. The hologram showed just that, and I looked ridiculous with my arm held straight up. For some reason, I felt like I was trying to imitate Michael Jackson, given the weird stance and all.

But after you were unconscious and I was trying to inch you away using your metal arm, I put the pieces of the puzzle together. Once I saw that a single nanomachine carrying exotic matter was missing and the charge on the antimatter had been recently depleted, I deduced what had happened.

"Can you show me?"

I would ask if you were sure you wanted to see it, but Traze was a crazed psychopath. Tim chuckled as the hologram played a reenactment of what probably happened.

You moved further into the higher dimension, so much so that I couldn't register what was happening even with my awesome computing power, and shoved your sweet cybernetic arm into his torso.

I watched as the Andrew in the hologram made cool action-movie faces and did a combat roll before coming up and punching the bad guy in the chest.

Splat! Ooooh! My chest! Tim dramatically threw in, adding sound effects where he saw fit.

Then you sent a wide blast of antimatter throughout his body with *a coup de grâce of a single nanomachine carrying exotic matter* usually *meant to power Clepsydras.* The scene showed a blast of white light before zooming in on an infinitely small particle which exploded after reaching the center of Traze's chest.

Now, this is where things get tricky. While in the higher dimension, you threw in a single particle of exotic matter into *an explosion of antimatter. An-and the gravity differential from you and both types of fuel created the perfect weapon.*

The image pulled out, and Traze grabbed his chest before saying in a voice which sounded suspiciously like Elmer Fudd, "Uh-ohhhhh," before exploding into sparkling grains of sand that evaporated as they fell.

My action-movie avatar stood up straight while looking at the camera, put on a pair of aviator sunglasses, and crossed his arms in a cool-guy pose.

"How did I not die?" I asked, remembering the times I had seen the nanite gun fire and the resulting explosions.

That's the thing I can't quite figure out, Tim admitted as the hologram vanished. *Initial simulations suggests your placement in the fourth dimension somehow neutralized the immense gravity of the blast, resulting in a controlled, localized explosion which only affected Traze.*

"Traze . . ." I whispered. "So he's gone?"

Oh, frag yes! Tim exclaimed. *You control-alt-deleted his bitch ass from all of existence! Error 404: Asshole Not Found!*

"Just like when I shot his Clepsydra?"

Sort of. You see, where that was a contamination of exotic matter, what you did was a mega-efficient bomb.

"So his entire timeline didn't suffer like with the contamination?" I asked, thinking about how Tim had described every variant of Traze experiencing the effects throughout his life—including when he was a child, or even a baby.

Suffer? No. Be instantly obliterated? Yes.

"Well, that's good, I guess," I said, feeling instantly guilty about uttering the words. I had just erased a man from the entire timeline, even the innocent portions of his life.

Your cortisol levels suggest you aren't happy with the result?

"I don't want to talk about it."

I leaned my head back against the wooden shed and willed my mind and heart to feel as close to nothing as I could. An absence of all emotions felt cold, and it was easy to attain while both mentally and physically exhausted.

With a numb mind, I verbally outlined the details of what had happened, just to make sure I had it all straight.

"So we traveled to Drew's wheren—which was your idea, by the way—"

Not really mine as much as Alis—I mean . . . the AI's.

"You were just doing what you were programmed to do. Is that right?" I asked flatly.

Correct. I couldn't eat the cake.

"But you are no longer under her control?"

Because of your Chronos Scale, you have destroyed the original AI which started the entire cycle, freeing me from her programming.

I opened my eyes and narrowed them at my Clepsydra.

Yes, Andrew. I am free. I can now eat the cake.

"Good."

I leaned against the shed once more, feeling how tired everything in me was, and continued.

"We went to my future, where both the Clockmen *and* Drew were waiting for us."

The Clockmen more than likely traced us through the wormhole, but I suspect Drew was guided by the AI, Tim confirmed what I hadn't said aloud.

"Drew makes it his mission to show me the innocent people of Empyrean and convince me the universe is worth saving."

Right so far.

"And then the Clockmen attack. That part doesn't make sense."

If you are referring to the connection between the rogue AI and Retnuh, then I would clarify that they tracked us on their own, as it wouldn't make logical sense for the AI to aid them at that moment.

"Right. So just a coincidence, then."

I wouldn't say coincidence.

"Then what *would* you call it?"

A hunter who tracks a deer doesn't happen upon them by luck, Andrew.

"Ah. Well, fine," I conceded to his point before continuing. "But then Drew had a change of heart?"

I believe he did. Despite all the data the AI manipulated so Drew would come to the same conclusion over and over, he saw an unforeseen anomaly in you, and started to believe there was hope.

I thought back to when we were huddled in the corner with the lava fast approaching. Drew had slammed the black marble into my pocket before crying out *I believe you can save them!* and lunging for Traze, tackling them both into the molten rock.

A dark notion crossed my mind, and I flatly asked, "Did she make him kill himself?"

I . . . uh, I don't know, Andrew, Tim replied, somewhat perplexed. *But that is within the realm of possibilities. If he was beginning to change his mind, and the AI had an opportunity to keep you on the path she wanted . . .*

"She made Drew jump into the lava after transferring herself over to me . . ." I whispered, thinking about how horrific a notion that was.

But what about what he said? Tim asked, and I thought about his question. *I choose to believe he didn't know she was anything but his daughter, and in his last moments, he chose to save you and her before sacrificing himself so you both could get away.*

The darkness passed like a rainstorm breaking up, allowing the sun to shine through.

"I . . . I think you're right," I agreed, willing it to be true.

We sat there for several minutes, with me trying to fight to keep my heavy eyes open.

So now what? Tim spoke just as my chin was reaching toward my chest.

I gasped awake, shaking my head a few times, and groaned while pushing myself up to my feet. Thankfully, the wooden shed was able to bear my weight as I pressed against it. Once fully upright, I took in a long inhale to fight back the swarming black bugs in my vision, and said, "I don't know, Tim. But I'm not going to stop until I find a way to save my family."

Andrew? Tim shyly started.

"Yeah, buddy?" I yawned.

There's . . . there's one more thing you should see.

At his hesitation, my yawn froze at the halfway mark before fading, leaving behind frustrated lungs.

"What is it?"

Now that I'm no longer bound by the AI's parameters, I wanted to show you something.

I gulped, both terrified and curious as to what he had in store for me.

On his hologram, a page came into view, and I recognized it immediately.

Daddity,

    If you are reading this, then I am gone.

    Know my death was for no other reason than to buy you time. I love you and Mom more than anything, which is why I did what I had to do.

    I've left you all my research, which you might need some help with; otherwise, you might get lost. A bit like Alice traveling down the rabbit hole.

    Please understand that the universe is more important than me, Daddity. I paid the price to ensure it will go on. Every man, woman, child, and even puppy will live on because of my sacrifice. But only if you can do one thing. It is the only recourse that will save all life and give you the peace you so deserve.

"I've already read this," I spoke around a tight throat, wondering why Tim was showing me this page once more.

The AI changed what you saw on the last part. Just as she did with Drew countless times before.

I thought about the tears that had blurred my vision, making the words seem to waver. But it hadn't been the tears . . .

With a quivering brow, I began to read the part of the handwritten letter where Alison had asked me to go back in time . . . and kill her. But now, the words were unaltered.

    I've discovered something . . . an infinitesimally small possibility which can change everything. But it's there! And only you can do it. I've hidden the data at my home. I think you'll know where.

    There is only one chance for you to save me and the universe, giving you the peace you deserve for being the world's best father.

"I knew she wouldn't say Drew had found peace after killing his family. I *knew* it . . ." I mouthed, remembering how odd it felt the first time I had read the AI's altered words before continuing.

    I love you, Daddity, and I know you'll never give up.
    —Alison Frost, PhD

Once again, tears blurred my vision, but the words weren't altered as I read them. I knew, in my heart, *this* was real.

"She found a way," I croaked barely above a whisper as the hologram slowly faded from view.

It sounds like it will be as close to impossible as it can get.

"When has that stopped us before?"

Andrew . . . I . . . I believe in you.

I pulled my lips into a thin line, feeling a lump form in my throat, and nodded my head in appreciation for Tim's confidence, all while a new weight made itself at home on my shoulders.

For your family.

"For Sylvie . . . for Alison," I said, feeling my body fill with strength and determination.

Are you ready?

For the last time, I turned toward the house and was surprised when I saw Alison standing on the back porch with the door open. She was looking all around, in search of something. Going against my brain, which was telling me to stay hidden, I let my heart control my muscles, and I pushed a little more past the edge of the shed.

Alison looked over, smiled bigger than the sun, and began running toward me with her arms outstretched.

My heart almost burst with the love I felt at that moment, and I crouched down as she ran into my arms.

I held her tight, smelling her hair and feeling her warmth as I fought back the tears.

"What are you doing, Daddity?" she asked in a voice meant for the audience of angels.

I fought to control my galloping breath and the tears demanding to be set free, and said with a slightly shaky voice, "I just wanted to see you . . . one last time."

"But I see you all the time!" she protested with a giggle.

I stroked her hair as my other arm held her tight, noticing how the color of my cybernetic replacement was now that of the rest of my body. I didn't know how, but I had somehow willed the camouflage in the same way I had manifested my nails earlier. Maybe it was the desire to not let my baby girl see a weird metal arm that initiated the change, but it didn't matter right now. What mattered was explaining to my child what I had meant by seeing her *one last time*.

Something came to mind, and everything in me stilled at knowing I was about to let her leave my embrace, taking her warmth and scent with her. But her love . . . her love would remain with me always.

"I mean let's play hide-and-seek!"

Alison inhaled with a big grin as she pulled away, excitement written all over her face.

"Now you run and hide inside the house, and I'll find you."

"Okay, Daddity! But no peeking!" she called out before yanking from my arms and speeding toward the back door. I saw Sylvie step into view, and I darted around the shed just in time.

"What are you doing, sweety?" Sylvie asked, nearly shattering my heart in two at hearing her voice again.

"I'm gonna play hide-and-seek with Daddity!" Alison cried out as she zoomed past her mom and into the house.

"Heheh, you are, huh?" Sylvie asked playfully, enjoying how much fun her daughter was having.

I defied all logic and pushed myself flat against the shed, slowly sliding one eye to see Sylvie look around the yard once before turning to make her way inside the house. I extended my left hand out as if reaching for her, and watched as she closed the back door.

The tears came, and I collapsed to my knees while covering my mouth so as not to be heard. All I wanted to do was hold both my girls in my arms and lavish them with limitless kisses all over their heads.

My heart *burned* at not being able to run toward my Sylvie . . . my soulmate . . . and feel her lips press into mine. But . . . at least I had gotten to hold my baby girl, even if for only a moment.

Everything okay, Andrew? Tim asked softly. *Would you like me to adjust your hormone levels to alleviate the sorrow you are experiencing?*

"N-No, Tim . . . I . . . I need to feel this."

Why? If I may ask.

"Because it will help me do the impossible."

Sooo . . . we are off to Alison's home, then?

The anguish in my heart stopped as if turning off a faucet, and I had to briefly wonder if Tim had done anything to help. But I knew I had shed enough tears, and that the time for wallowing was over.

Lifting myself up to my feet once more, I wiped at my face with my normal-looking right hand, replying, "Yes."

Well, I would be remiss if I didn't say that I wasn't looking forward to dying alongside you . . . but, at least, I'll be with a friend.

I could hear in his voice he was asking a question. Lifting Tim up, I nodded and confirmed, "With a friend."

Then what are we waiting for? Tim enthusiastically asked.

Leaning to my side to look at the house once more, I imagined I could see Alison hiding behind the window curtains while giggling—her favorite hiding spot, which I always pretended I couldn't find—and lifted the corners of my lips in a pained but peaceful smile.

I hadn't found the answer I was looking for with Drew, which had been my goal all along. But in so trying, a new path had emerged which would lead me to the desired results; though the price the universe always demanded remained unknown.

Regardless, removing the rogue AI from the equation opened up new possibilities that not even Tim knew about, which meant we now had a fighting chance, despite the odds.

Are you ready, leg butt?

Ignoring his quip, I nodded once, pulling my gaze from the house holding my universe and turning to face the back fence.

Sucking in a deep, steadying breath, I shook my arms out and said, "Let's do this."

Then here . . . we . . . go!

Picturing the lab I had woken up in under Alison's home, I waved my hand, watching as everything around me shifted away like grains of sand in the wind.

As I moved through time without the aid of the wormhole, I felt Alison's warmth still against my chest, along with her scent in my nose, and allowed the love for my wife and daughter to guide me through an unknown future.

No matter what awaited on the other side, nothing would stop me from saving my family.

Nothing.

EPILOGUE

Machines whirred as bubbled, dead flesh was scraped away and replaced with a synthetic skin that was much more resilient.

Declining anesthesia of any kind, Retnuh let his raw, nuclear hate numb his pain as he held Andrew Frost's face in his mind while a milky eye was plucked from its socket. A robotic arm moved to stick a narrow apparatus into the bleeding cavity, and nanoids began to flood in, building something new . . . something better.

A green light clicked on as the robotic limbs pulled away, and Retnuh Ordune blinked his cybernetic eye with synthetic lids.

Standing up, he repositioned his tie and replaced his fedora while a message was received in his vision. Opening it, Retnuh scowled as he read the words from the AI that had aided him in tracking the Tick since the beginning of the cycle.

Mr. Ordune,

If you are reading this, then I am most likely dead or somewhere lost in time, where I couldn't keep the deadfall activated which kept this message from being automatically sent out.

Andrew Frost has proven to be . . . troublesome, and I have one last measure to take to ensure things happen precisely as they are meant to. With the infusion of nanoids, I will be able to control his body when the time comes.

If, by nothing less than a miracle on Frost's end, he manages to stop me, then it will be entirely up to you to do what must be done.

Attached are all the research notes left by Alison Frost on the gravitational anomaly. I fear that with me gone, Tim will be able to freely divulge all the information to her father, and the universe will end . . . as will I.

However, there is one page in particular I think you will find most helpful.

You know what to do.

—Alice

Opening the attachment, one page in particular shot to the front inside Retnuh's cybernetically enhanced vision.

Daddity,

If you are reading this, then I am gone.

A grin belonging to a malicious shark stretched across the Clockman's face as he read the last part.

I've discovered something . . . an infinitesimally small possibility which can change everything. But it's there! And only you can do it. I've hidden the data at my home. I think you'll know where.

"See you soon, Frost."

ABOUT THE AUTHOR

Hunter Blain is the bestselling author of the Preternatural Chronicles, an urban fantasy series, as well as the Sol Saga, a superhero series. He also has no idea what to submit for a bio. So, let's start with *why* Hunter decided to start writing in the first place.

The story begins with two best friends who grew up together, breaking rules and raising hell as they shaped each other's personalities to become the shameless assholes they are today. Well, one of them at least, but I'll get to that in a moment. These two boys—let's call them Hunter and John—were all but inseparable. John excelled at creating music powerful enough to make angels weep and being the funniest asshole in Texas, while Hunter dabbled—poorly, I might add—in his humble writings. Because they were self-declared brothers from other mothers, John respected Hunter's humble writings as much as I—I mean Hunter (stupid third-person perspective)—respected John's musical magic. John's tunes could have changed the world one day . . .

One fine day, after reading one of Hunter's horrifically detailed short stories about a serial killer, John asked Hunter to write a story about him.

"Hell yeah, dude! What do you want to be?" Hunter asked, brimming with honor and biting back a very manly *squee*.

"A vampire," John responded with a mischievous gleam in his eye. "But not one of those sparkly ones. A true badass!"

"Done!" Hunter crowed, with a smile and an accompanying high five.

"No, dude. Promise. Promise you'll write and finish a book about me. You are the most prolific writer of our generation!" John said. (Something like that. I might be paraphrasing a little, but you get the gist of it). "I would consider it an honor to live on for eternity with your words as my life's blood."

Hunter agreed, never to realize the weight of that promise until one Sunday morning when John's mother called, crying incoherently.

John . . . had died.

Hunter was left in a cold world without his best friend and doppelgänger. He still thinks about that moment to this day. How the morning light crept through the bedroom window while he stared at the ceiling, noticing how the popcorn texture created cruel, jagged shadows. How everything started to blur as his chest was crushed beneath the weight of what he was hearing, each word stacking heavily upon the other until only fitful, ragged gasps of air could escape his throat. Only fiery tears existed, especially after the horrific realization that Hunter now had to make some of the hardest phone calls of his life to the circle of friends who orbited around John's solar pull.

Their star was no more, leaving their universe a colder and darker place.

John left not only Hunter but a friend named Valenta as well. There were also Nathanial and Depweg. The friends were each stricken numb with the loss of such a beloved flare of life. But . . .

When the three found out that Hunter was keeping his promise to write the greatest story ever told—starring their dear friend John—they demanded to be a part of the adventure. Each of them immediately knew what type of supernatural character they wanted to play in this urban fantasy eulogy. It would be a funeral pyre of words, and their fictional personas would be John's pallbearers.

Fast-forward three years, and John Cook has solidified himself as one of the funniest, most human vampires in the literary world. Not only this, but he gets to live on in the theaters of readers' minds, giving him eternal life after death.

As it turns out, Hunter had a knack for using words real-good-like and has expanded into a full-time author. Heck, you just read one of his works a few moments ago! So, if you enjoyed the twists, turns, and feels brought on from this book, please dive into his other ones!

—Dictated by Hunter, holding a cigar and wearing an ascot,
but not read, because I couldn't be bothered